praise for
Hunter: Apocrypha
by Tim Dedopulos

"The needle screams upwards and places [**Hunter: Apocrypha**], with its style, tenacity, and mythopoetic heroic grip, right at the top…"
—Chuck Wendig, *Ex Libris Nocturnis*

"**Apocrypha** is written by the esteemed Tim Dedopulos, who delivers as usual. If he's guilty of any crime in the work, it's not making it longer."
—*RPGnet*

Vampire: The Masquerade Fiction from White Wolf

The Clan Novel Series

The Clan Tremere Trilogy

The Clan Lasombra Trilogy

The Victorian Age Vampire Trilogy

The Dark Ages Clan Novel Series

Also by Tim Dedopulos

For all these titles and more, visit www.white-wolf.com/fiction

SLAVE RING ™

TIM DEDOPULOS

Book One of the Clan
Brujah Trilogy

Cover art by John Van Fleet. Book design by Mike Chaney. Art direction by Richard Thomas. Copyedited by James Stewart.

ISBN 1-58846-814-3
First Edition: May 2003
Printed in Canada

White Wolf Publishing
1554 Litton Drive
Stone Mountain, GA 30083
www.white-wolf.com/fiction

For George and Ben,
With much love, for a whole lifetime's worth of reasons.

"Come fill your cup, and in the fires of Spring
The winter clothing of Repentance fling:
The Bird of Time has but a little way
To fly—and Lo! the Bird is on the wing..."
—*The Rubaiyat of Omar Khayyam*

prologue:
The Trade

Rob wandered through the small park surrounding Lake George, bored out of his skull. St. Cloud, Minnesota had turned out to be every bit as pleasant and relaxed as Rob had feared. It was just like being back in St. Paul, only smaller and with even less money to play with. He should have been in Minneapolis with Mike and Richie, scoping out the town and having some laughs. Angry at himself, he kicked at a small wooden post next to the path. *Loser.*

Still, St. Cloud State was better than no university at all. He looked around at the park, irritated. The lake was still visible through the trees, despite the fading light, but the place was practically deserted. The city was supposed to be one-third students, but if that was true, then most of them were hiding.

Earlier in the evening, he had spent a few minutes exploring the campus mall before heading out to see what the town had to offer. Someone had pointed him up Fourth Avenue, toward High Banks Place. The mansions were beautiful, no doubt about it, but they weren't exactly fun, and it wasn't as if they played host to a cool street scene or anything.

The lake was a few blocks west, and it wasn't any better. Rob hadn't really had much hope of finding a bandstand, but he had expected to see a few kids knocking about or something. He headed back toward Division Street and briefly considered walking up to the Crossroads Mall, but it hardly seemed worth wearing himself out. Maybe downtown would have picked up a bit.

Twenty minutes later, he was standing around indecisively on West St. Germain, wondering whether he was more likely to get carded in Rox or the Tavern, when he realized someone was looking at him expectantly from across the street. Someone cute. He ruthlessly stamped on the quick flare of hope. She probably wanted to know the time or something. The girl smiled as Rob noticed her.

"Hey." Her voice was cute too, light and relaxed, with a hint of laughter around the edges.

"Hi there," said Rob warily. "Can I help you?"

"You from the U?"

"Fresh in," said Rob, unable to keep the hint of bitterness out of his voice. "Lucky me."

The girl smiled and crossed the street. "Lucky me, more like. I'm Ginny. Wanna play guide?"

Up close, Ginny was a few years older than he'd first thought, somewhere in her early twenties. Her hair was pulled back loosely into a long auburn ponytail. Tight jeans and an equally snug black top did nothing whatsoever to hide her figure. Her eyes sparkled with delicious mischief. He shook his head to try to clear it, confused. This sort of stuff just didn't happen. Ginny arched an eyebrow quizzically at his apparent rejection.

"No, that's not, uh, that is…" Rob floundered to a halt, suddenly feeling panicky. Ginny grinned at his expression, and he got a grip on himself. "Let me try that again. Hi Ginny. I'm Rob. How can I help?"

"Hi Rob. Like I said, I need a guide. A friend of ours just started up here, but, well, we got kinda turned around. Can you help out?"

Rob sagged a little, disappointed despite himself.

"Sure, I can tell you where to go."

Ginny laughed. "You don't get off that easy, Robbo. I told you, I want a *guide*. Come hop in the back of the van, talk Bill through it, and then tag along to the party. You seem cool, and I figure Lucy would just love you. That is, unless you're scared of having a good time?"

"Really?" asked Rob eagerly. "That'd be great." Maybe St. Cloud would pick up yet.

"Any new friends you wanna drop in and bring along? More the merrier."

Rob shook his head sourly. "Not yet."

Ginny smiled. "Well, you'll meet some folks tonight."

A nasty thought crossed Rob's mind. "You sure your boyfriend isn't going to mind you bringing me back?"

"Who said anything about a boyfriend?" She flashed him a dazzling smile. "Bill's my cousin, and he's seeing Sammie. They're back in his van. Anyway, it's all part of the plan. C'mon, big guy, we're parked just round back."

Ginny looped her arm through his and started down the street. Rob lurched to keep up with her, desperate not to break contact. Her arm was electric against his skin, and it made his whole body tingle. Thinking about anything else seemed impossible, but he tried to find something to say. *Get her talking about herself*, he thought wildly, the original source of the advice long forgotten.

"So, where'd you come from anyway?"

She glanced up at him, still smiling. "Minneapolis. Nicolet Island, actually. It's a funky place, all regenerated bits mixed in with atmospheric old warehouses and stuff. Some of them are great for messing around in, too. You ever get out there?"

"Not to the island, no. Minneapolis, some. Not as much as I wanted to. It sounds cool, though."

Ginny pulled a bit closer, and Rob's head swam. "You should come down there some time. I think you'd like it."

"Yeah," he managed, his throat suddenly dry.

She guided him round into an alley. A big, off-white panel van was idling a short way up, the blank rear doors facing them. She steered him toward it.

"Here we are, Robbie. I'll have to pop you in the back for a couple of minutes, but you'll be fine, just grab hold of the front seat or something." She looked back at the street for a moment, then grabbed the handle, twisted it easily, and pulled the door slightly ajar.

Suddenly, she pushed him against the van, one hand on his chest, the other sliding down to her hip. "I wouldn't want you to get cold or anything back there on your own though, so..." To his amazement, he discovered that she was pressed up tight against him, her breasts squashing into his chest. She shot him a grin that was pure mischief, then went up on tiptoes and kissed him, hard.

He barely noticed the sharp pressure against his side, and then everything went black.

***

Ginny watched the kid—the merchandise, she corrected herself—slump back against the van. She looked at him critically for a moment and gave him another brief blast, just to make sure he stayed well and truly zapped. She turned the taser off, slipped it back into the pocket of her jeans and rapped twice on the back of the van. An arm came out through the rear curtain, and she let go of the merchandise, allowing it to slip toward the open doorway.

Alex caught it with a grunt, and started to tug. Ginny crouched quickly, wrapped her legs around its knees and lifted—heavier than she expected—and it slid smoothly into the back of the van. She climbed in after it, breathing a little harder, and heard Alex curse softly. She shut the door, and the van immediately lurched off down the alley. Four minutes from start to finish. Not bad at all.

Alex looked disgruntled. "You know I hate having to haul big bastards aboard. I'll have to up the tranquilizer dosage, too. Why d'ya have to get such a fat one?"

Ginny shrugged. "That was the order. One chubby freshman. They probably want him going down as a first-week runaway or something."

"There's chubby and there's chubby. He didn't have to be that size."

"You'd rather I hung around the area for twenty minutes trying to find someone a few pounds less? Don't be an asshole. He's not that big, anyway." She shot Alex a wicked little grin. "Besides, he was kinda sweet."

He rose straight to the bait and scowled blackly at her. "Yeah, what the hell *was* all that about back there?"

"Oh, I figured that it'd be a real tragedy if he went through his whole life without ever getting to kiss even one girl. I thought I'd be generous. Give him something to remember." She smiled sweetly at Alex. "Surely you're not jealous?"

Alex made a disgusted-sounding noise and changed the subject. "Did he give you any trouble?"

Ginny laughed, genuinely. "You have gotta be kidding me. He practically fell over himself telling me he had no friends here. Open and shut."

"Good. Help me get him locked in, will you?" Alex still looked pissed, but he managed to keep it out of his voice.

Between them, it wasn't that hard to haul the merchandise over to one of the cages along the left side of the van, and tip it in face first. Once in place, its own size and weight kept it more or less upright, and it was only a moment to lock the holding bar in place. Ginny reached for a couple of self-locking plastic restraints. "You gag and hood him, and I'll get him tied."

Alex grunted and grabbed the ball gag and hood that were hanging from the cage door. Ginny wrapped a restraint around the merchandise's ankles and pulled it savagely tight, then repeated the process with its wrists, pinioning its arms behind its back. It moaned faintly as the restraint cut into soft flesh.

Alex had heard the moan too, and once he'd locked the gag in place and covered the head, he quickly reached for his bag of tricks and started preparing an injection. Ginny left him to it and checked on the others. All quiet. The little junkie was horribly skinny, with arms like pincushions and a scarred, bony ass, but at least she didn't smell as bad as the two hobos. To make matters worse, one of them had pissed himself under the influence of the anesthetic. She sighed and made a mental note to get Alex to disinfect the van once they'd unloaded.

She glanced around at him. Alex was putting his medical kit away, and looking longingly at the case bolted to the right-hand wall of the van. She shook her head. "Don't even think about it."

"What?" He sounded indignant.

"It's a special order, remember? No playing."

Alex pulled a face at her, then sat down on the bench, watching the new merchandise with a nasty glint in his eye. Ginny left him to it. She knocked twice on the driver access panel. "Miles, open up." After a moment or two, he obliged.

"Well?" Miles was terse, as usual.

"Whacked, racked and packed. We're solid."

"Is that it?"

"Yeah, back to the barn."

"You got it." The partition slammed shut again.

Ginny sat down on the bench, letting the tension drain out of her. She suddenly felt exhausted, and rested her head in her hands. "Alex, keep an eye on number two and make sure she doesn't come around. Apart from that, just keep quiet and don't bother me unless something happens. And remember, no playing." She ignored his pout and drifted off.

Ginny woke up once, briefly, and glanced around to check what had disturbed her. It was Alex. He'd rolled up the left sleeve of his shirt and was making small, delicate cuts in his forearm with one of his scalpels. It looked like he was trying to draw some sort of design in his own blood. He flinched each time he made an incision, mumbling obscenities and grimacing strangely in what might have been a smile. He was doing this with the van moving? Ginny resolved to cut him a bit of slack for a while, then blocked out his soft grunts and muttered curses, and went back to sleep.

***

The factory was unusually busy when they finally made it back. Once the van had been cleared through the security check and allowed through the access tunnel, the place proved to be surprisingly hectic. Ginny sighed. Alex glanced over at her incuriously, then went back to picking his nails. Miles backed up into the bay he'd been directed to and cut the engine.

"It sounds like it may be a while before we get to unload this evening, Alex. Keep an eye on things, will you? I'll find out what the score is and let you know as soon as I find out." She made an effort to sound conciliatory.

"Sure, whatever."

"Thanks."

Ginny opened the back door of the van and hopped out. The factory was chaotic. Back in the sixties, it had been a vegetable processing and packaging plant for one of the major retailers, and traces of its old purpose were still visible. Grooved tracks led from each of the loading bays out toward where the main hoppers and storage tanks had once been, and the floor of the central area was pitted with holes that indicated the path of the conveyor tracks. That was then, of course. Things were a lot more advanced now.

Three small trucks were parked in bays alongside the van. Ginny didn't recognize any of them, as usual. She knew the other resident teams, but they never rubbed shoulders—it was a strict rotation, one week on, three out-of-state.

Liam Wickman was standing in front of the second truck. He looked harassed—his thinning hair was less tidy than usual, and his suit looked like he'd been sleeping in it. He was going over some piece of paperwork with a lean Chinese guy. He caught sight of Ginny and beckoned to her. "Will you come over here a for moment, Ginny?"

She made her way round to the front of the truck, passing the lean guy as he moved to the back of the vehicle. "Sure thing, boss."

"Did you come across any problems on your run?" His voice had a faint lilt, always more noticeable when he was under pressure. "Nope." She smiled. "It all went like clockwork."

"How about that special request I had for you?"
"Easy."

"You're a good girl, Ginny. Thank you. We'll get you unloaded as soon as we can, but as you can see, things are a little busy right now."

"Anything I can help with?"

Liam shook his head. "No, that's okay. We've got plenty of people on hand. It's just taking a while to get everything smoothed out. You know what devils the Triads are for formality and paperwork.

The cargo think they're getting jobs making sportswear, and I'd rather they didn't catch on until after someone's had a chance to get them all split up and horsed out of their heads. It'll make their trip to LA that much easier."

Ginny's heart sank. "You're not going to want us to take any of them out there, are you? I don't think I can handle another two-week road trip with the boys just yet."

Liam grinned at her expression and shook his head. "No need to worry. They're going to the 1%ers, and they'll be sending people here to collect them. They'll do the distribution to the various chapters themselves."

"That's a relief." Ginny smiled.

"Yeah, I don't like long-haul exposure any more than you do."

"Any unnecessary exposure is foolish." An unexpected voice cut in, making Ginny jump. She turned, hand reflexively twitching toward the taser.

Matthew Flock was a little over six feet tall, with shoulder-length honey-blond hair, chiseled cheekbones and blue eyes that seemed to glitter in his pale face. He always dressed as if he were about to head out somewhere spectacular for dinner. Very good looking, but hard and cruel with it. He had a creepy habit of staying really still too, like he only moved when absolutely necessary. She briefly wondered how he'd managed to get so close without her noticing—she was supposed to be better than that—but the factory was pretty noisy, and she'd been distracted.

"Good evening Matthew. Everything okay?" Liam seemed at ease. How the two of them had ended up working together was beyond her.

"Indeed." The voice matched the man perfectly: cold, elegant, unpleasant. He gestured at Ginny. "This is your active operator?"

Liam nodded. "Yeah, this is Ginny."

"Good." Ginny wondered if he'd even heard Liam speak her name. "Is she reliable?"

Ginny started to make some sarcastic comment, but Liam leaped in and cut her off, shooting her a strong warning glance.

"Yes, she's reliable."

Matthew turned to her then, and his eyes seemed to bore into the back of her skull. "Very well. I have a task for you, girl. Do not fail at it, and your worst nightmares will not be forced upon you. Do you understand?"

Ginny had to fight a sudden, inexplicable urge to look at the floor and shuffle her feet like a frightened schoolgirl. She tried to work out why she wasn't spitting fire. "I get the picture. What do you need?"

"I require ownership of a specific pair of young women. Sisters. You are to befriend them swiftly, lure them into your custody and bring them to me unsullied. My partner will provide you with the requisite details."

"That shouldn't be too tricky."

"Pray it is not. Their acquisition is considered important by my superiors. I have assured them that it will be a simple matter. To have it prove otherwise would be embarrassing. I do not like to be embarrassed, girl."

Ginny nodded nervously. "I understand."

Matthew turned abruptly and stalked off toward the main offices. Ginny let out a huge sigh of relief. Immediately, fear and resentment started to surface in roughly equal amounts.

Liam looked at her sympathetically. "Is that the first time you've spoken to Matthew?"

She nodded, not trusting herself to answer.

"He can be a bit forceful. Try not to take it personally. It's just the way he is."

Ginny wrestled her emotions back under control. "Okay, boss. Whatever you say. I still think he's a prick, though."

Liam looked a bit uncomfortable. "Well, keep that to yourself, all right?"

She nodded again.

"Good. You can go and unwind once you've unloaded the cargo. I'll give you the details on this next collection just as soon as I get them. There'll be a bonus in it for you, too, so don't worry about that. Be careful, okay?"

"Of course."

"Thanks, Ginny. Looks like the Triad boys have finished delivering their takeout, so you can dump the rest of your catch first, if you want."

"Will do."

Liam smiled. "Great. Talk to you tomorrow. Sleep well." He headed off toward the main offices.

Better him than me, Ginny decided. Matthew was in there somewhere.

A couple of porters unloaded the hobos and the battered junkie, and carted them off to the pens. Once they were clear, Alex looked at her expectantly. "What about King Kong there?"

She smiled. "Tell you what. Wake it up, and then *you* can tell it. Okay?"

He grinned nastily. "I can live with that."

Ginny nodded. "Make sure you do."

It took a couple of minutes to wrestle the merchandise out of the cage and lay it out on the floor of the van. They propped it on its side, ankles and wrists still locked together. Ginny took the mask off while Alex prepared an injection to throw off the effects of the tranquilizer that he had administered earlier.

It was only a short wait before the merchandise came round. It looked pained, confused and scared, and, when it caught sight of Ginny, it also managed to look hurt. It started to try to say something through the gag, but Alex was ready for that. He slapped it hard round the face.

Ginny made her way to the door. As she left, Alex looked into the merchandise's eyes, grinned nastily and recited Speech Number Three. "Keep your mouth shut, you piece of shit. If you cause any trouble whatsoever, you'll fucking regret it. I'm not going to damage you unless I have to—"

A muffled scream indicated that Alex had thumped the merchandise hard in the nuts to illustrate the point. "But that doesn't mean that I can't cause you a hell of a lot of pain if I feel the need. You want to make sure I don't feel the need, loser. I bet you're wondering what's going to happen to you, right? It's good news, asshole. We're not going to kill you. We're not even going to rape you. No, we're going to sell you. For a rather impressive sum of money, you'll be glad to hear. No one will find you or come to your rescue. Forget your hopes and dreams, forget your family and friends, forget your name and home. You'll never, ever know any of those things again. You'll wish for death a million times or more before she finally comes for you. Have a nice day."

chapter one:
A night in the life of...

Someone had been busy causing some spectacular trouble over the last couple of weeks.

On August 22nd, a two-man police patrol called for backup to deal with an armed mugger who'd been distressing the residents of Aurora, Illinois. When the second car arrived, the four officers followed the man into a small network of service alleys, and then vanished. They were found two hours later by a nervous fellow officer investigating their disappearance, who eventually had to be taken care of. The mugger was splayed out in the middle of an alley with his eviscerated intestines draped around him in a particularly tasteless imitation of a crime scene chalk outline. One officer was impaled on each of the mugger's limbs, with the hand (or foot) having been forced down the officer's throat to the shoulder (or mid-thigh). As an apparent afterthought, all ten eyes had been removed and piled inside the mugger's gaping mouth. The chief of police obediently ordered a news blackout regarding the atrocity, and although rumors spread, no one really knew anything for sure.

But the next incident had been impossible to cover up. Four days later, a number of individuals broke in to the local zoo and slaughtered approximately half of the assorted sheep, goats, pigs, foxes, otters, llamas and elks that were available. None of the birds were harmed. All of the carcasses were beheaded, and the heads were hidden around the zoo grounds—behind bushes, under benches and so on, like Easter eggs. Some of the carcasses were crucified and carved with meaningless but unpleasant-looking symbols. Surveillance equipment was destroyed in the raid, but examination of the carcasses suggested that the carnage had taken several hours. Local journalists naturally described the raid as satanic.

Aurora remained peaceful until September 7th, but that night more than made up for the respite. An hour or two after sunset, one of the more popular local coffee bars went up in flames. Despite the best efforts of the local fire department—and the fact that the bar was glass-fronted—none of the customers managed to escape the blaze. In fact, none of them even got out of their seats. The official reports suggested that fumes had overcome the unfortunate victims before the fire became obvious. The fact that all fourteen had been killed by a single brutal slash to the throat (so savage that two of them were almost decapitated) was not made public. The city was shocked and traumatized— only three of the victims had been older than twenty-two—but even so, it might not have been disastrous.

Just a few minutes before dawn on September 8th, however, a prominent merchant banker named Brendon Douglas was stabbed through the heart with a two-foot long oak stake and left in the middle of one of the more popular commuter routes into Chicago. Rather than simply run the body over, some Good Samaritan stopped and called the police and ambulance services. Officers were unable to reach the scene before the sun rose, and Mr. Douglas, a who had quietly been a resident of Illinois for more than one hundred and fifty years, was consumed by fire. Police enforced another news blackout, rounded up as many of the witnesses as they could find, and explained all about modern terror techniques, incendiary devices, booby traps and so on.

Three doubters required extensive memory modification, and one unhappy local journalist had a tragic accident that night, but some witnesses must have already made off, because the story started to spread. Some of the wilder rumormongers were linking it to the other incidents and suggesting that Aurora was haunted, or that a bunch of kids were under demonic possession. The Prince of Chicago asked for urgent assistance later that night, and was granted the immediate services of the nearest archon.

Lucky me, Theo thought sourly. Four weeks of investigation into the Milwaukee incident straight down the drain. Paschek had not been sympathetic, however—"I'm not interested in your theories, *Archon* Bell. Mortals are mortals. Your job is to enforce the traditions, not to invent new enemies. We have more than enough of those as it is. Find the idiots responsible for this mess and kill them before they make things even worse. That's an order."

When Theo got to Aurora on September 9th, he discovered that a couple of the locals who fancied themselves as sleuths had been poking around over the last twenty-four hours and already had some good leads. They were as concerned as the rest of the city's vampires, and seemed genuinely pleased to see him. Their prime suspect was—surprise, surprise—an anarch group, supposedly holed up in a disused commercial building on the Aurora-Naperville border. The locals had even drawn Theo a little map, to show him where the unit was. They'd stopped short of decorating it with doodled hearts and flowers—but only just.

The unit wasn't anything special to look at from the outside. Some distance away from its nearest neighbors, there was nothing about it that would attract attention. Its shabby chain-link fence surrounded a big, concrete yard, already a bit straggly with weeds. The gates had some weather-stained signs warning trespassers away, but no logos or other identifiers. The building itself sat to the back of the yard, long and fairly low. The windows and doors were all boarded up, and twelve-foot metal shutters sealed off a loading bay or warehouse entrance. A tall Dumpster stood in one corner of the yard, near a stack of empty wooden pallets, bits of scrap metal and other miscellaneous crap.

A guard walked slowly around the front of the unit. He wore a tacky brown-and-khaki uniform—particularly nasty in the piss-yellow light of the streetlamps—and carried a nightstick and a flashlight. He looked like a standard rent-a-cop, slouching around bored with stooped shoulders and a bit of a paunch. Theo had been watching him for thirty minutes. The man spent a little over ten minutes loitering near the front corner of the building looking out over the yard, then walked along the front, checked round the back briefly—only the front had windows—and then returned to lurk at the other corner.

As soon as Theo was satisfied that the guard had his back to him, he crossed the road and crouched down by the edge of the fence keeping the Dumpster and pallets between the guard and him. He put his shotgun down, then grabbed hold of the bottom edge of the fence, and peeled it up from the ground very slowly, to minimize the noise. It was a lot tougher than it looked. He could feel the blood seething in his muscles as he strained to open a gap he could fit through. When the space was finally big enough, he slipped through, pulled his gun in after him and then forced the fence back down into some sort of rough approximation of shape again as slowly and silently as he'd opened it. Absently rubbing a grumbling shoulder, he scuttled behind the stack of pallets.

The guard had paused in his pacing and was looking over in Theo's direction. That settled it; his senses were uncannily sharp. The guard pulled out his flashlight, thumbed it on and shined it toward the

Dumpster and pallets, shading his eyes from the glare of the streetlights with his other hand. Theo cursed softly to himself and froze in place. The guard took slow, uncertain steps toward his hiding place. An almost overpowering urge to leap up and rip the enemy into bloody shreds surged through Theo, but he crushed it ruthlessly. *Softly.* After a long, lingering stare, the guard sagged a little, then turned round and continued his walk.

As soon as the guard went round the side of the building, Theo leaped up and ran across the yard. The blood burst into his muscles, hot and fierce, filling him with its power. At the edge of his vision, the fence blurred as he shot forward like a bullet. He held his shotgun tight against his side, to stop it from bouncing, and went straight to the left-most window. Thirty seconds didn't leave much in the way of slack. He looked around cautiously, then put his gun down and pushed on the board blocking the window, softly at first, but quickly piling on pressure. After a few moments, it started to give way with a soft screech of tortured nails.

As soon as one edge came loose, Theo grabbed it to stop the board falling and kept the pressure on. With a small popping noise, the board gave way, slipping back against what felt like thick drapes. He braced his forearm on the empty window frame and managed to keep the board from hitting the floor. He lowered it gently, grabbed his gun and slipped inside. He pushed the drapes aside and propped the board back in place.

Theo checked his watch. Twenty-two seconds total.

It was darker inside the building, but not pitch black. The drapes covered both windows—even more of a giveaway than the ghoul on patrol out front—but the door to the room was open, and a dim light shone in from the corridor.

The room he was in appeared to be a disused office.

There was a desk and chair, and a bookcase, but all of it was covered with dust and cobwebs, and there was no sign of paperwork or personal effects.

Theo leaned up against the wall for a moment, closed his eyes and concentrated on the feel of old, dusty rooms and disused emptiness. His mind calmed, and the world seemed to take a slow, reluctant step back. The impression solidified into a strong sensation of dislocation, and he opened his eyes, feeling a little more secure.

He moved to the doorway, keeping out of the light just in case, and listened for any sounds of activity. After contenting himself that there was nothing to break the silence, he stepped back into the shadow of the room and looked out into the hallway.

The corridor ran for a hundred or more feet of cheap green-checked vinyl flooring and institutional yellow walls. A number of dead light fixtures hung from the ceiling. Only the one at the far end was actually working, but the naked bulb was just about enough. Every twenty feet or so, a door opened up to the right, toward the front of the building, helping to break the monotony a little. Theo waited quietly for a moment or two, then started down the hallway cautiously, holding a mental image of the empty corridor, checking the hunting knife in his belt as he did so.

Most of the doors along the hallway were open. Theo approached each carefully, looking through the doorways as much as possible before passing the open space. The rooms all looked as neglected as the one Theo had broken into, a succession of dusty, crap-filled offices and storerooms. When he finally got to the end of the corridor, he waited for several minutes. There were occasional faint noises, but even he couldn't make them out, so he tried the door slowly. It opened easily, and he slipped through and into the broad hallway beyond.

The new area marked the obvious transition from office space to commercial activity. The floor and walls were bare concrete, adorned here and there with a variety of graffiti tags, scrawls and signs. Some sort of glass-fronted control booth was a short distance off to the right, and to the other side of the doorway, a flight of concrete steps led upward. The hallway itself terminated in a large, solid-looking door, and there were definitely voices somewhere on the other side. After the quiet of the last quarter hour, the noise grated on his nerves like a scream.

Theo paused for a moment to build an image of an expanse of plain concrete, then crossed quickly to the control booth and looked around. Several banks of miscellaneous switches were obviously connected to a variety of systems around the building. An old fire route chart on the back wall of the booth gave a stylized layout of the building.

It appeared that the sturdy door at the end of the corridor led straight out onto a large, open work space. Smaller rooms opened off it along the far wall. It would probably have been used as warehousing originally, or as a site to base an assembly line of some sort. A high balcony wound around three sides of the space, leading to a long room that ran the length of the far wall, above the smaller rooms below.

Satisfied, Theo left the control room and started quietly making his way up the stairs. He was just past the halfway landing when something made him nervous—a scent in the air perhaps, or a sound he hadn't quite noticed. He froze in place, listening carefully. A quick, faint rustle of clothing informed him that someone had just shifted position, some feet past the top of the stairs by the sound of it. Theo gently lowered his gun to the floor, pulled his knife out and tucked himself in against the left-hand wall of the staircase. He then continued up slowly, as soundless as a ghost, the image of empty stairs held firm.

When his head reached the level of the top stair, Theo froze again and looked for the source of the noise he had heard. A door maybe ten feet away led out onto the balcony. A man lounged in the doorway, all black leather, silver chains, spikes and wild hair, casually dangling a light automatic weapon of some sort from one hand. He was watching something going on in the room downstairs, looking vaguely disgruntled. He didn't breathe.

The guard had his back to the stairs, so Theo continued up silently, coming into a crouch as he reached the top. Staying close to the wall, Theo crept toward him. As Theo got close to the door, the guard turned idly on some half-perceived awareness, and shot a glance back down the stairs. Theo froze, just a foot or two out of optimum strike range, and thought about concrete walls, and being an unobtrusive part of the background. The guard's glance swept right over him, and the vampire turned back to watching the proceedings below.

Two more steps, and Theo suddenly forced himself into top gear. It was as if the blood instantly boiled throughout his body. He felt the pressure of it, raw energy bursting out into his muscles and filling him with power. The world crashed down around him, slipping into slow motion. He shot straight up out of his crouch, clamping one hand round the guard's mouth and effortlessly plucking the gun away from his loose grip with the other. He then pulled back away from the doorway and toward the stairs, dragging the guard with him. Before the punk had even had time to blink in astonishment, Theo had him pinned flat on his back at the top of the stairs, the blade of the hunting knife pressing cruelly into his throat.

Theo put a bit more pressure on the knife blade, letting it cut skin and draw a few beads of blood, and stared into the guard's frightened eyes, his gaze drilling holes in the back of the punk's skull. The vampire's will was flabby from years of thoughtless self-indulgence, and further weakened by fear, shock and lack of conviction. It was pathetically easy to crush the veneer of rebellious ego and get through to the frightened little child beneath.

"Stay exactly as you are until I release you no matter what happens, without moving a muscle or making a sound, and I might let you live." The guard nodded once, softly, already terrorized into obedience. Theo eased off him a bit, and when the punk didn't react, he cautiously took his hand from his mouth, ready to slam it back down if he started to call for help. The guard just lay there, as mesmerized as a rabbit caught in headlamps.

Theo took the clip out of the vampire's gun and left him there, went back to get his shotgun, and then focused inward again, stilling his mind and thinking about the dark concrete floor. Everything seemed to go soft around the edges again. He crossed to the doorway, looking out. The balcony was concrete-floored, with a flimsy metal fence along the open side. Beneath the balcony, the warehouse floor stretched out for quite some distance. The big metal doors were visible at the far end, still closed. The place had been decked out like some sort of slumland studio apartment. Off to one side, a mess of old sofas and chairs surrounded a battered TV, stereo and other bits and pieces.

Further in, several large workbenches held all sorts of bits of electrical, mechanical and chemical equipment, a mad scientist's personal junkyard. There even appeared to be a microwave oven. Nearer to the door, about a dozen people sat in some sort of meeting around two tables run end to end. By the way they moved, maybe five or six were vampires, the rest presumably ghouls. At the far end, a pair of terrified-looking mortals were gagged and bound to their chairs. Theo settled back into the shadow of the wall and crept around the balcony, crouched almost out of view, his mind full of shady concrete.

"I've had word from one or two of the usual sources. The inbreds are absolutely shitting themselves—running around like headless chickens. They don't know what's going on, and they're scared to move in case they make things worse. One more push, and they'll agree to anything to head us off."

The speaker stood up, leaning over the table to emphasize her words. She was a tall, slender woman with long red hair that cascaded down to her waist, blond streaks running from each temple down her mane's entire length. Her face was deceptively angelic, and something fascinating about her suggested power. She wore a tight-fitting black one-piece with a sharply studded belt fastened around her waist, with a billowy white shirt thrown over everything.

"We're taking a hell of a risk, Polly. What if they decide to fight back? I've got a real shitty feeling about this." This was from a tall, heavy-set man with cropped black hair and a face heavily tattooed with mock-Celtic spiral designs around his eyes and cheekbones. Despite the tattoos, his accent sounded local, and his voice was deeply concerned.

"What are they going to do? They don't know where we are, how many of us there are, or even that we're definitely responsible, and on top of that, the Minneapolis Triangle is making them all nervous. They're not going to risk their precious asses. We're perfectly safe. Besides which, don't forget that Janos is watching the Aurora Elysium. If they started mobilizing or anything, he'd call. If they do anything, we'll just split, nice and easy. We've still got that squat up toward Milwaukee. They'd never find us there."

"I dunno," said a slim, blond-haired young man in jeans and an Iron Maiden T-shirt. "I reckon Rod's got a point. The zoo was fun, and those cops had it coming, but we shouldn't have cacked that blue-blood. Not like that. The fucker was gagging for it, but leaving him out like that... I don't like it. We went too far.

We should get out while we can." Some of the others around the table were nodding in agreement.

Theo came round the balcony to a point just a short distance from Polly and froze in place, his nerves singing their tension. He forced his thoughts still, and let the world wash over him.

"If you're scared, maybe you *should* fuck off." Polly's voice was dripping with scorn, and even up on the balcony, Theo could feel the force of her willpower crackling behind it. "I don't have any use for little boys who don't have the balls to stand by their decisions. We agreed. *You* agreed, Mark. I thought maybe you were enough of a man to teach those fuckers a lesson."

The blond guy squirmed uncomfortably. "I got what it takes, Polly, it's just…" He trailed off, cowed by her glare.

"It's just what, Marky?" She sounded threatening. "D'ya want me to kick you out? You want me to make you go back to sucking dick for the inbreds?"

"No Polly, don't do that. Please." Mark's voice was suddenly small and broken.

"Pull it together then, you spineless bastard. Tomorrow night is going to be hard enough as it is. Rod and I will need everyone on their A-game." Polly let some of the scorn—and compulsion—fade from her voice. "You're all clear on how to turn someone into a vampire, yeah? Drain 'em dry, then feed 'em some of your blood, and wait around for half an hour. Doesn't take much. Easy as pie. We've got plenty of blood left over from that donor van still, and I've got backpacks for all of us. They're not particularly 'street' I'm afraid, but they'll hold a dozen bags easy."

"How many should we do?" The new speaker sounded meek, as if she were unwilling to risk aggravating the redhead any further.

"Three or four each will be enough. Leave them three bags of blood, show them how to seal their place up, and tell them not to venture out under any circumstances. Make up some bullshit about it being fatal or something."

"We're going to be dangerously exposed if you expect us to go back to their homes to drop supplies off every night." Rod still sounded concerned.

"We'll have the inbreds over a barrel. There'll be something like twenty clueless newbies hidden all around the city, with no idea of what to do, how to behave, or how to hide what they are. If they take one of us out, that'll be four time bombs waiting to explode as soon as the hunger gets strong enough." A cold shiver ran down Theo's spine at the thought of it.

"They could make us talk," pointed out Rod reasonably.

"They'd never be able to be totally confident they got all the newbies," replied Polly smugly. "There's no way they'd risk it. Not when they're already this scared. They'll give us the border territories here without a fight, and our new recruits will give us the manpower to hold them off. We'll be totally safe by midnight tomorrow. Freedom from the fucking Aurora Mafia at last."

The plan was dangerously clever, up to a point. Theo sighed silently to himself, but Justicar Paschek's orders had been absolutely explicit. The people responsible were to be killed. The way Theo saw it, that meant the leaders. Paschek hadn't said anything about balky lackeys. He brought up his shotgun with glacial slowness. The trick was to do it slowly and casually, so that everyone else—who'd so willingly convinced themselves he wasn't there—had no reason to go back on that decision. It wasn't something that came naturally to Theo, but long nights of practice had paid off.

"What about the Justicars?"

Maybe Rod had a touch of second sight. Theo took aim at Polly's head.

"What about them? They won't dare risk it either,

and once it's done and we've apologized, we'll be almost thirty strong. We can't—"

Theo braced himself and pulled the trigger. There was an immense roar and a cloud of smoke as the pellets tore down and struck Polly in the face. She didn't even have time to scream. Her face pulped, and her body fell to the floor like a puppet with severed strings. A moment's shocked silence followed. Theo could feel the fierce urge to lose himself in slaughter, but he pushed it down ruthlessly, cocked his shotgun again, then cursed. The mechanism had jammed.

As the floor below erupted into a chaos of screams and babbling, Theo leaped up, vaulted the banister and landed with a loud thud in the middle of the table. There were a number of further screams.

Theo's blood surged, white hot, and his muscles blazed, screaming their protest at being forced to move at such speed. He ignored the discomfort and launched himself at Rod like a missile, catching the astonished vampire high in the chest with a fist like a hammer. As Rod fell backward in his chair, seemingly moving through molasses, Theo darted round behind the vampire, grabbed his head and snapped it down toward the back of the seat. There was a loud crack as Rod's neck broke. Theo then ducked back out of the way of the falling chair, bared his fangs and tore at the paralyzed vampire's throat, biting down hard across it and ripping it out with all his strength. Rod was truly and finally dead before his chair hit the ground.

Theo stood up, blood dripping down his chin. The shocked vampires and ghouls reacted now, backing away and drawing weapons. The fury roiled within him, and the urge to leap at the next victim built with every moment. He wanted to rip and tear and shred, to destroy these stupid children, to pile their skulls… Theo fought it with all his will, and managed to lock the feeling down. He wiped the gore from his mouth absentmindedly.

"Your leaders have been judged guilty of breaking the first, second and sixth traditions by Jaroslav Paschek, Justicar to the Inner Circle of the Camarilla. They have duly been executed." Theo watched the group tensely, the blood within him screaming its need to rend and tear. He fought hard to make his voice slightly more conciliatory. "You do not need to follow them."

The survivors facing him paused, uncertain. One or two seemed to think about bringing weapons to bear, but others were more reluctant, and he could clearly hear someone whisper his nickname, Killa B. Sometimes notoriety had its advantages.

Off to one side, an unknown voice spoke up, heavy with scorn. Theo risked a quick look away from the main pack, but he couldn't see the speaker. "Asshole. We don't have leaders. We're a collective."

There was a crash of glass, and a ball of flames erupted at Theo's feet. He leaped, but not before feeling the fire bite into his flesh. The burning flames seemed to ignite the rage in his mind, and then his carefully erected barriers crumbled, and everything went red.

... *a sense of movement and speed... blood pounding through his veins... a fleeting pain in one shoulder... enemies, all around, to be destroyed... tearing and rending... a splash of wetness... the dance of hectic battle... the feel of flesh and skin lifting away from bone... targets falling... a fresh victim cowering... a reluctant thought intruded: Defenseless prey was no challenge.*

The red mist wavered, and Theo remembered himself enough to fight to get his control back. Slowly, grudgingly, the battle madness parted and cleared.

The thin, blond vampire, Mark, cowered on the floor in front of him, sobbing brokenly. Theo looked around. The room was a charnel house of broken bodies and torn limbs. Apart from the mortals trying desperately to escape their chairs at the end of the table, and Mark in front of him, everyone else was dead. Theo's thigh and stomach both blazed with pain, but his right shoulder was absolute agony. He was dangerously low on blood, so hungry he could hardly think. He must have been burning it like it was going out of fashion. Ironic, given that he was drenched from head to toe in the stuff. A wave of weakness rippled through him, and he swayed before regaining his balance.

"Get up, kid. Mark, whatever. Get up."

Mark broke off his litany of pleas and looked up uncertainly.

"Go on, get the fuck out of here. Leave the area. Go out west or something. If you hook up with any more damn fool idealists, tell them what I'm like when I'm pissed off. Now go on, get. Now!" Theo barked the last word, and the kid finally leaped to his heels and ran as if hell itself pursued him.

Theo walked slowly down the table to where the two mortals—teenagers, boyfriend and girlfriend probably—were still wriggling frantically against their ropes. He walked round behind them and crouched down, putting his hands on their shoulders.

"I'm sorry, folks. You shouldn't have had to see that." He sounded shockingly tired, even to himself. The kids looked at him, somewhere between petrified and hopeful.

He considered trying to crush their memories, but with no real idea of how much time they'd been imprisoned, it was going to be risky at best—and he was a long way from best. There was no choice. He sighed, then stood up, took hold of the girl's head and twisted it around almost a hundred and eighty degrees in one sudden, violent action. As she slumped back dead against her restraints, he leaned down and sank his fangs into her boyfriend's neck, and drained him dry.

***

Later, when the punk-ass guard had been released, and he and his ghoul companion outside chased off, Theo turned the site over to the grateful locals to clean up and went back to the room that they had set aside for his use. He had a long, hot shower, trying to drive away some of the night's memories with scalding water, and left his clothes outside for cleaning during the day. Finally, he fastened the door, pushed some furniture against it and prepared a few nasty surprises for any intruder. He was just about to settle down to sleep when his cell phone rang. He answered it without even glancing at the caller.

"Bell."

"Good morning, Archon Bell." It was Paschek.

"Good morning, sir. Do you require my report?"

"I have been fully briefed regarding the night's events, thank you. I wanted to congratulate you on your enthusiasm." Paschek's voice was cold and mocking. "I understand from the local primogen that you left quite a mess for them to clean up. They were particularly impressed that you somehow managed to scatter an arc of brain tissue across a twenty-foot high ceiling, and to distribute another victim over four thousand square feet of floor space. That is quite an achievement, even given your predilections. You should be proud."

Theo didn't trust himself to answer.

"I assume that there were no, ah, loose ends?"

"No mistakes," said Theo coldly. "Those responsible have been executed, and witnesses pacified."

"Good. I want you out of there first thing tomorrow night. You've got an old friend to visit."

Theo paused, confused. "An old friend? I don't understand."

"Your presence has been requested. In Minneapolis. Personally, by a certain Angus Abranson."

Angus? Theo's mind whirled. "Thank you, sir. Goodnight." He cut the phone link and lay back down, stunned. *Angus*.

chapter two:
rough handling
(london, 1888)

"The thing to remember, Theophilus, is that the English have made a virtue of their repression and suspicion. No, not just a virtue. They actually take pleasure in it, as if it were a fine brandy, to be savored at leisure." Don Cerro smirked at Theo from across the gently rocking carriage.

Theo nodded, not knowing whether his sire expected a response or not.

"Ah, but you are confused as to my purpose in this instruction, I see. Look out across Hyde Park, Theophilus, and tell me what you observe." Cerro pointed out of the right-hand window.

Theo shrugged. "Gaslights. Grass. Trees. Several wealthy couples strolling around on the paths."

"That is correct. Now, tell me what you do not see."

Theo paused, confused. "I don't see…" *Daisy's bloody face, dead eyes staring out accusingly.* "There's all sorts of things I don't see."

"You do not see groups of friends, laughing together and taking pleasure in the warm evening. You do not see children playing. You do not see any lone women. You do not see the poor. You do not see any person actually enjoying himself."

"Are you saying that they don't know how to relax?"

"It is more than that, Theophilus. They are taught that they may be observed at any time, and that it is a great matter of shame to be visibly having a good time. Their Queen Victoria does not approve of such foolishness, so they concentrate on keeping their personal inclinations hidden away, where others cannot see them. That means that they have had to learn to gain pleasure from the act of hiding their emotions away."

"So the implication then is that they are used to lying and manipulating, and that they cannot be trusted?"

Cerro laughed, a rich, pleasant sound. "No one can be trusted, Theophilus. But the English will not show you how they are truly feeling—and if they do, then beware, for the exposure makes them feel vulnerable, and they can become vicious in an instant."

"I'll be careful," said Theo, slightly offended. "It's not as if this is the first party I've been to over here." He bounced around a little as the coach pulled out of Hyde Park, past a large, gleaming archway, and down along the main thoroughfare of the Park Lane.

"I know you will, Theophilus. Just remember their repression. Displays of emotion are considered boorish, and they will derive pleasure and status at your expense if they can make you betray your feelings openly."

"This party is starting to sound better and better," said Theo dryly.

"Ah yes, that reminds me. One last thing, and London is very different to Paris: The English loathe intelligence, difference, anything above the ordinary. It reminds them of their own inadequacies, and they become extremely jealous. The French are always delighted to meet someone with a keen intellect— proud even—but the English will hate you for it passionately, so do not be too quick to demonstrate your wit. Let them feel superior about your humble beginnings instead, and they will love you for the opportunity to improve you."

"I will not be patronized by overprivileged

dandies," said Theo, face like stone.

Don Cerro arched an eyebrow. "Then I suggest you do your best to ensure that no one speaks to you, for even the mortals there will mostly be under someone's protection." He leaned forward, swaying with the coach, his voice turning earnest. "Seriously, Theo. Do not underestimate these English. They are extremely dangerous, and will knife you in the back as soon as look at you, telling their friends how charming you are even as they do it. They are vicious and devious manipulators, and hide their spite perfectly, behind exquisite manners."

Theo shook his head in disgust. "I'll be polite, I promise."

"I know this is a trial for you, Theophilus. Trust me, however. These weeks will stand you in excellent stead. Our kind is ever given to plotting and malice. Once you have experienced London, you will be ready for any situation."

The coach pulled up outside an expensive-looking residence. A sign declared that this was Merritt House. Through the tall iron gates, Theo could see a stretch of lush garden isolating the house from the road and from its neighbors. A tall servant of some sort stood attentively by the gate, wearing a formal black and gray uniform. As soon as the coach came to a halt, he came over to the door and opened it. His eyes flickered over Theo's face and hands before he turned his attention to Don Cerro.

"May I announce you, sirs?"

Cerro handed over the beautifully prepared invitation that he had received, and with a faintly mocking grin announced "Don Cerro de León and Mr. Theophilus Bell, to see Doña Merritt."

The servant smiled blandly. "Welcome to Merritt House, gentlemen. If you'll follow me?" He turned, opened the gates and led them along a pebbled path that led around between the finely trimmed rosebushes and down along the side of the house. Small gaslights set at ground level ran along the path, providing plenty of light to navigate by. They turned a corner and came out onto the edge of a large paved terrace. Maybe a dozen over-dressed guests stood milling around in small groups, talking quietly. Past the edge of the terrace, ornamental gardens stretched out some distance, with a tightly trimmed hedge maze lurking past the flower beds, bushes and pieces of statuary. The grounds were an extravagance in crowded London. A few small knots of people could be seen out in the gardens, past the terrace.

The whole yard stank of opulence, and Theo found himself wondering how many people were forced to live in slums so that their hostess could have all this space, and how many more of them were kept in near-slavery to tend her property. The familiar anger rose within him, and he forced his mind away from the subject.

The servant who had led them to the terrace stepped forward and clearly announced "Don Cerro de León and Mr. Theophilus Bell." There was a sudden hush as everyone on the terrace stopped talking and turned around to look at the two of them. After a moment or two, the conversations resumed, but most of the guests continued staring, seemingly thoughtful.

The servant bowed once and retreated. A blond, wasp-waisted woman in an obviously expensive wine-colored gown stepped up into the space that the servant had vacated, smiling brightly at them both. "My dear Don Cerro. I am *so* glad you could make it tonight. You're looking as dashing as ever."

Cerro took her offered hand and kissed it extravagantly. "That is a great compliment indeed, coming from the loveliest rose in all of London. You honor us. We are indebted to you for your hospitality. May I present to you my protégé, Theophilus Bell?"

Lady Merritt turned to Theo with a dazzling smile that did not even get close to her eyes. "My, you *are* a big one. Most impressive. I have heard all sorts of extraordinary things about you, Mr. Bell. Welcome."

"Thank you, ma'am," said Theo, a little uncomfortably.

"Come, let me introduce you to some people who I know are simply *dying* to meet you." Lady Merritt's gaze encompassed both men.

Don Cerro smiled. "But of course."

Lady Merritt led them over to a small group of kindred near the back of the terrace. "My dear friends, allow me to introduce Don Cerro de León and Mr. Theophilus Bell. Don Cerro, I'd like you to meet Lord Palmer, Mr. Angus Abranson, and Miss Juliet Parr." They were a diverse group. Palmer was tall and thin, with an arrogant face and a pinched nose, and carried a silver-topped cane. Abranson was a little shorter. He looked rather like an artist, with lively eyes and a long shock of wavy brown hair. If his appearance was eccentric, it was nothing compared to that of the third member of the group. Miss Parr was almost as tall as Angus Abranson and wore a man's tweed suit, cut in a fashionable style. Her hair was pulled back severely away from her face in a simple ponytail.

"Charmed," murmured Don Cerro with a smile. "Hello again, Sheriff Parr. I trust you are well."

Juliet Parr nodded to him formally. "Archon Cerro."

"Do forgive me," said Lady Merritt insincerely. "I didn't realize that the two of you were already friends."

"We've run into each other before," said Miss Parr coolly.

Lord Palmer shot a quick glare at Theo, then turned to Lady Merritt and bowed elegantly. "Lady Merritt, Mr. Abranson, forgive me, but I shall take my leave. I did not come to Merritt House to fraternize with Negroes and Spaniards." He walked off, ignoring Theo's angry stare, and Don Cerro put a restraining hand on Theo's arm.

There was a momentary silence, then Angus shrugged and said, "Personally, I'm just as happy milord Palmer has chosen to retire. I didn't come here to socialize with self-important fools."

Don Cerro smiled deprecatingly, and said, "Every man is entitled to his feelings."

Juliet Parr raised her eyebrows. "Every man, Archon Cerro? What about every woman?"

Don Cerro let his eyes flick over her outfit. "What indeed, Miss Parr."

Her eyes narrowed dangerously, and Angus stepped in quickly. "Surely, the worth of any person is dependent upon his—or her—potential. Wouldn't you agree, Don Cerro?" He shot a meaningful look at Theo.

"Of course," replied Don Cerro pleasantly.

"And one's potential, of course, is dependent upon getting the best start in life," said Lady Merritt with a smile, clearly enjoying herself. "The poor unfortunates we have littering the streets have very little scope for potential, by virtue of the position they find themselves in."

"It could be argued that wealth and privilege lead to softness and complacency, while hardship breeds resilience and talent," said Theo, unable to keep silent any longer.

Lady Merritt laughed indulgently, and patted Theo's arm. "What a novel idea." She seemed about to say more, but stopped for a moment, listening carefully. "Please excuse me for a moment." She pushed past Theo and crossed the terrace, to where the tall, gray-clad servant was escorting another guest in.

Don Cerro seemed distracted by the new arrival, but Angus and Miss Parr were looking at Theo with interest.

"I think history would probably agree with you," said Angus. "Empires are built by hungry, aggressive generals, and lost by pampered nobles and small-minded bureaucrats. The bottom line is that the disadvantaged need to make themselves strong in order to advance, while the elite are only actually interested in maintaining things as they are, and often become weak. Those at the top may be the least useful in a crisis. Troubled times require troubled champions."

Miss Parr frowned. "That's by the by. Any society that denies opportunity and responsibility to one half of its population merely because of a simple accident of gender is in a great deal of trouble already."

Theo started to say something, but Don Cerro tapped him on the arm, and motioned him to follow. "Come, Theophilus."

Theo smiled an apology to Angus and Miss Parr, and reluctantly followed his sire to where Lady Merritt was talking to the new guest, a young noblewoman with flowing brunette curls.

Don Cerro smiled a predatory smile. "And just who is this fine addition to your fiesta, Doña Merritt?" The girl turned to look at him, and stopped, awestruck by the impact of his presence.

"This is Regina, a fine exemplar of English womanhood," said Lady Merritt, and laughed nastily. "Please excuse her gaping."

"Don Cerro de León." He bowed extravagantly, grabbed Regina's hand, and pressed it lingeringly to his lips.

"A pleasure…" mumbled Regina. She was barely able to speak.

"Oh," said Don Cerro, taking hold of her arm. "You have scratched yourself." He ran his fingers across the scratch, lifting the droplets of blood from her skin. Regina trembled. Theo shifted uncomfortably, then shrugged to himself. One less spoiled little girl was hardly a tragedy.

Lady Merritt snickered, and said "Please excuse me a moment. There are some things I must see to."

Don Cerro smiled dazzlingly at Regina, and said, "May I introduce my protégé, Theophilus Bell of the United States of America." The girl glanced at Theo obediently.

"Ma'am," said Theo, nodding briefly.

Don Cerro glanced at him mischievously. "Mr. Bell had the misfortune to be born in bondage, but had the wherewithal to escape and even seek justice against those who put him chains. To the plantation owners he was a monster, but to me a prize student."

Monster indeed. Theo didn't remember much about the night he killed his former master. Most of it was buried under a thick, red haze of frenzy. The one moment he could not forget, no matter how hard he tried, was coming to his senses in the slave compound. Daisy looked straight at him accusingly, her corpse torn open from sternum to navel like an overripe fruit. He was drenched in her blood. Theo tried to banish the memories and stared coldly at his sire. Spreading his story was one thing, but tormenting him in order to amuse an overprivileged meal was something entirely different.

"Mr. Bell does not enjoy it when I discuss these matters so casually. He finds it crass." Don Cerro smiled at the girl again, and she swayed even closer to him. "But he forgets our duty to serve as exemplars to others. His story is a powerful one, don't you think? Triumph over the limitations of race and society?" Regina gazed up at him mindlessly, and Theo realized that Don Cerro may as well be reciting cargo manifests for all that the words were registering in the girl's mind. He decided to get out of the way and leave his sire to his amusements.

"Excuse me," he said politely, then turned his back on the pair of them and walked across to where Angus and Miss Parr now stood, just inside the house.

"Sorry for departing so rudely," said Theo. "Don Cerro needed me to, uh, illustrate some points."

Miss Parr frowned slightly. "I hope he's not going to do anything rash."

"He is always mindful of the traditions," said Theo.

"That may not be enough," said Miss Parr bluntly.

"I'm sure everything will be fine," said Theo, more out of loyalty than conviction.

"Don Cerro seems to be an interesting person," said Angus mildly. "I sense an independent, even subversive mind under his charm. What is he like to know?"

"Perceptive, fair and without bigotry," said Theo wryly. "Passionate and quick to act too, though. He has taught me a lot, and I will always be in his debt for the tools he gave me to help me fight my former masters."

Angus nodded thoughtfully, and then glanced over to his left.

Theo followed his gaze and saw an attractive woman with long black hair making a beeline for him. She was wearing a red and cream gown, almost as tightly corseted at the waist as Lady Merritt was. She smiled invitingly at him and stepped up, putting a hand familiarly on Theo's forearm and drawing him slightly away from the others. He shot a wry glance at Angus and Miss Parr, and followed the girl, smiling politely.

"I am Amelia Downing, and you are Theophilus Bell. There, that's the introductions taken care of. Come, you may call me Amy, and I shall call you Theo. I've heard so much about you that I feel I know you already. It's a pleasure to meet you."

"A pleasure to meet you too, ma'am," said Theo politely, feeling nonplussed.

"Amy," said Amy firmly.

"A pleasure to meet you too, Amy."

She smiled at him. "There, that's better." Amy ran her hand along Theo's forearm and up to the shoulder, and murmured appreciatively. "You are strong, aren't you. I'd heard of course, but…"

Theo looked at her blankly, and she shook her head quickly.

"It's of no matter. Tell me Theo, I've heard you traveled in Europe before coming to England. Were you there long?"

"Several years," said Theo. "Madrid, Vienna, Florence, Prague, Berlin, Amsterdam and, most recently, Paris."

Amy smiled indulgently. "My! Quite the grand tour. How does London compare?"

"I'm not really sure yet," replied Theo diplomatically.

"You must have some first impressions," said Amy.

"Well, it's certainly very grand," said Theo, trying to stay on safe ground.

"Yes," said Amy thoughtfully. "I suppose it must be, for someone of your, well…" She waved a hand absently in his direction. "Heritage."

Theo's hackles rose, and the rage surged within him briefly, turning in its sleep. "Are you referring to my color, my pedigree or my nationality?" he asked coolly.

Amy laughed brightly. "Well, all three I suppose. It's no wonder you've become so strong, living under such *savage* conditions."

Theo blinked in surprise.

"It must have been terribly exciting though," she said eagerly. "You must tell me all about it."

"What must have been exciting?" asked Theo warily.

"Why being a slave of course, silly. I'd imagine being a Negro is quite dull."

Theo fought to keep his face still, determined not to let the fury show. He told himself firmly that he could do this, that he'd endured worse a thousand times over. He fought the anger back down, so that it almost didn't thicken his voice. "I'm not sure that exciting is the right word. Horrific is probably closer."

Amy nodded eagerly, and when Theo didn't go into detail, she grabbed him by the hand and pulled him toward the stairs. "Come with me, Theo. There's something you simply *have* to see."

"I'm not sure that's a good idea," said Theo cautiously. "I should wait here for Don Cerro."

"No, you must come along now, or I shall get dreadfully offended. Come along. You should be used to taking orders." She smiled at him.

Theo fought down a low growl, and looked around him, but there was no one else in the room to use as an excuse.

"Come *along*, Theo," said Amy, starting to sound petulant.

Remembering his promise to Don Cerro, Theo reluctantly let himself be dragged upstairs. The furnishings and decorations were lavish, but he wasn't given any time to stop and look at them in detail. Amy pulled him along a corridor and into a small bedroom.

Theo looked around, puzzled. "What did you want me to look at?"

"Is it true?" asked Amy, an odd glint in her eye.

"What is going on?" asked Theo suspiciously. Amy stepped up close, and pressed her body against his, leaning her head on his chest. "Don't you want to kiss me, Theo?"

"I'm not sure that would be proper," he said carefully. He could feel the warmth of her flesh. She was no kindred. *Even the mortals*, Cerro had warned.

Amy surprised him by pulling him forward and then throwing her weight against him. Caught off balance, he stumbled back against the bed and fell onto it, Amy still clinging onto him. "What do you care about proper for? You're not one of us."

"You're very right about that," said Theo, openly angry now.

Amy shifted her position so that she was lying on top of him fully, and kissed him rapidly several times, on the lips and cheek. The fury was getting harder to control, and he wanted nothing more than to drink the bitch dry. Don Cerro's warning came back to him though, and he resisted the urge to rip into her. She kept kissing him breathlessly, talking through the kisses, her voice slurring.

"Come on, slave. They say that niggers have cocks as thick as a baby's arm, and that you're so rough, it's like fucking a wild animal. Show me."

Theo tried to push her off, but she wrapped her legs around one of his, darted inside his arms and continued with her fevered kissing. "I want to taste that black skin of yours. They trained you to talk better than I expected, but I want to see the real savage." She bit him, hard, on the shoulder.

Reflex took over, and he slapped her away before she could draw blood, knocking her back onto the bed. He rose up immediately, took a couple of paces and turned away from her, clinging to his self-control with the last shards of his willpower.

"That's better," purred Amy, panting hard. "That's a good little nigger. Now do as you're told, slave, and come here and fuck me like a beast." He didn't move, and she paused for a moment, and rustled as she adjusted her position. *"Look at me!"* she shrieked, and Theo turned round, nervous of attracting attention from elsewhere in the house.

Amy was lying back on the bed, her skirts hitched up to her waist and a bruise already forming on her cheek where he'd slapped her. She had no undergarments at all, and her legs were spread wide open, exposing her wetness. Theo froze, astonished.

"I bet you've never even fucked a white girl before," said Amy, reaching down to stroke herself. "Come on, what are you waiting for? I'm better than any saggy nigger bitch. Come on, slave. Obey your betters."

Theo was moving before he realized it. He leaned down and hit her again, across the mouth this time. Hard. He finally stopped fighting the fury and welcomed it instead. He could feel his face contort with the loathing he felt, lips pulling back into a savage snarl. When he spoke, he barely recognized his own voice. "If you don't get out of here right now, I'm going

46   SLAVE RING

to rip your heart out of your chest and stuff it down your throat." He stood up and pointed at the door. "Go."

Amy wailed wordlessly, leaped up off the bed, and dashed out of the room. For a moment, the urge to chase the fleeing prey and hunt it down was so strong that Theo's nails drew blood from his clenched fists. He stood in the same spot for a long time then, slowly regaining some mental equilibrium.

Eventually, Theo left the room and headed for the stairs, Amy's frenzied behavior running over and over in his mind. As he headed down back toward the parlor, there was a faint scuffing noise from above him, and then something extremely hard smashed into the back of his head. Theo fell forward and crashed down the stairs, tumbling head over heels. He finally landed at the bottom, too dazed and pained to move, and two pairs of hands grabbed him and dragged him a short distance. Then they threw him down another staircase, and the world went away.

***

A thin line of agony erupted across Theo's back, bringing him back to full consciousness. He heard a loud crack, and a second line joined the first, suddenly horribly familiar. It felt like fire. He bit back a howl, and tried to move, but he was restrained. He realized that his arms were stretched up over his head, chained tightly to a thick wooden beam. There was a third crack, and a new bar of pain. He was having trouble focusing his eyes, and he blinked several times, trying to see what was going on. Slowly, the room swam back into view. He was in a dimly lit cellar of some sort, barefoot and naked from the waist up. He tried to see who was whipping him, and caught a glimpse of a small crowd of unfamiliar kindred standing behind a tall figure in a black formal suit, with a black hood pulled over his head. The hooded figure swung his whip again, cutting deeply into Theo's back.

"Look, I think it's awake." A woman's voice, unfamiliar.

"About time too." This voice was male.

"We don't like niggers," said a third voice, male again, rougher than the first two. "We especially don't like vile slime who try to rape our girls."

There was a particularly loud crack, and Theo's back blazed. He tried to protest, and realized that his mouth was firmly gagged with a wad of cloth.

"We seen what you did to poor Lady Amelia," said the rough voice. "It's a miracle she managed to escape you. I'm just glad she came to us to sort it out."

The whip-wielder continued striking, time after time after time, the pain in Theo's back getting steadily stronger and more urgent. Someone in the crowd had started clapping a little with each stroke, and if the lash was particularly vicious, it might even raise a small cheer. The hooded whip-wielder paused for a moment, and walked in front of Theo, who was sagging, exhausted and agonized, against his chains. He stepped back and lashed Theo hard across the chest, cutting into him. Theo moaned in pain, jerked back reflexively, and then jerked forward again as the movement made his back blaze with agony.

The hooded man raised his whip handle and waved it at Theo's face. "Do you know what we're going to do, nigger?" It was the same rough voice as earlier. "We're going to douse you in brine in a minute, once I've cut you up a little more, and then we're going to whip you back into your stinking grave for once and for all."

"No," said Don Cerro, his voice coming from over to one side. "You are not."

Theo barely had time to register that help had arrived before there was a blur of motion, and then Don Cerro was in front of him, with the hooded man's arm twisted behind his back, and one hand clamped around his throat. A murmur of dismay rose from the small crowd behind Theo. "You are evidently not Prince Mithras. You do not have the right of destruction. I, however, do. I have found you in the act of breaching the sixth tradition, and that entitles me to end your pitiful existence." He looked up at the rest of the crowd, who were muttering angrily, and turned the full force of his awesome personality on them. "You are all complicit. Interfere, and you will die." He gave the whip-wielder's arm a savage wrench, and the man howled in pain as his arm shattered at the shoulder, elbow and wrist.

"That's enough, Cerro." Theo looked round, and saw Juliet Parr standing in the doorway.

"You again," spat Don Cerro.

Miss Parr ignored him. She pointed at someone in the group behind Theo, and said "You, release him." As someone leaped to obey, she turned back to Don Cerro. "Give that one to me. This is my territory, and he falls under my authority. Both he and the girl will be punished."

"Go to hell," snarled Don Cerro.

The blazing pain in Theo's shoulders suddenly abated as his arms were freed, and he dropped to the floor. As his mind cleared enough to think about his wounds, the blood inside him rushed to his back, and the skin started knitting together. It felt uncomfortably like worms burrowing through him.

"If you spent more time looking after your own protégé and less time feeding off other people's, this would never have happened," Miss Parr said coldly. "As I seem to be pointing out a lot tonight, if you do not watch over your companions, then others will. This is my jurisdiction, and if you act, you will bring all sorts of trouble down upon your head. More than you or your protégé can survive, perhaps, and certainly more than I want to be bothered with. Do not make more of a fool of yourself than you already have."

"Thank you for your advice," said Don Cerro

angrily, dropping the moaning whip-wielder and standing up. "Come, Theophilus. It is time for us to leave." He walked out of the room without so much as a backward glance, deliberately treading hard on the masked man's shattered elbow as he did so. Theo forced himself upright, and gingerly followed his sire. Several pairs of unfriendly eyes watched him go.

chapter three:
A parliament of crows

The basement was filthy, and it stank of decay. The little paint that remained was cracked and flaking, the wall underneath streaked with black waves of damp rot. The dust and debris of chronic neglect littered the floor. Someone had squatted in the building at one point and had left behind a small pile of trash and some miscellaneous stains. Still, the door down into the room was sturdy, lockable from both sides, and there was nothing about the building to attract any attention. The neighborhood itself was largely disused, so Kristine could come and go as she pleased without attracting any attention. Besides, she'd stayed in worse. Much worse.

She looked down critically at the pile of assorted papers and other bits spread out over the floor—old leads, used-up clues, information that she no longer required—and spread it around a bit with her foot, just double-checking that nothing important had slipped in. She spotted a photo from New Haven, a smug-looking Meonia blue-blood coming out of an office, and smoothly picked it up, adding it to the file of still-current data under her arm. That was it though, so she put the file with the few personal things she still had and scooped the rest of the crap into a trash bag.

Kristine had been in Minneapolis for just

under a week, and had been productive so far. Four objectives successfully dealt with. She checked the time and decided to make her way to the phone booth. She grabbed the sack of old papers, locked the door on her way out, pushed past the piles of old bedding and slipped out the back door. She vaulted fences easily, crossing several backyards before reaching the sidewalk past another dark, boarded property.

The streets were quiet, few cars and no pedestrians, but she kept to the shadows as much as possible anyway, stopping only to toss the sack into a handy trash can. She arrived at the booth with several minutes to spare, and the chances of anyone else coming to use it were very nearly zero, but she went over to it anyway. The whole booth was so covered with graffiti that it took her a moment or two to verify that the telephone hadn't been vandalized. She waited impatiently until exactly 10 p.m. She dialed the number she had been given.

"Speak." An electronic filter made the voice utterly unrecognizable. Kristine couldn't even tell if it was male or female.

"One aim." She smiled grimly at the irony.

"I am one," replied the voice, completing the exchange.

"So, what you got for me?" asked Kristine.

"It has become known to me that members of the society will be at a warehouse on Nicolet Island tomorrow at 1 a.m. to close a deal involving a pair of mortals, red-haired twins. It is important that the deal should not go ahead."

"It'll be a pleasure to piss on their fireworks," said Kristine with feeling. "Do you know anything about the security arrangements?"

"There will be little or none. They are relying on stealth."

"Good. It's done."

"Excellent. The address is 1026 East Island Avenue. Good luck."

"Won't need it," said Kristine as she put the phone down.

***

The Minneapolis Institute of Arts was a natural choice for Elysium. It was a beautiful, sprawling white building with elegant columns in a neo-classical Greek style, attractively worked and set in lavishly tended grounds. Just as importantly, however, late-night comings and goings went unnoticed among the cleaners, researchers and so on. Tasteful frescoes showing a range of artistic endeavors hung above the main entrance, reinforcing the impression of cultural dominance. Soft spotlights set around the building at ground level cast just enough illumination to make the institute glow. Very symbolic. *This is art*, the building declared arrogantly. *Everything else is inferior*. Theo rode round to the parking lot, left his bike in a disabled-access bay and went round the back, to the staff entrance.

The back of the building was less illuminated and had a more practical feel to it, although it was still impressive. Following the instructions that Paschek had passed on, Theo crossed to a plain wooden door and pressed the third buzzer in a column of seven. A panel slid back, and a thin-faced vampire peered out. He eyed Theo up and down slowly, and arched an eyebrow.

"Yes? May I help you?" The vampire's voice was reedy and nasal. Whoever it was who'd embraced him, it wasn't for his charm.

"You've got that the wrong way round, friend," said Theo flatly.

"That seems unlikely," said the vampire, sneering faintly.

"Look," said Theo coldly, "I'm tired. Just let me in."

"I hardly think so." The sneer was open now. "The prince is in court, and doesn't want to be bothered by riffraff off the streets."

"So will *you* tell him that you refused to admit the archon he requested?"

"*She*—and please, do you think me a child? Any cheap madman can put on a Yankees hat and a pair of sunglasses and claim rank."

Theo sighed, then flashed a hand out, grabbed the offensive doorkeeper by the chin, and pulled his head hard into the door. The vampire yelped and tried to pull away, but Theo held the doorkeeper fast, his muscles seething with blood and power as the vampire tried to escape the grip. Theo then bent down and looked the fool straight in the eyes. He felt the rage boiling within him, the urge to rip the offensive idiot to shreds, and could feel it thickening his voice, darkening his stare. "Do you really think there's anyone in the world stupid enough to pretend to be me?"

The vampire suddenly became even more pale, and stopped struggling against Theo's grip. "Archon Bell, I'm so sorry. Please forgive me. I never dreamt that... if you'd forewarned..." He trailed off nervously, and there was a loud click as the door lock was released.

Theo pushed the door open hard, letting go of the vampire as he did so. There was a dull clatter as the man fell over. He walked in, slamming the door behind him. "Didn't they tell you I was coming?"

The vampire shook his head, and stayed where he was, sprawled on his back. "No sir, I had no idea. I'm extremely sorry. No offense was intended."

"It's my fault, I'm afraid." A cultured, deeply mellow voice suddenly spoke up from behind Theo.

Theo spun round, a smile flickering across his mouth, his anger already subsiding. "Angus!"

"Hello, old friend. It's good to see you. How the devil have you been?"

"Busy," said Theo dryly. "I like to make sure Paschek doesn't have any excuses to ream me. How about you?"

"Enjoying the quiet life," said Angus, smiling. "Minneapolis is a good place to be, and my kindred here seem to like me well enough. I'm sorry about Gary. I had a number of calls to make this evening, and I forgot that I hadn't told him you were expected."

Theo shrugged. "He seemed to remember his manners eventually."

Angus glanced over at Gary, still sprawled on the floor. "I'll bet." He gestured at the doorkeeper irritably. "Go on man, get up."

"Of course, sir." Gary scrambled to his feet.

"That's better," said Angus. "Theo, my friend, you must be exhausted. Come on, let's get the formalities over with so you can unwind. It's quite a drive."

Theo followed Angus down a corridor and through into a wing of offices. The corridors were blandly institutional, occasionally punctuated by presumably expensive works of art. Theo and Angus walked past a number of deserted offices, and a small refreshment area complete with water cooler, kettle and fridge, before Angus pressed his palm against a small scanner and led them through a security door.

The prince turned out to be holding court in a fairly small boardroom, a beige office dominated by a locking nest of pine desks that formed an island in the center, surrounded by padded chairs. The prince sat at the head of the table, flanked by a selection of other vampires. Like Angus, the

Prince of Minneapolis was of Toreador lineage. And like most kindred of that line, she was almost uncannily beautiful. Long, straight black hair cascaded to below her waist, framing a face that managed to combine sweetness with intelligent reserve. Her eyes were a deep, soft brown, with a sparkling hint of unspoken promise. She was shorter than average, but Theo felt as if her size was proper, and he was the one who was at fault. She... Theo took hold of himself, and forced the impact of her presence down by sheer, stubborn force of will. Angus shot him an amused glance.

"Ladies and gentlemen, this is Archon Theo Bell, representing Justicar Jaroslav Paschek for Clan Brujah. He's here to help out with our little problem." Theo nodded politely to the collected primogen, and the prince inclined her head, gravely. Angus gave them a moment, then continued. "Theo, welcome to the court of Elizabeth, Prince of Minneapolis."

"It's a pleasure to finally be able to meet with you in person, Archon. Thank you for responding to our call so quickly." Elizabeth had a lovely voice, dark and smoky, with a hint of a foreign accent.

"All part of the job, ma'am," said Theo.

The prince smiled warmly. "Welcome to Minneapolis. I hope we shall have an opportunity to talk while you are here. You are certainly welcome to make use of our facilities for the duration of your visit. I'm certain that Angus will make sure you are well taken care of."

"Thank you."

"Enjoy your stay, Archon Bell."

Angus touched Theo's shoulder and led him back toward the doors. "Okay, that's done. Now we can see about setting you up with a guest room." He led Theo back toward the doors, but a tall, slender vampire in an expensive suit got up from the table and crossed the room to intercept them. He smiled mirthlessly as he approached. "I do hope you weren't going to whisk the archon off without giving the rest of us a chance to say hello, Angus."

"Christopher. Good evening." Angus didn't sound particularly pleased to see the newcomer, and turned to Theo. "Christopher represents Clan Tremere."

"Indeed," said Christopher. "Lovely to meet you, Archon. I must say that you seem even more formidable in the flesh than your reputation had led me to believe. Your vigilance and zeal is a great comfort in these troubled times."

Theo's eyes narrowed, and he stared at the Tremere piercingly, looking for any hint of sarcasm or mockery. Finally, he shrugged and said, "You'd be surprised at the things some kindred think they can get away with."

Christopher smiled coldly. "Perhaps I would, Archon. Tales of your exploits seem to reach us up here with a surprising regularity. The reports of your adventures in Memphis were most impressive."

Theo glared at the Tremere.

"Forty-three dead, including four of the blood," continued Christopher, ignoring Angus's hiss of disapproval. "No survivors, am I correct? Not even the captives."

"They were killed before I could get to them," said Theo flatly.

"Of course," said Christopher insincerely. "You deal with a lot of very twisted individuals. It must be difficult to stop all that corruption from rubbing off on you. I commend you for your resilience."

"I'm stronger than I look," said Theo, his voice like ice.

"Yes," said Christopher. "I imagine that you would be."

"You'll find it's a common feature of our clan," said a short, flamboyantly dressed blonde man from behind the Tremere.

"No doubt you consider that a virtue, Simon," said Christopher, not bothering to turn round.

"An asset," corrected Simon, smiling at Theo. "Archon Bell, I do hope this tiresome old windbag isn't boring you too much. We try to keep him safely restrained in a quiet corner when guests drop by, but sometimes he slips his leash."

Theo grinned nastily. "I'm sure it's just the long ride catching up with me."

"Of course," said Simon. "We should leave you to refresh yourself. Come along Chris, there's a good boy. Elizabeth sent me to fetch you."

The Tremere scowled at Simon's retreating back, then followed him at a certain distance.

"Sorry about that," said Angus. "Simon is right. The Tremere *is* tiresome. It's nothing personal, though. He's like that with everyone."

"Perhaps he's a frustrated harpy," said Theo, with a tight smile.

Angus laughed. "You know, I think you could be right on the mark there. Sharp as always, eh?"

"Years of practice, old friend. Years of practice."

Angus headed out across the galleries, and Theo followed. "I'll sort you out with somewhere to stay. The prince keeps a set of guest suites within the building, hidden away under the staff area of the institute. They're totally secure, and none of the mortals who work here during the day even suspect their existence. Acceptable?"

"That's great," said Theo. "Thank you."

"Before I leave you to it, I need to brief you on the problem we have here."

"Yes," Theo said wryly. "That would be useful."

Angus paused by a door clearly marked "No Access," thumbed a code into the keypad, and let Theo through. The corridor beyond was as plain as the rest of the office suite. They continued deeper into the building, passing offices, meeting areas and other rooms, then going down a couple of flights of stairs to a sub-basement. Off to one side, Theo could make out several large workrooms, cluttered with long benches, crates and boxes, and all sorts of craft tools. Angus punched a code into another keypad, and then pressed his palm against a sensor plate.

The door clicked, and Angus led Theo through into a functional reception room. The carpet was deep green rather than brown, thankfully, but the overall effect was still like something out of a highway motel. The painting hanging above the small pine desk was almost certainly original, but it might as well have been a cheap 3D effect print of a leaping tiger. The furniture looked perfectly serviceable, however, and everything seemed fairly new.

"This is the main guest suite," said Angus, sinking into a comfortable armchair. "Not the most beautiful surroundings ever, I'm afraid. The other suites are more or less the same, though."

Theo shrugged. "It's all the same when you're asleep." A thought occurred to him. "Hey, Angus, tell me something, will you?"

"Of course," said Angus immediately.

"What in the name of hell is the Minneapolis Triangle?"

Angus blinked, and his face fell. "How did you... Um, look, it's nonsense, just hearsay and idle speculation."

Theo arched an eyebrow. "So there's no harm in filling me in on it, then."

"I suppose not," said Angus, resigned. "It's just not something that any of us want to encourage."

"I'll bear it in mind as you explain," said Theo.

"Very well," said Angus. "Cutting to the core of the matter, certain statistical reports appear to indicate that the Minneapolis-St. Paul region has seen a sudden rise in missing persons over the last twelve months."

"Is that it?" asked Theo, slightly incredulous.

"Well, more or less. There have been a number of rumors surrounding vampires vanishing from the area, particularly transients, but there's nothing unusually sinister about that. Minneapolis isn't the only city, either. Half a dozen places across the country have seen significant rises in cases of missing mortals."

"So how come it's got its own nickname?"

"Who can tell? It's one of those peculiar byproducts of the modern imagination. Some lunatic or other somewhere must have got a bee in his bonnet and started publicizing his theories, which were then taken up by the credulous, the bored and the stupid. It's probably all over a website somewhere, whatever that entails."

Theo laughed. "I take it you haven't spent much time getting acquainted with the Internet, then."

"Why should I bother? It seems an ugly, blunt thing, full of lies and advertising. If there's any difference. It certainly can't help me hunt, or guard me when I sleep."

"It is a good source of reference information," said Theo.

"Perhaps, but I have an excellent library of my own. It's all too much effort for too little return. I don't have the patience for mortal toys any more."

"I've found it useful," said Theo mildly.

"Of course," said Angus, "You always did like to keep in close contact with your relations. I'd imagine that this email thing is extremely handy for that."

Theo nodded. "Very. It lets me keep an eye on things from afar. You might like to consider it for that reason alone."

Angus shook his head. "I lost track of my descendants a very long time ago."

"The Internet could probably find them for you again. I've made mine useful."

"In all honesty, my friend, I couldn't care less. Too small a potential return again."

"Of course," said Theo, letting the matter drop. "Anyway, I assume that the problem you've called me here for is nothing to do with this Minneapolis Triangle, right?"

Angus nodded. "Absolutely nothing. We've got a rogue in the city who seems determined to tear the place up, and we're having difficulty pinning her down."

Theo looked at Angus, surprised. "One rogue?"

Angus smiled at him. "Well, we're not at full strength at the moment. Elizabeth has a couple of scourge packs out and about at the limits of her territory, and that's depleted our general pool of enforcers. The rogue seems to be a bit better organized than most, but she's distressingly noisy. Even so, she's not leaving any trails, and we can't find out where she's lairing. Still, none of that would necessarily be a problem. We've set a number of people out looking for her however, and she's avoided them all, almost as if she knew they were there. I'm worried that she's being fed information by someone on our side, so turning to someone on the outside—someone impeccable—seemed like a sensible decision. I know you're incorruptible."

Theo decided to let that pass. "You have a description?"

"Yes. We've spotted her a couple of times. She's about 5'4", slim, with shoulder-length black hair. She's rather striking."

"But you haven't been able to follow her?"

"No. She's extremely fast, and she seems skilled at throwing off pursuit."

"Do you have any leads at all?"

"It's not much, but yes. Apparently there's a rumor that suggests she may attempt to break into a warehouse on Nicolet Island tomorrow night."

"Really? Why?"

"We're not sure. It's not associated with any activity that we know of."

"I mean where does the rumor come from?"

"A couple of street types claim to have sold her information."

"But why tomorrow in particular?"

Angus looked a little uncomfortable. "I don't know. That's just what the rumor says. Maybe something is scheduled there."

Theo's eyes narrowed. "Okay. I assume you haven't called me in just because she hasn't presented herself to the prince like a good little girl. What's this so-called rogue been up to, anyway?"

"Ah, yes. Well, she's been rather prolific. Over the last six days, she's killed one kindred—a Ventrue, high-ranking—along with a total of six ghouls associated with a number of different individuals, and two mortals who were foolish enough to get in her way. She's also destroyed two houses, both in the better parts of the city, both linked to kindred interests. We're doing what we can to keep public reactions under control, but that's quite a spree in anyone's language. On top of that, last night she also broke into a set of offices downtown, killed two cleaners and one executive who was working late, burned some files and destroyed more than $15,000 worth of computer equipment. She threw it out of a fifteenth-story window into the street, in fact."

"I'll need details on the attacks—the victims, the properties and companies, and so on. How confident are you that this warehouse is a solid lead?"

"I really can't sensibly guess. Either way, it's the only useful information that I can offer you."

"I suppose I should go stake it out a bit, check the insides, see if I can get a bead on her."

"There seems little point tonight, to be honest. It's getting late. I'd leave it until tomorrow."

"If you say so," said Theo. "Anything else I need to know?"

"I don't think so," Angus said. "We've been unable to find any links between the victims— the attacks seem random—but I'll get as much information as I can brought down for you. Oh, there is one thing actually."

"Yes?"

"The keypad to get in here. The code is C5XY, and then you have to press your palm against the sensor to complete the action."

Theo frowned uncertainly. "How did you get my palm print into the system?"

Angus grinned. "Oh, we didn't. It's thermal. It looks for any hand, and if that hand is above room temperature, it doesn't open."

"Clever," said Theo.

"It can be useful," said Angus. "We have quite a lot of utterly clueless staff here during the day. Speaking of which, the door does have several sturdy bolts on the inside, to enable you a reasonable guarantee of security. This entire institute is considered Elysium, but you can never be too careful."

"Oh, I'll be careful," Theo said. "That's a promise."

"Then I'm happy," said Angus. "I know what your promise is worth."

"You should," Theo said with a smile.

"No one better," replied Angus. "Right, I'm going to leave you to relax for a while. You must be keen to unwind after the long journey. I'll have those files sent down for your attention, but if you want anything in the meanwhile, the telephone on the side there will connect you to the prince's hospitality staff."

"Thank you, Angus," Theo said. "Good to see you."

Angus paused in the doorway. "You too, old friend. Welcome to Minneapolis."

chapter four:
monkey business

Nicolet Island had been home to industry and commerce during the sixties and seventies. Sometime during the late seventies though, conditions had changed. The companies moved out, leaving a whole load of empty warehouses and factories behind. Most of these buildings looked as if they'd remained empty ever since, a ghost town of boarded-up windows and weed-filled yards. There were signs of change though. Population pressures and the constant need for more accommodation were making redevelopment profitable at last, and one by one, the old warehouses were being converted into apartment blocks or condo developments. The old and tired being dressed up in a shiny new suit and pressed into service once more. Still, plenty of units remained untouched, and the derelict and the fashionable rubbed shoulders in high contrast.

East Island Avenue was still mostly undeveloped, with large patches of parkland and other greenery breaking up the old warehouses. It looked a bit tattered, worn around the edges. *Too many years and not enough care*, thought Theo wryly. The unit in question was a large, hangar-like warehouse with a nest of offices and other buildings close in along the near side. No lights were visible, and the gates looked as if they'd been open for the best part of twenty years. There wasn't anything in particular to distinguish it from any of the other units. Theo stopped a couple of hundred yards down the road, coasting his Yamaha into the tree line on the opposite side of the road from the warehouses. He used the cover of the bushes and trees along the strip of park to push the R1 back to a position almost opposite the open gates. When he was satisfied that neither he nor the bike were visible, he settled down to watch.

The warehouse seemed to be a surprising choice of target for the rogue. Her previous attacks had been against local kindred and their property, but there was no suggestion in any of the material that Angus had provided that the warehouse had ever even seen a vampire. It had belonged to a construction company in the sixties, who had used it to store lumber and other materials, but they had gone bust by the end of the decade. The building was now owned by a large life insurance firm, held against potential land values in the future. No one would care if she torched the place. In fact, she'd probably be doing the owners a favor. Theo shrugged and settled down to watch. He closed his eyes and concentrated for a moment, building up a careful picture of bushes and trees, and slowly felt reality slip away from him a notch. He opened his eyes again, confidant that he'd effectively vanished from sight.

It was almost midnight when the rumbling drone of approaching engines warned him that several vehicles were approaching. He checked his cover and continued waiting. Two minutes later, a small convoy of vans drove up the road and pulled steadily into the warehouse. They headed round the side, stopping somewhere just out of view. Theo was perversely pleased; while they muddied the waters a lot, at least they indicated that the warehouse was used for something, which made the rogue's interest a lot more understandable. He immediately decided against investigating the vans. The rogue wouldn't be among them, and whatever the new arrivals were up to, it wasn't his business.

Flashes of movement indicated that the occupants had posted at least two sentries. That would make it a bit trickier to get into the building when the time came.

It was approaching half past midnight when Theo heard the steady crunch of footsteps approaching from the parkland behind him. They were cautious and deliberate, but almost comically loud, as if an elephant were trying to sneak up. It didn't fit with the way the rogue had been described. Puzzled, Theo turned slowly and scanned the area. A tall, skinny, gray-haired man in camouflage pants and a bulky hunter's slicker was heading toward his general location, eyes fixed on the warehouse. There was a chill in the fall air and his breath was clouding just a bit—a mortal. That explained the lack of stealth. The man gave no sign of having seen Theo, and eventually crouched down in the shadow of a tree less that eight feet away.

Theo sighed to himself, shook his head, stood up slowly and stalked over to where the man was studying the warehouse. Then he reached down and snapped an arm tightly around the man's throat. "Give me one good reason why I shouldn't just kill you right now," he hissed.

The man bit back a startled yelp. "Where the hell…" He paused and gathered his thoughts. "Listen asshole, I'm wired with enough explosive to blow your fucking factory to smithereens, and I'm holding the detonator. Kill me, and you're paste. Now back off, slowly."

The mortal sounded sincere. Theo released him and took a couple of slow steps back. "What the hell are you doing out here?"

The man stood up and held his closed hand out

from his side so that Theo could see it clearly. He was certainly holding something that could have been some sort of crude switch, and wires ran from it up into the sleeve of his slicker. He reached down to his side with the other hand, pulled up an automatic pistol, and pointed it straight at Theo's face. "I'm going to go get my daughters back, you stinking piece of shit, and there's nothing you can do to stop me."

Theo reached out for the man's mind and grabbed it, smashing his will down into it. "Lower that gun and sit down."

The man obeyed instantly, cowed.

"Right, let's get some things straight. One, I have nothing to do with whatever is going on in that warehouse. Two, I don't give a shit about you or your threats. Three, I'm busy. Four, you're in my way. Five, I can stop you or kill you before you even have time to blink. Six, you're going to fuck off back to wherever you came from. Right now." Theo reached out mentally and piled crushing pressure onto the man's thoughts as he spoke the last two words.

The man started to rise, then stopped half-crouching, shaking slightly. His face paled and his eyes dilated, but he shook his head stubbornly, and his mind flared hard with diamond edges of desperation. Theo looked at him, astonished.

"N... No. No way." His voice got stronger. "No way. You're going to have to kill me. I'm dead anyway, if I let those sickos take my girls. Fucking slavers is what they are, can you believe it? Besides, what's it to you?"

Cold fingers of ice stroked their way down Theo's spine. "Slavers? What do you know?"

The man spat on the grass, and when he spoke, his voice was thick with fury, disgust and grief. "The fuckers abducted my daughters two days ago. They're planning to sell them tonight. As slaves. I'm not going to let that happen. Can you imagine what they must be going through? Knowing they're going to be sold into Christ alone knows what sort of torment, no idea of where in the world they are, no way to escape, forced to…" he broke off with a choke, and spent a couple of moments regaining his composure. "They're seventeen, man. Can you imagine what they must be going through?"

Theo nodded quietly. "Yes. As a matter of fact, I think I can."

"Then you know why I'm going to get them out at any cost," said the man. "*Any* cost."

"How do you know they're there?"

"A sympathetic whistleblower. He called me last night and told me what had happened, and where and when the fucking *sale* was taking place. Said that abducting my girls was going too far, and he wanted to help me stop it."

"Are you certain he was genuine?"

"He knew stuff that he couldn't have known. Details about the girls. Where and when they vanished. Stuff like that. I went back to where he said the snatch happened." His voice faltered, and he paused for several seconds, breathing deeply. "I found a ribbon of Nathalie's."

"No cops?"

"I called 'em but the fuckers won't even open a file till they've been gone forty-eight hours or some shit like that. Runaways is what they called my girls."

"What else did this whistleblower tell you?"

"Not much. Just that these perverts sell people as fucking slaves to clients all over the globe, and that this is just a drop site for them, nothing more."

Suddenly, the convoy of vans seemed a lot less irrelevant, and the Minneapolis Triangle came back to mind. Eventually, the mortals would be forced to pay attention, and if some idiot vampire was behind it, as the rogue's interest suggested... "Did your source give you his name?"

The man shook his head, weary. "You've got to be kidding me. Even his voice was all garbled and shit. Look, I'm running out of time here. I'm going in." He looked up at Theo plaintively. "You look pretty good in a fight. I could really use your help. They're just kids. Please?"

"You can't go in," said Theo. "You have no idea of what you're up against, and you'll screw up my work."

The man grimaced, resigned. "I don't have any choice, buddy. I can't stay here and let my girls become slaves. You might as well kill me right now, because that's the only way to stop me." His voice hardened a little, getting colder and more defiant. "Remember their names, though. Delphine and Nathalie. You'll be the one responsible for the shit they're going through. I want you to think about that from time to time. If you survive the blast."

Theo stared deep into the man's eyes, crashing into his mind, trying to crack through his will power. "Stay here," he thundered.

The man cringed back and started trembling, but he shook his head again, first slowly and reluctantly, and then with mounting conviction. "No."

Theo shook his head in wonder. The man had to be borderline suicidal. Although he was thin, he looked comparatively fit. If the bomb was real and not just a fantasy, trying to disable him was a risk, particularly if it was a dead-man switch. Theo shook his head irritably, frowning. "All right, tell you what, I'll get them for you. I need to go in there and look around anyway. But you have *got* to stay here. You'll make my task impossible."

The man looked nervous and uncertain. "I don't trust you. Sure, you're a big guy, but that doesn't count for much. Why should I leave it to you? I did my time in the forces."

"Remember how you didn't notice me until I had my arm round your throat, hero?" Theo's voice was sarcastic.

"Hey..." the man suddenly sounded awed, and some of the confusion and fear lifted from his face. "You're some sort of special forces Op. That's why you were asking... I should have guessed."

Theo simply looked at him flatly, saying nothing either way.

"Hah! I knew it! Well, it just so happens I remember what you bastards are like," said the man, his voice suddenly going cold again. "Accidents happen, eh? Promise. Promise me you'll see my girls safe, and I'll keep out of your way."

Theo nodded his head, reluctantly. "Fine."

"Say it," said the man. "Like you actually think I should believe it."

Theo hesitated for a long moment, reluctant to commit. Getting two girls from a bunch of mortals didn't sound all that hard though. And being sold into slavery... He drew himself up to his full height. "I swear that I will do all I can to bring your daughters to safety."

The man sagged, fear, desperation and hope mingling visibly across his features. "Okay. But if you're not out in half an hour, or anyone tries to leave, the deal is off."

"What do your daughters look like?"

"5' 7", slender, shoulder-length red hair. Pretty, and it's not just me who says it. They're identical twins, but Delphine wears her hair straight, while Nathalie has hers wavy."

"All right," said Theo. "You'd better give me your name too, so they know to trust me."

"Pierre," said the man. "Pierre Decourt."

Theo stared down at the man, and nodded

grimly. "Okay, Pierre. Now wait here silently for me without taking any further action, however long it takes." He drilled the words down through the mortal's suicidal desperation, forcing them in deep. This time, there was no resistance. Finally.

Theo turned his back on Pierre and walked a short distance next to the sidewalk, staying within the tree line. He paused, calming himself down and focusing on the empty scene in front of him, and the night gradually slipped out of phase. Then the blood caught fire inside him, filling him with power, and he shot across the road.

The wall was only seven or eight feet high, so Theo took advantage of his momentum and leaped, vaulting it. He caught the top edge as he cleared it and used the grip to stop himself. He hung from the wall for a moment, then silently dropped the couple of feet down to the ground, crouching down into the shadows as he did so. He looked around carefully, watching for guards or signs of alarm, but there was nothing to suggest he'd been spotted. Staying low, in the wall's shadow, he slowly made his way round the far side of the warehouse, away from the offices and vans.

The rear of the unit was all much the same—no doors, but plenty of windows. Theo picked his way along cautiously, staying silent. About halfway along, he caught a shred of quiet conversation drifting through a broken window and spotted a glimmer of light. He ghosted over to the window.

"I am not comfortable with this arrangement, Liam." The voice was cold, and despite the low volume, Theo could still hear an unmistakable note of power behind it. Kindred, probably. The situation was getting worse and worse by the minute. Theo cursed bitterly to himself.

"What's wrong? We chose this place, so it can't be a setup." A second speaker, nondescript, with a slight accent. Probably mortal. Liam, presumably.

"I am not certain. Something here is not right."

"Well, a special order as well as a mixed bag of standard merchandise is certainly an unusual choice for a private collector, but then your lot often do make some pretty wacky purchases."

"Do not presume too much." The cold voice got even icier. "You may lack the wit or education to see subtle patterns, but our association does not give you the right to mock me."

"I'm not mocking anyone, *old friend*," said Liam, with a surprising hint of steel. "Merely pointing out the facts. But any time you want to break off our partnership, you just help yourself. You'll be stuck right back where you started."

"Fool. I could own your soul."

"Yes, Matthew, you could, and then I'd be dead within twenty-four hours, and you within forty-eight, so it wouldn't get you anywhere. If you fuck with my brain, my boy will pick it up straight away, and then it's all over. Look, this is silly. Just relax, will you? I'm not poking fun at you. Your sort are driven by a wide range of compulsions."

Theo scowled unhappily. Matthew was definitely kindred and unless this Liam was too, there had been a significant breach of masquerade. He could be a ghoul—a mortal fed on vampiric blood—but then he should be a subservient toady, not a lippy motherfucker. This was turning into a shit storm.

There was a long pause. "Very well. I shall allow it to pass. It does not change the fact that I am feeling uneasy about this deal." Matthew sounded considerably less icy.

"Do you want to call it off, then? I trust your intuition, particularly when we're dealing with selling—or selling to—your sort."

Another pause. "No," Matthew said. "The total

sale is worth more than one quarter of a million dollars. It is a generous price, particularly for the stock cattle, and red-haired twins are a very specialized requirement. We would be able to obtain sixty thousand for the pair on the general market I suspect, given their physical appearance, but that would still be a considerable loss. We stay, until it is certain that we have been misled."

The memory of bile burned painfully at the back of Theo's throat as he struggled to control his nausea and rage.

"Whatever you say. That reminds me. Do we have any other special requests coming up? It's always good to give the teams some advance notice."

"Nothing that requires your involvement. You can be sure that I will advise you if anything is needed. How trustworthy is that girl of yours?"

"Ginny? Utterly. She's extremely good, too— just the right look and manner for a bagger."

"I think perhaps we should have her killed."

"What? Why?" Liam sounded offended.

"This was a highly sensitive acquisition. Mortals get particularly outraged about female adolescents. It may be safer to eliminate your operative and make it appear as if she was working alone."

"I don't think that's necessary. Ginny's a valuable resource, and it would be a shame to waste her. If you really want to hide the trail a little, we have someone similar in the pens who could take her place."

"I suppose that will do. Kill this substitute, have your operative's driver shot, and leave the corpses in an empty van. Make it look like one of your gang betrayals."

"Sure, why not," Liam said. "Miles is expendable. I'll get the license plates switched too, just in case."

"A very sen… Wait. I hear something. Silence."

Matthew paused for a moment. "There's an intruder!" Theo shrank back from the window, horrified. "There," continued Matthew urgently. "Out by the vans. Quick, see to the stock."

The vans? Theo relaxed momentarily as he realized that they weren't talking about him. It had to be the rogue. He looked through the window carefully. There were people running around at the far end of the warehouse, but no one near. Very well. He sprinted down toward the side of the building. As he approached the corner, the offices that he had seen from the park came into view. He could hear people running, and the quiet babble of excited voices. He risked a quick peek around the corner.

The doors to the warehouse were open, and three vans were parked up inside, in a roughly triangular formation. Several figures were darting around them busily, trying to stay behind cover. Others were out in the main yard, close by, some heading toward the office buildings while others seemed to be milling about. There was a general impression of urgency, confusion and threat.

A procession of figures filed out despondently from between a couple of offices. It was a slow column of individuals, locked into line. They were wearing fetters around one ankle, linked to a thick metal chain that stretched the length of the column, and their hands were shackled behind their backs. Everything swam red for a moment, and Theo had to concentrate fiercely to fight off the urge to just charge in. The column was being escorted, and one of the guards was haranguing the captives to pick up their pace, punctuating his hoarse curses with vicious slashes from a long, switchlike cane. Theo took a step forward before he'd even realized it.

"Hey! You in the corner!"

Theo looked round to see a tall, well-muscled figure standing at the edge of the office buildings, pointing directly at him. "Fuck," he muttered.

Suddenly three figures were running straight for him. Theo immediately slammed into overdrive, time stuttering as the blood ignited in his veins and energy flashed through his body. He looked around quickly for a makeshift weapon, something long, but there was nothing useful within range, so he whipped his hunting knife out of its sheath, readying it in a backhand grip.

He leaped forward in a long, rolling dive, slipping under the arm of the nearest enemy, who was a few heartbeats ahead. He came up in a crouch just a short distance in front of the two slower opponents, between them, and lashed out with both hands. He rose as he did so, aiming for the throats. To the right, the knife ripped straight through neck and lower jaw, blood immediately fountaining in a wide arc, but to the left he only managed a glancing blow to a shoulder. Theo was turning to face the man on the left even as his companion sank to the ground, gurgling nastily.

A faint noise alerted him that the first opponent was approaching again, from behind. Theo judged the distance, and made a feint toward the second enemy, his ferocious stare slashing through the man's already shredded nerves. The fool stepped back, and Theo ducked, grabbed above him for the arm he knew was coming and rolled forward, pulling his startled attacker with him. There was a muffled yelp, and the man flew into the other assailant, hard. Both went down in a tangle of limbs and curses.

Theo pounced, smashing his heel down into one throat and grinding it against the concrete of the yard, while his hands sought and found the other's head and twisted sharply. There was a moment of terrible resistance, and then Theo straightened his body, tightening his muscles and pushing all of his power into his hands and feet. An almost

SLAVE RING

simultaneous double-crack told him that both necks had snapped.

There was no time for taking chances. He dropped the one he had been holding, and then swiftly bent down and ripped both throats out with his fangs. A quick taste of the blood reassured him that both were fully mortal. He glanced over at the third figure. He was writhing feebly, crimson hands around his ruined throat, making unpleasantly soft gurgling noises. Theo left him to it.

The slaves were being herded beyond the vans. Theo darted toward the door, trying to catch up. There was a sudden disturbance from that direction though, and one of the overseers staggered back into view and collapsed. Theo slowed down cautiously. Something clearly wasn't right. He paused. There was a shockingly loud scream from behind the vans, followed by another and then another. Theo crouched and looked around the door, keeping his head at knee-height. A burly enforcer of some sort was standing behind it, holding a big, wicked-looking crowbar. He was glancing toward the vans, looking for the source of the scream. Theo flicked his knife to his left hand, then stood up smoothly and snatched the bar from the enforcer's startled grasp.

The man started to say something, but Theo whipped the crowbar up into a ready stance, and then smashed it down the man's chest and belly, ripping a long, deep tear, which he immediately followed with a savage crosscut of his knife, slicing across the man's gut. The words turned into a howl of pain, and the man doubled over, trying to clutch at his entrails as they spilled out of his abdomen in greasy, blood-soaked coils. Theo brought the end of the crowbar back up as fast and hard as possible, crunching up through the enforcer's lower jaw and deep into the back of his head in one smooth movement. The corpse collapsed, and Theo paused for a moment to wipe some of the blood off his hands and arms before pulling the bar back out of the shattered skull and hefting it thoughtfully.

Automatic gunfire chattered loudly nearby, and Theo's back erupted in a line of pain. He dove to one side immediately, the walls blurring as the blood screamed inside him, and looked back. A man was standing a short distance behind him with a small, snub-nosed SMG, pumping rounds into the spot Theo had just vacated. Mortal, by the way he was panting wildly. Theo dove as the gunman finally started to turn to follow his previous movement, slashing a wide backhand circle with his knife as he came up into a crouch. There was considerable resistance, but the blade didn't break. The gunman screamed, blood erupting in jets from his groin and upper thighs, and then he was falling in on himself.

Theo flicked the crowbar out as the body fell, caving the man's head in as if it were eggshell and cutting his scream off like a light. "No one shoots me, motherfucker."

He stood up again, hot blood worming its way into the wounds in his back and forcing them together again. The flesh crawled and writhed as the bullets were slowly pushed out. He shuddered a little, and looked around cautiously, ready to spring for cover. There was the sound of gunfire from behind a stack of wooden crates and pallets off to one side in the main warehouse. Theo went in cautiously, wiping blood off his face as he did so. A low gurgle came from behind the crates. Theo headed in that direction slowly, the blood within him singing its tension and filling his mind with tempting visions of slaughter.

As he came round the side of the crates, Theo heard a worrying gargle, and he paused for a long moment before carrying on. Behind the crates, the warehouse stretched back unobstructed for quite a distance. A man was lying on the floor, covered in blood. He was writhing about feebly, clutching at a deep rip in his chest and stomach. A striking woman was straddling his abdomen, holding him down. Her hair was black, reaching down to her shoulders, and she was wearing snug dark clothing. She looked up as he approached, and surprise flickered across her face. She arched an eyebrow.

"You? These goons really *must* have been naughty."

Theo shook his head. "I can't comment on the situation here, but you've certainly caused me all sorts of problems."

"Come on, the leaders are still out there." She stood up with a fluid, graceful movement. "I'm Kristine." She paused thoughtfully, then turned to look at Theo. A wry smile played over her lips, and she took several very swift steps backward, then darted over to a low crate at the side of the warehouse. "Ah, of course. You're not here for them at all, are you? You're here for me. I'm flattered."

"Yes ma'am, I'm afraid it's you I'm here for."

She flipped a catch on a long case resting on top of the crate and lifted the lid. "How on earth did you know I'd be here? I suppose that bastard set me up. No matter." She drew a long, elegant sword lovingly from the case. "I have to say, I'm a little disappointed to find the mighty Theo Bell running wetwork errands for a corrupt conspiracy. I'd heard you put some store in honor. That'll teach me to believe fairy tales."

"I just go where I'm told," said Theo guardedly, slowly circling around the corpse toward her.

Kristine laughed moving to keep the corpse between them as she closed the distance. "Ah yes, the famous SS defense. I'd have expected better, clansman. Did they even tell you why they murdered my coterie and wanted me silenced?"

"I know nothing about your coterie, but you have broken several traditions in this domain, and you endanger the masquerade in Minneapolis. You have been judged guilty and sentenced to execution by Justicar Jaroslav Paschek." Theo started stepping the other way, to cut off Kristine's line to the door.

Kristine circled away from Theo again, looking mortally offended. "Minneapolis? What about New York, Hartford and the rest? Do you really mean to tell me you've come to kill me for just a conspirator, some mooks and a database? Oh boy. You really don't know jack shit about this, do you? You're in well over your pretty little head, *Archon*."

Theo shrugged. "Like I said, I just go where I'm told."

"Like a good little drone," said Kristine mockingly. "They like a man with no mind of his own, I guess." She shrugged. "Come on then, big boy. Let's dance."

She leaped over the corpse on the floor like a streak, landing in a crouch at Theo's feet and whipping around in a blur. He jumped instinctively, blood flaring white-hot as it burned within him, filling him with power. Everything slowed, but even so he was still barely able to see her sword slashing round where his ankles had been. He landed immediately, snapping the crowbar forward to cut at her eyes as he brought his knife up into a parry. Kristine swayed backward at the last possible instant and turned the momentum of her spin into savage slash at his chest. He continued bringing the bar down and turned her blade aside with a clash of glacial sparks, his knife licking out at where she had been a moment before.

Kristine grinned. "You're superb," she said, taking a half-step back then lunging at his throat. Theo caught her sword with his knife and landed an ineffectual blow on her hip with the crowbar, and then felt a sudden, hot pain in his left leg. He glanced down at where she'd kicked the side of his kneecap, hard enough to almost dislocate the joint. He stepped back a pace, testing the leg and cursing himself for falling for the feint. "But I'm better," she continued. In the background, Theo could hear heavy doors slamming.

Kristine launched into a flurry of attacks, cutting high, then using the momentum of his knife-block to come down and probe repeatedly at his torso, breaking the pattern to nick at the back of his hand. Theo tried to keep up, the blood raging within him, muscles burning, but she was at least as fast as he was, and considerably more skilled. He jumped back toward the pallets, taking a moment to regroup, and discovered he was bleeding from four different shallow cuts.

"I've been wanting to go up against an archon for over a century," said Kristine, taking the opportunity to talk. "I hear Don Cerro was an exquisite fencer once. Your knife should more than make up for the lack of edge on your cudgel. You really should have studied more."

Theo made some quick estimates of distance, speed and weight. "Oh, we're full of surprises."

"I've heard that before," said Kristine, pressing forward once again. Theo fell back toward the crates, desperately using both blade and bar to parry her flickering onslaught. She smiled triumphantly as Theo got close enough to the wood to be restricted, and surged forward. Theo saw the movement start, dropped into a spinning crouch and darted sideways, then surged up behind her, dropping both weapons. She was turning even as he came upright, but he swayed inside her slash and smashed his forearms hard into the center of her chest, jumping up to put all of his weight and strength behind the blow.

Kristine was flung back into the side of a crate, which crushed under the force of the impact. Overbalanced, she fell back into the wreckage.

Theo followed her down, adding his weight to hers so that when they landed, the impact stunned her for a moment. As she tried to recover, he grabbed a shard of broken wood and rammed it down through the top of her left breast and into her heart, then stepped back. Kristine was frozen with her arms reaching out, a look of horror on her face.

Theo shrugged. "I did warn you, ma'am. Now, just you stay put please. I'll be back to collect you in a little while." He dusted himself down, then grabbed his knife and her sword—it really was exquisite—and sprinted round the crates. The vans looked prepared to go, drivers already in their seats. Two of the vans were closed, but outside the back of the third one, a tall, balding man was struggling with a young woman, who was flailing at him wildly. He looked up and saw Theo, and his eyes widened. He pushed the girl back and then leaned back against the van, pulled his legs up and kicked her hard in the chest, toward Theo. He then leaped into the back of the van and slammed the door. Immediately, all three engines started. The girl staggered backward, straight into Theo's path, and he had to drop the blades again and catch hold of her. As he did, the vans tore off screeching, out through the warehouse door.

Theo looked at the vans, then back at the struggling girl he was having to work to restrain. Long, straight red hair. Fairly tall. Slim.

Fangs, drenched in fresh blood.

"Oh fuck," said Theo.

chapter five:
principia Discordia

Theo cradled the sobbing girl gently, trying to make appropriately reassuring noises.

"I *ate* him," she wailed. Again. "He tried to grab me, and I just ate him. I *drank* his *blood!* I killed him!"

"I know," he said quietly, patting her awkwardly on the back. "Didn't he taste great, though?"

She paused at that. "Yeah. Yeah, he did. Better than a mud pie, even." The tears stopped momentarily. "But it was blood. I mean… eww. Blood. That's revolting. I want more." She suddenly burst into tears again. "What's happening to me? Oh god, I've gone crazy. First I go all gay, and now I'm a freaking blood fetishist murderer. Oh god, oh god."

"Shh," said Theo gently. "It's okay. It'll all be okay. Just tell me what happened."

"You promise?"

Theo winced. "What happened, Delphine?"

She looked up at him, suddenly scared. "How do you know my *name*? Oh god…"

"You father sent me. Pierre Decourt. To rescue you." The words tasted like ash. Great job he'd done so far.

"Is he…" She couldn't complete the sentence.

"He's fine," said Theo kindly. "I'll take you to him in a few minutes. I need to know what happened first, though. Please, tell me everything."

"All right." She sniffed, and wiped her cheeks.

Theo grabbed hold of her hand gently before she could see that she was crying blood, and held it, safely out of sight. "They brought us here. They were going to *sell* us! God, that makes me mad. How fucking dare they? I want to rip them to fucking little shreds. I want to…"

"Delphine," said Theo quietly. "Calmly."

She fought for a bit of control. "Yeah. Okay. They brought us here, and they locked us in a small room with some other prisoners, kinda unhealthy-looking mostly, and there was this one guy who was *really* pale and freaky, like half dead, and he was just sneering all the time. Nat and I were trying to keep away from the others, as much as the chains would allow, and praying for some sort of miracle. Oh my god, they've still got her. We have to go get her. We *have* to." She glared up at him. "We have to go get her *now*."

"Do you know where they were holding you?" asked Theo, gently. "Do you know where to go?"

She sagged against him, tears welling up in her eyes again. "No. Oh, Nat. No."

"It'll be okay," said Theo. "Please, carry on while I tidy up here a bit." He started going around the warehouse quickly, arranging bodies into plausible positions, distributing weapons and generally trying to make the carnage look like some sort of gang battle.

"Tidy up? Jesus. This is fucking freaky."

"It's my job, and I really need you to tell me what's going on so that I can do it."

Delphine sighed bitterly. "*All right*, already. So they were holding us in this room, and we were totally shitting ourselves and trying to hide it from each other, and all this noise and stuff starts erupting outside, screams and everything. We didn't know whether to hope or hide. Then a couple of the goons blast in, and they drag us all up and herd us out. There was loads of chaos and people running around shouting, and they took us into that warehouse.

"They were about to start loading us back into those creepy vans when this woman just strolled up to the goons and smacked them about like they were nothing, and then she practically ripped one of them apart, man. She was awesome, totally beautiful, really fit, and stacked too—you know, she was actually *hot*, and that freaked me out, because I don't dig chicks like that. I couldn't stop staring at her."

"I can imagine," murmured Theo, stashing his knife back in his belt, and putting Kristine's sword back in its case.

"Yeah, well, then she came over to me and snapped my chains like string, which was really weird now that I think about it. She looked straight at me, and I could hardly breathe, and then she smiled at me and said 'I'm sorry about this my dear, but I have to muddy your waters.' That didn't make any sense either, but then suddenly I was in her arms, and nothing seemed to matter." Delphine paused, and looked at Theo. "Everything?"

Theo nodded gravely, kicking the ruined crates around a little to disguise the obvious impact.

She sighed. "All right. She started kissing my throat, and oh my god, I've never felt anything like it. It was incredible, just *so* horny, and I couldn't think or anything. All I knew was that she felt like fire. I think I even came. I certainly blacked out a little." She paused. "Oh god, I'm gay, aren't I?"

Theo smiled despite himself, amused. "I don't think you need to worry about that."

"But she blasted me away man, and a minute ago you were holding me and like you're a total rock, *and* you're drop-dead cute, and I didn't feel anything."

"Like I said, I wouldn't worry about it."

She squinted at him suspiciously. "Something freaky's going on here, isn't it? What aren't you telling me?"

"Just trust me for a few minutes more, okay?"

She frowned. "Hm. Well, when I came round, the babe had her hand over my mouth, and I felt *really* shitty. I don't know what happened, but everything hurt. Then the pain sort of went away again, and the world seemed sharper and harder and more real suddenly. Then this goon stumbled around the corner, and..." She stopped and sniffled a little. "And I leaped on him and pushed him to the ground, and just bit into his chest. All this blood spurted into my mouth, and it tasted like nothing I've ever tasted, and I just sucked and sucked and sucked, until no more came. Then this other guy came by and tried to grab me, but he was too slow this time, and we were struggling, and then he kicked me away, and you caught me." Her voice turned angry. "Right, that's everything. So then, Mr. Just Tell Me What Happened, what the *fuck* is going on?"

"I'll tell you more later, but we're in a hurry. My name is Theo. The quick version is that something has been done to you that was done to me too once, and you're in a lot of danger now. You're going to have to hide from everyone. What was done was, well, illegal in effect, and if you are caught, you will be killed. You're going to have to leave this area completely right away, get away from all your former friends. Staying would be immensely dangerous. Do you understand?"

"No. No fucking way."

Theo shrugged from across the warehouse. "Fine. You will be dead within a few days at most, and your father will probably be killed as well, and there will be no one left to save your sister."

Delphine stared at him, horrified. "What?"

"I can only help you to help yourself, child. If you won't listen, you will undoubtedly die a horrifying death."

"Why?" She sounded stunned.

"People like us have to keep secret, so we have to eliminate all breaches of security. If you will not do as I say, you will be caught and slaughtered."

Delphine sounded disgusted, tired and pissed. She paused for a long moment. "Is it really that bad? They'll kill me and Dad?"

Theo nodded. "As soon as look at you."

Tears welled in the corners of her eyes, but she blinked them back defiantly, and when she spoke, there was a note of challenge in her voice. "And you'll help us make it if we do what you say."

"As much as I can," said Theo.

"So there's no choice then, is there?"

"None whatsoever. I'm glad we reached an understanding."

"You think? I don't fucking understand any of this shit. Still, I guess I'll have to cope for the moment."

"Good. I've done all I can here now. Follow me, and keep quiet." Theo headed out of the warehouse, Delphine in tow. He moved cautiously, keeping an eye out for possible assailants or police come to investigate the disturbance, but everything seemed quiet. They crossed the yard, and then Theo led Delphine over to where he had left Pierre. They entered the tree line on the far side of the road, and Theo looked around for the girl's father. The man was lying sprawled on the ground beside a tree, his head twisted at an unnatural angle. He was clearly dead.

Delphine howled something and ran over to where he lay, sobbing through her frantic calls. Theo left her to it for a moment, his mind whirling. He cursed, softly.

Delphine was clinging to her father's corpse, weeping brokenly. He crossed over to her and put a hand on her shoulder. "I'm really sorry, but you'll have to grieve later. We don't have much time."

She looked up, streaks of red running down her face. "Just fuck off and leave me alone."

"No. If you do not come with me now, you will not live to see tomorrow night."

"What do you care?"

"I gave my word," said Theo simply. "Plus you may be useful. Now come on. Don't you want to save your sister?"

She flinched at that and spoke bitterly. "So what do I have to do, oh great master?"

Theo winced. "I guess I deserved that. Just stick to 'Theo,' okay? I know it's distasteful, but to start with, you should retrieve your father's wallet and any identification or keys he is carrying. You may need them, and a car would be very useful right now."

Delphine's eyes widened, and she stared at him, shocked. "You want me to loot my father?"

Theo shrugged. "Would you rather I did it?"

She shuddered. "Fuck you."

"That's what I thought."

She closed her eyes for a long moment and took a deep breath, then started going through her father's pockets, keening softly as she did so. After a few moments, she paused, puzzled. "What the fuck?" She started to unzip the bloody slicker, hands trembling.

Theo cursed silently to himself. "Oh yeah, that's…"

"Why the fuck has Dad got bags of flour strapped to his chest?"

"What?!"

"You deaf? He's got bags of flour strapped to his fucking chest. Is this some sort of sick joke?"

Theo shook his head wryly. "Your father was a very brave, determined man, and he loved you and your sister more than anything." Delphine started crying again, a low sob full of regret and pain. Theo let her weep for a short while, then rested a hand gently on her shoulder. "Delphine…"

"I know," she said quietly. "I know. No fucking

time." She retrieved Pierre's wallet and keys, then stood up, turning her back on the corpse. She was trembling.

Theo nodded approvingly. "Good girl. Thank you. Now, when he approached, you father came from that way—" He pointed off across the park "—so chances are, that's where the car is. Come on. Let's see if we can find it. We've got a number of things that we need to pick up."

Fifteen minutes later, Theo and Delphine had the car, a station wagon, parked outside the warehouse. Theo's bike was in the back, with his shotgun and Kristine's sword.

"There's another thing we need to get," said Theo. "I don't want you losing control, either. I have a feeling that it could be useful in the long run. You better not damage it."

"What are you talking about, Theo?"

"The woman who did this to you."

A wild jumble of emotions chased across Delphine's face, and when she actually saw Kristine, her eyes widened and her breathing quickened. Theo tensed, ready to restrain her if she dashed forward.

"What's wrong with her? Is she dead?" She sounded concerned.

"No," Theo said. "Just paralyzed."

"Oh," said Delphine thoughtfully.

Theo bent down and lifted Kristine easily, resting her stiff body over one shoulder like a plank, outstretched arms pointing down his back, and started moving toward the car. "Delphine." She turned to look at him. "How long have you lived in Minneapolis?"

"We moved here from Quebec when Mom died. I was seven. Why?"

"Do you know the city well?"

"I guess."

"We need to find somewhere discreet. An abandoned building or unit ideally, something lightproof."

She looked a bit uncertain. "I guess I can go into hiding."

Theo shook his head and gestured at Kristine. "It's not for you. It's for her. You're going to have to be presented to the others."

"Hey hey hey, wait a fucking second. You just got through telling me how everyone would zap me if they found me, and now you want to go and just hand me over?"

"The situation has changed. You're too important to my investigations, and you don't have anyone to look after you. I won't let them take you."

"Oh yeah? So how come you couldn't have done that anyway, then?"

"You weren't my responsibility then."

Delphine frowned at him, looking hurt. "Oh gee, thanks. Beforehand, I was Dad's problem, and now I'm a charity case?"

"Something like that."

"Screw you." She reached for the door handle.

Theo grabbed her shoulder. "It's a cold world, child. I'll tell you this, though—leave this car, and you'll be dead within forty-eight hours, and you will be unable to help save your sister. Stay, and I will see you both safe if I possibly can."

"You're an asshole," said Delphine angrily, but she dropped her hand.

Theo shrugged. "You're not the first person to say so. Now, to get back to what I was trying to say, we need to find somewhere to store the woman. Do you know anywhere suitable? It has to be abandoned, somewhere people just don't go."

Delphine thought for several minutes. "Yeah, I guess so. There are a heap of places out north. One or two of them are hang-outs or shit like that, but the rest of them are just crappy."

"Can you guide me there?"

"Yeah, I suppose so."

The journey took about twenty minutes, heading off Nicolet Island and out from the center of the city.

Once they were on the right route, Delphine looked at Theo icily. "I've waited about as long as I'm prepared to. What the fuck is the score here?"

Theo shot her a sympathetic look. "Brace yourself, Delphine. I'm really sorry, but I'm afraid you didn't make it. You're dead."

She stared at him, disbelievingly. "What lame-ass bull is that? Like this is some sort of really crappy low-rent afterlife?"

Theo shook his head. "No. This is the same world it's always been. You died—murdered, technically—and have been reanimated. You're dead, yet you live on. You'll never age, never grow ill. If you're careful and lucky, and you have enough time before the world ends, you might live for centuries, always ageless and beautiful. But you have to drink blood to survive, feeding off your former species like a leech, and if you ever go out in the sun again, it will burn you to ash where you stand."

She blinked. "Like some sort of fucking *vampire*, you mean?"

"Exactly like that," said Theo flatly. He reached out, took her hand, and raised it so that she could see it easily. "See that blood? That's the tears you wiped away earlier." He lifted her hand further, to her mouth. "Have a feel. You have fangs."

"This is bullshit," shouted Delphine angrily. "How are you supposed to know so much about it?"

Theo opened his mouth and bared his fangs. "I died almost 150 years ago, Delphine. Think about it. How do you think you sank your teeth into that man's chest? You haven't noticed yet, but you're only breathing to talk. You don't have any pulse. If you lay still, you'd be indistinguishable from any other corpse."

She froze, stunned. "Oh, fuck."

"That's almost exactly what I said," said Theo.

"So now you're going to tell me that vampires all become gay? Is that why you're so ripped?"

Theo grinned, amused. "Good guess, but no, it's nothing to do with that. Kristine was supernaturally beautiful, her appearance enhanced by the force of her personality."

"Kristine?" Delphine sounded outraged. "She some kind of friend of yours?"

"Not exactly. She told me her name while we were fighting."

"Oh. Okay. That's not so bad." She sighed heavily, looking thoughtful.

"You're too kind," said Theo wryly. "Anyway, the same is true for when she was feeding from you. It feels wonderful when a vampire drinks your blood, and it can be an intensely erotic experience for some mortals. Finally, the reason that you are not experiencing any sexual interest in me, assuming you think you ought to be, is that vampires no longer possess strong sexual feelings. We can love, in a way, but we do not gain much pleasure from sex. You're not lesbian; you're dead."

Delphine looked at him pensively for a long moment, and then her eyes widened. "No fucking way," she said, quietly horrified. "Oh my god. I held my breath all the way through that, and nothing happened. No discomfort. Nothing. I don't want this crap. I don't want to be some sort of fucking nightstalker parasite. I want to go to my prom, go to college, ball a football player or three, and have some fucking *fun*, and now you're telling me I'm gonna be a dead, gazillion-year-old, blood-drinking *virgin*? Turn me back. Turn me back."

"There is no way back," said Theo sadly. "You are already dead. One more statistic. There is this, or there is your final, true death. There is nothing else."

"There is one thing, Theo." Delphine sounded icy.

"What's that?"

"Revenge."

"Yes," said Theo sadly. "There is always revenge."

They rode in silence for a while, then Delphine glanced back over at Kristine for several long moments, before turning back to him curiously. "She looks like a big-boobed novelty coat-rack back there, or some kind of really expensive sex toy. Isn't it uncomfortable for her?"

"Not really," said Theo. "Her muscles are frozen in place, so she is not exerting any effort to stay like that."

"That bitch has *really* fucked me over." The anger rose in her voice again, hot and hard. "I should…" She paused, confused. "I should *want* to rip her fucking head off. Why do I want her to hold me like that again?"

"We all feel something for the vampire who created us. It's perfectly natural."

"There's absolutely nothing natural about any of this shit, you freak."

"You get used to it," said Theo. "It's not as if there's much of an option."

Delphine just sighed and glared moodily out of the window. Theo let her brood.

Eventually, they came to a rundown district littered with boarded-up factories and office blocks. One or two showed signs of use, but most of them appeared utterly disused, victims of some earlier shift in the economic markets. Theo cruised the area for a few minutes until he found a promising unit, a small factory comprised of a cluster of squat, solid buildings with few windows. He pointed it out to Delphine.

"That place. Is that one of your hangouts?"

"Nope. Don't know anything about it."

"Fine, that'll do. It's getting toward 2:30, and we don't have a huge amount of time to be messing around with."

Theo pulled up outside the factory and got out of the car. The door was closed, but one good wrench opened it easily enough, and no alarms went off. He paused for a long look but couldn't spot anything out of the ordinary. He went back to the car and pulled Kristine out of the back, slinging her back over his shoulder again, then opened Delphine's door.

"Come on, let's move it."

She scowled at him. "You want me to come with? All right, I guess."

"I don't want you sitting in the car out on the road."

Delphine shrugged. "Whatever."

Theo led Delphine into the factory. The floor was covered with a thick layer of dust, and cobwebs lurked in all the corners and crannies. There was some furniture remaining, but most of the equipment had been removed. Apart from a few broken windows, the place looked surprisingly unvandalized.

"Hey, it's not as dark as I thought." Delphine sounded surprised.

"Your eyes are more sensitive to light now. Your senses are all sharper, in fact."

"How does that work? Die, and go twenty-twenty?"

"That's just the way it is," said Theo.

"Maybe being fully alive distracts you from using your senses properly. All those physical processes might get in the way, or something."

"Maybe," agreed Theo. "I've never really thought about it."

Delphine looked at him, surprised. "In a hundred and fifty years?"

"I've been busy," he said grimly.

She arched her eyebrows but wisely let the matter drop. "So, what are we looking for?"

Theo shrugged. "A storage locker, or a broom cupboard, or a cellar, or any other space where no light can get in. Let's split up and try to find a place quickly."

After a few minutes of searching, Delphine called Theo over. "I think I've got something."

It was more like a small vault than a large room, a secure storage area of some sort with a heavy metal door, leading off from a large office area. The area inside was featureless concrete. The large bolt on the outside of the door even had a padlock hanging from it, key in the lock.

"It's perfect," said Theo. "Thank you."

"You're welcome," said Delphine, smiling for the first time.

Theo took the padlock off the bolt, and tried turning the key. It was rusty, and the lock was sticky, but he put some force behind it, and it turned. He closed the lock and tried again, and it opened fairly smoothly. He nodded to himself, satisfied. He went and fetched Kristine from where he'd left her, leaned back against the door, and carried her into the vault.

A thought suddenly hit him, and he leaned her against a wall, face first, her outstretched arms supporting her. When she was securely positioned, Theo went round behind her and starting pulling her sweater up over her back.

"What the hell are you doing to her, you fucking pervert?" screeched Delphine from behind him, outraged.

Theo looked round at her flatly. "Searching for any sort of identifying mark."

"Yeah. Right."

"I told you once already, we don't have the same sort of sexual drive that mortals do."

"In that case," said Delphine disbelievingly, "you won't mind if I do it instead, will you."

"Help yourself," said Theo, stepping back.

Delphine looked at Kristine's taut body, and moistened her lips nervously, then slowly ran her hands up Kristine's sides, trembling slightly. Suddenly she pulled away and turned round quickly. "Um, no, it's okay actually. I'll believe you."

Theo grinned at Delphine's retreating back, then stripped Kristine naked, pulling her sweater up over her head and down her arms, and tugging her pants down to the floor. He checked her over closely, paying special attention to typical tattoo sites like shoulders, butt and ankles, and then turned her round to start examining her front. Delphine made a strangled noise somewhere between a gasp and a sigh from behind him. He ignored it and continued his inspection. When he was absolutely sure Kristine didn't have any particular identifiers, he pulled her clothes back on and smoothed them down.

He laid her out on her back in the dust, grinned down at her, and tipped the brim of his cap. "Sorry about the rough handling, ma'am. You'll be safe here, and I'll bring you a snack soon. Sleep well." He left the vault, swinging the heavy door shut behind him and then locking the bolt shut. He pocketed the key.

Delphine looked at him shakily as he came out.

"It's okay. She'll be fine in there," said Theo. "No one can disturb her, and no light will get in."

"Won't she freak out in there like that?"

"Nowhere near as much as if we left her somewhere that might be open to the day," said Theo grimly.

"How about food? Will she starve?"

Theo shook his head. "No. We don't starve. When you use the last of your blood, you get all shriveled and sink into a... well, it's like a coma. You can be revived though."

"It sounds horrible!"

"It is," Theo said, flatly. "I have no wish to do it again. Anyway, I won't let her get that bad. She should be fine on her own for a week or so, and then we'll see about feeding her a bit to keep her going."

"Oh, okay," said Delphine. "I guess I don't like to think of her like that, all stiff and dead, lying alone in the dark."

Theo nodded. "Try not to worry. She'll be okay there."

"You promise?"

He shook his head. "No. She *is* a criminal, and a multiple murderer, and I was assigned to execute her. I may need her knowledge, though. I will probably have to kill her in the end anyway."

"Oh." Delphine sounded subdued. "What are you then, some sort of assassin?"

"I'm more like a SWAT team," said Theo, grinning ever so slightly.

"What, the whole team?"

"Yes."

Delphine shook her head. "Jesus. This is just too much."

"I will promise that I won't cause her any undue suffering. Okay?"

"I guess."

"Good. Now, come on, we've still got a lot to do tonight, and there's only a few hours left until dawn."

"There is? Now what?" Delphine sounded tired and scared.

"We're going to have to abandon your car somewhere neutral, at least for a while."

"Why, for Christ's sake?"

"It's too easy to trace. There's a significant risk that the people behind the operation that abducted you are going to want to try to recapture you, or to eliminate you entirely. We have to make sure that doesn't happen."

She looked at him wordlessly, her eyes wide and vulnerable.

Theo tried to soften his voice a little. "Look, this is one hell of a mess, but if there's any way to keep you safe and sound, I'll do so. I gave your father my word that I'd see the both of you safe."

"But he's dead," said Delphine, voice quavering a little.

"That has nothing to do with it," said Theo.

"What am I going to do?" She was close to tears.

Theo put his arms around her and held her comfortingly. She let herself be drawn into the embrace, and started crying again, softly, her head on his chest. "You're going to trust me," he said gently. "And between us, we'll get you out of this mess and rescue your sister."

"I can't go home, can I?" Delphine sounded young and scared.

"No, I'm afraid you can't. You can't contact anyone you knew. You have to forget your old life, particularly for the moment. Anything else would be dangerous, both for you and for anyone you made contact with."

"I'll need clothes," she said, sounding a bit stronger.

"Good girl. We'll sort that out tomorrow. Before we do anything else though, we're going to go see the head vampire in the city, the prince." *Where I'm going to have to plead for your existence*, he added silently.

chapter six:
Fiat Nox

By the time that Theo had made it to the Amtrak station, left Pierre's car in long-term parking, and then ridden his bike back into Downtown Minneapolis with Delphine clutching on grimly behind him, it was getting uncomfortably close to dawn. It was far too late to address the prince tonight. So much the better. He pulled into the Institute of Arts, and rode round to the staff parking lot again.

"You've got to be joking," muttered Delphine.

Theo shook his head. "You'll see. Some of our kind have a lot of influence over mortal society."

He parked and shut the engine off, then turned round to look at Delphine. "Wait here for me. I'll only be a minute."

She glanced up at the sky, and then looked at him, clearly doubtful. "I don't know… I'm feeling kinda jumpy."

"It's perfectly natural. I really won't be long. You'll be fine here for a moment longer. I promise."

"That means you really mean it, right?"

Theo nodded. "Yeah."

"Okay. I'll trust you. Don't take too long though."

"I won't. Wait here until I call your name, then come over to me."

Theo strode over to the plain door and pressed the buzzer. The panel shot back, and the gatekeeper, Gary, looked out. He seemed relieved to see Theo. "Archon Bell! We were getting concerned. Please, come in, come in." He opened the door.

Theo caught the door as it opened. "Thank you. I need you to do me a small service. Is Angus in Elysium anywhere?"

"Yes, I believe he's staying in his rooms here tonight."

"Excellent. I want you to go tell him that I'm back, and that I'd like to see him first thing tomorrow, in the suite he has set aside for me."

"I'm not sure I…"

"Quickly, man, if you don't mind," said Theo with a hint of menace. "You'll want to catch him before he turns in. I'll close the door, don't worry."

"Yes, Archon," said Gary with some resignation.

As soon as the thin vampire had bustled off, Theo called Delphine over. She came quickly, looking uncomfortable. He ushered her through into the building, closed the door securely, and then led her swiftly back to the rooms that had been set aside for his use. As soon as they were in, he closed and locked the door, and secured all the bolts.

Delphine seemed slightly stunned. "This place… it's yours?"

"Think of it as a hotel room."

"The MIA makes one hell of a hotel."

"Yeah," agreed Theo. "That it does."

"I don't understand any of this, you know." Delphine sounded tired and plaintive.

Theo nodded sympathetically. "I know. You're being thrown in right at the deep end, kid. You've been great so far. It'll all make more sense tomorrow."

"I hope so. What now?"

He pointed toward the bedroom, with its large double bed. "You go in there, lie down and go to sleep."

"Don't leave me. Please?" She sounded very young again.

"I'm taking the couch," said Theo. "Never did like those big fancy-ass beds anyway."

"Oh. Okay. Thank you, Theo. For everything." Delphine smiled at him wanly.

"You're welcome. Sleep well. If you need me at

all, I'll be right here."

"Do you promise?" Her voice was small and vulnerable.

"Yes. I promise."

***

As soon as the van made it through security and access and into the factory proper, Liam directed the driver to pull up in one of the bays, then hopped out, hammering on the hood of the next van even as it pulled up beside him. As the teams assembled, he started barking orders.

"Right, listen to me. Get the cargo unloaded and back in storage immediately, then go back to the vans and wait for me to give you the thumbs up. Don't talk to anyone about this evening. In fact, don't talk to anyone at all. Just get it done as quickly as possible, and keep your bloody mouths shut. Understand?" The teams nodded and bustled into action.

Once they were busy and out of earshot, Liam turned to Matthew angrily. "What the *fuck* happened back there?"

"There was an intruder," said Matthew coldly. "You ought to have noticed."

"Two intruders," said Liam. "We were supposed to be able to take care of an intruder or two. You gonna explain?"

Matthew's eyes narrowed. "They were kindred, highly skilled. I believe one may have been one of our kind's chief enforcers. The other I have never seen or heard of before."

"How the hell did they know we were there? What did they want?"

"I do not know."

Liam spat on the floor. "That's just not good enough. They're your department. You're paying this shitty little city enough of our profits to fund a small army. You're supposed to know what your *kindred* are doing. Find the fuck out before they crash *this* party, too."

"You do not give me orders." Matthew sounded icily furious.

Liam stared at him, equally angry. "Yeah? Pull your fucking weight, *vampire*, or you'll get a real good reminder of what midday feels like, this time of year."

"My organization…" Matthew began.

"…needs mine far more than mine needs yours, and don't you forget it. We can make almost as much money without all this undead crap. We have had a number of problems caused by your bunch, and it wouldn't take much more to push them right over the edge. My interim report is going to be as vague as always, but if you push me, you're going to discover a whole new world of pain. How would you like to be personally responsible for screwing up this deal?"

Matthew snarled at Liam, teeth bared savagely.

"I thought not," said Liam coolly. "Find out where those assholes came from, why we didn't know they were planning to raise hell, and what they're likely to get up to next. In case you hadn't noticed, one of the twins is missing. What the hell is the use of a single fucking twin? We'll be lucky to get thirty for her now. That's a big motherfucker of a loss."

Liam turned his back on Matthew, ignoring the vampire's apoplectic splutters, and looked around the factory. He called out to one of the men clustered by the vans. "Hey, Roland. Come here."

"Sure thing boss." Roland walked over, eyeing Matthew nervously.

"Tell us what happened back there, Roland. I thought you were going to keep the merchandise together."

"It was this crazy chick. She ripped Mark up and kicked me into the middle of next week. She was dusted or something."

Liam nodded, pulled a small pistol out of his pocket, and shot Roland in the stomach, three times. He fell to the floor, writhing and screaming. Liam ignored him and turned his attention back to the men around the van. "Greg."

A big, blond bear of a man, Greg blanched. "Boss." He sounded very scared.

"The promotion is yours. Don't *fucking* lose any *fucking* priceless *fucking* redhead virgin *fucking* twins."

"Y-yes, boss. Thank you."

"Oh, and have the little bitch broken. She'll be worth more as a sub. Maybe we can claw a bit back."

"Broken?"

Liam ground his teeth together. "Mentally, idiot, not physically. No permanent damage, no Class A. Have them start the full program immediately."

"Right away boss," said Greg nervously.

Liam didn't bother acknowledging him. He looked down at Roland, irritated by the man's loud moans of pain. "You shut the fuck up and die, will you?" He glanced up at Matthew, pitching his voice low so that only the vampire would hear. "Why don't you do something useful and fucking eat him or something?" He turned on one heel and stomped off toward the offices, trying to blot out the whole damn mess.

***

Theo hadn't been up long when there was a loud knock on the suite door. He stood up, walked over to one side of the doorway and called out "Yes?"

"Good evening, Theo. It's Angus." Angus's voice was muffled by the heavy door but still clearly recognizable.

"I'll just open up," called Theo. He slid the bolts back, the metal thumping loudly into place, then unlocked the door and opened it. Angus looked pleased to see him.

"Come on in, Angus. Thanks for dropping by so promptly."

"It's a pleasure," said Angus, smiling. "Is everything okay?"

"I'm fine," said Theo. "I wanted to bring you up to speed on things. I'm also going to need you to call the council of primogen together. There's a few things that I need to discuss with them."

Angus nodded. "Of course. Is this to do with the rogue?"

"It's all interrelated, yes."

"Did you manage to get any leads?"

Theo shook his head. "It went a bit beyond leads, actually. I've dealt with her."

"Already?" Angus looked impressed. "That's fantastic news. What happened?"

"Well, I'll deal with things one area at a time. I came up against the rogue in the warehouse you pointed me toward. She initially thought that I was there for the same reason she was, to uncover some shadowy conspiracy that had murdered the rest of her coterie."

Angus shook his head sadly. "Tragic. Her delusions have been immensely destructive."

"She also implied that she'd been causing trouble in a number of places, including Hartford and New York," said Theo.

Angus shrugged. "I suppose it's possible. Are you going to follow it up?"

"No, I don't see the need for that. She may have been telling the truth as she saw it or not. Anyway, we fought. She was tough, but I managed to nail her in the end. Problem over."

"Thank you, old friend," Angus said, smiling. "I never had any doubts that you'd be able to solve the problem swiftly for us."

"There is more, though."

"Oh?"

"I mentioned that the rogue thought I was there to assist her."

"Yes, I did wonder about that."

"There was a deal going down in the warehouse," said Theo grimly.

"Drugs?" Angus sounded slightly confused.

"Slaves."

Angus's eyes widened.

"Worse than that, I heard two of the slave traders talking. One kindred and one mortal."

"Ghouled?"

Theo shook his head. "No. They seemed to be working in partnership. The mortal knew far too much. Enough to know that he could be controlled—and he implied that he was being monitored by his allies for signs of domination."

Angus looked horrified. "That's terrible."

"How much do you know about mortal criminal organizations?"

"Gangs are not a specialty of mine."

"Then you may not be aware of it, but over the last few years, the large groups have corporatized. These are not street thugs. They're vast, international criminal businesses, run by management experts. The organizations have more money—and more soldiers— than some countries. They're starting to work together, sharing resources and trade routes to minimize overhead and exposure. The leaders of the theoretically rival groups even strategize together now. Mortal governments can't even touch them. All the police can do is pick up the crumbs and keep the herd ignorant. The organizations already directly control several Eastern European countries, and they are gaining more power from other world governments all the time."

"Dreadful," murmured Angus.

Theo frowned at him. "It is when you consider what it would mean if these transnational criminal organizations came to understand our presence. We're looking at ruthless, strongly regimented, highly armed predators, often above or in control of the law, who wouldn't think twice about slaughtering anyone or anything who stood in their way. Sound familiar? Well, unlike the kindred, there's tens of millions of them, and they can move around by daylight as well as at night."

"My god."

"Exactly," said Theo. "So it's imperative that we find out how much kindred involvement there is in this slave operation and what the scope of the slave trade actually is. I know for certain that they are working with the Hong Kong Triads, and that means they are probably working with everyone else, too. Oh, and they're selling to kindred as well as mortals."

Angus was stunned. "And these slavers are here, in Minneapolis?"

"I'm prepared to lay a wager that they're your famous Minneapolis Triangle, Angus."

"I can understand why you need to speak to the primogen. I'll get it organized at once."

"Actually, it's not that so much. I will of course explain the situation, but that's not my main reason for calling council."

"It isn't?" Angus couldn't seem to decide between worry and bewilderment. "Is there something worse?"

"I wouldn't say worse, necessarily," said Theo. "Delphine, you can come out now."

Delphine opened the door to the bedroom, and came out into the room. "Hi."

Angus stared at her in absolute horror.

"Angus, this is Delphine. She was embraced last night. Delphine, Angus is an important person here, and a very old friend of mine."

Angus turned to look at him, still staring. "Not you, surely?"

Theo laughed bitterly. "Hardly. You know me better than that. She was one of the would-be slaves and was embraced by the rogue as some sort of attack against the conspiracy."

Angus visibly pulled himself together. "Ah. I'm starting to understand. Child, forgive me. You must have had a dreadful time recently."

Delphine nodded fervently. "That doesn't even come close. Um, sir."

"I'll notify the prince that you wish to make an

introduction as well as to brief her on this worrying new development," said Angus.

"Thank you," said Theo.

"I have to warn you now though that the council is not usually lenient with breaches of the third tradition. If it were down to Elizabeth alone then perhaps things would be different, but on this matter, the situation is a little strained."

"Leave that to me," said Theo flatly.

"Of course," said Angus. "I'll go and make preparations. I'll send for you as soon as we are ready. A pleasure to meet you, child."

"Thanks again, Angus," said Theo. "I knew I could count on you."

"Always," said Angus, already on his way out of the door. As soon as he was out, Theo slid the bolts back into place. He turned around to see that Delphine was looking at him crossly.

"What exactly did he mean by 'breach of the third tradition'?"

Theo sighed. "No vampire may bring another into being without the advance permission of the prince of that city. If the law is broken, both sire and childe are killed. Your sire had no authority to create you. That is why I initially told you that you would have to keep away from our kind."

Delphine collapsed into a chair bonelessly. "So that's it then. I'm fucking dead. Oh god."

"Stop that," said Theo sharply. "You are a vital material witness in a critical investigation. I am confident that I can secure you leniency in this situation—after all, you were just a pawn. Just remember what I told you, and leave most of the talking to me."

"Yeah? Exactly how confident is confident?" asked Delphine suspiciously.

"Ninety percent," said Theo reassuringly.

Delphine's eyes narrowed. "That's crappy odds to bet your life on. Why don't I just make a run for it?"

"Because then you'd be hunted down and killed. You'll be much better off getting legitimized."

"Providing your prince doesn't just kill me."

"She's not *my* prince," said Theo. "Actually, technically she's your prince. I work for someone else. I do have some authority, you know."

"Enough to make them leave me alone?"

Theo paused. "No. Not quite."

Delphine grimaced. "I was right. You *are* an asshole. You're playing games with my fucking life, Theo."

"I'm doing everything in my power to save you, child. It would be a lot easier if you'd just trust me. You know nothing about any of this. Nothing."

"Jesus, it's always 'Tell me all about it' with you isn't it, and never 'Here, let me explain.' You're being a jerk. If I'm ignorant, fucking bring me up to speed then."

"I will, don't worry about that. Just as soon as we've sorted your status out. Just say what I told you to, okay?"

"I don't have much choice, do I. Why are you lying about Kris, anyway?"

"Kris?"

"My—what'd you call it?—*sire*. Don't you think she looks like a Kris?"

"Uh…"

"Well, she does. So, why did you lie to your friend?"

"I didn't lie," said Theo. "I hardly ever lie."

Delphine looked at him flatly. "It sounded like you were lying to me."

Theo shook his head. "I told him that she had been taken care of, and she has. She poses no further threat to this domain. If he chose to interpret that as my having killed her, that is his business."

"You're being a weasel, Theo. That's lying by omission."

Theo sighed. "Look, I was called in to solve the problem, and I've solved it. It would have proven difficult to explain to him why I needed to keep her intact. I suspect she is insane, but she may actually know something useful about this slavery operation. It's always good to have an ace or two up your sleeve, too."

"Would you get in trouble if I told on you?" Delphine sounded mischievously eager.

"I'm afraid not," said Theo wryly. "But you'd probably cut our chances of finding your sister."

"You're not playing fair," said Delphine with a pout.

Theo glared at her. "I'm not playing at all."

A knock at the door stopped Delphine as she started to make some retort or other. She actually got a little paler, though it hardly seemed possible. Theo rested a hand on her shoulder sympathetically. "Come on, kid. It'll be okay." She nodded vaguely and stood up, letting herself be drawn toward the door. Theo halted before the doorway.

"Yes?"

"You are summoned before the council, Archon Bell." The voice was unfamiliar.

Theo unbolted and opened the door. A stocky vampire with short, blond hair stood a couple of paces away, looking politely attentive.

"Would you follow me, please?"

"Sure," Theo said. "Lead on."

They walked through the corridors of the museum in silence. Delphine was wrapped in her own thoughts and hardly seemed to notice the surroundings. Theo understood her feelings, but there was little he could do to set her mind at ease, and the risk *was* real.

The stocky vampire palmed open the security doors that Theo remembered, and stopped before the closed boardroom door. He waited until Theo and Delphine were standing behind him, then knocked on the door.

"Come," called Elizabeth from inside the room.

The vampire pulled the doors open and stepped

back to let Theo and Delphine into the room. The doors closed behind them with a very solid click, and Delphine jumped slightly. The desks were laid out in the same configuration as before, with Elizabeth at the head, looking out across the table at the pair of them. The force of her beauty washed out over them, demanding respect and adoration. Delphine looked visibly cowed.

"It's a trick," hissed Theo. "She's not *that* beautiful or awe-inspiring. Keep telling yourself that. We'll be through with this soon. Just don't underestimate them. Don't underestimate *any* of them."

Delphine nodded, nervously.

Elizabeth stood up and took a couple of steps around the end of the table. "Good evening, Archon Bell. Do come in." Her voice rang like music.

They walked forward a few steps, then Theo stopped and nodded pleasantly to the prince. One bow was more than enough. Delphine remembered her instructions properly and bowed deeply.

If Elizabeth was put out by Theo's lack of deference, she didn't let it show. "Welcome, Archon. I'm grateful to you for taking care of our troublesome intruder so quickly. Thank you."

"You're very welcome, ma'am," said Theo.

Elizabeth gestured at the vampires sitting around the table. "You already know Angus, but I'd like to take a moment to introduce you to Christopher Houghton, Gloria Astor, Simon Crieff and Angela Vincenze.

Theo nodded to the primogen in turn, receiving smiles from Angus and Simon, and a less than effective withering stare from Christopher.

"Ladies and gentlemen," said Theo firmly. "Thank you for getting together for me." A couple of the vampires bristled visibly at the implication. "I have some news which you may find disturbing."

"So I see," said Christopher, eyeing Delphine coldly.

Theo ignored him. "A syndicate of slave traders with links to major organized criminal groups is active in this domain. The syndicate is headed by a partnership of kindred and uninfluenced mortals. They prey on both kindred and kine."

None of the primogen looked particularly surprised or horrified. The dominant expression was one of guarded disapproval.

"The dangers posed by this situation are intense. One mortal already gives evidence of knowing more about our condition than many neonates and is working with others of his kind to circumvent our powers of dominance. If this information should filter up to government circles or, even worse, to the heads of the major criminal organizations, we would all be at extreme risk."

"While I naturally deplore any breach of masquerade, Archon Bell, I hardly see a need for panic." Despite her pretty, doll-like face, Gloria Astor sounded like a rather fussy schoolmistress. "Surely we have nothing to fear from these thugs."

Theo fought down a growl. "In the mortal world, *Gloria*, criminals are the new aristocrats, even more so than CEOs and bankers. Maybe that's the way it's always been, but this new generation of scum are better organized, better armed and better financed than many governments—and they are considerably better at taking effective action."

Gloria's eyes narrowed dangerously, and she made her tone deliberately patronizing. "Maybe you're suffering from battle fatigue if you're scared of shadows. Perhaps Paschek should give you some time off."

"That's upward of forty million shadows worldwide," said Theo. "Well-trained, well-armed, ruthless, regimented, unconstrained, with de facto access to just about all the information there is, and the ability to hunt during the day. Yes, I'm scared of what could happen if these people were to hear of us without being held back. You should be too." That got to them. Theo could see it.

"People disappear in the country surrounding the Twin Cities," said Angela. "That much is true. We've all been aware of it for a while. These stories of white slavery and global mafias working with kindred are new, however."

"It's happening. Believe it. The important thing is to find out how far it goes, and then take steps to deal with the problem, whatever its scale."

"So far, all I hear is words," said Christopher. "What evidence do you have for any of this?"

"Are you calling me a liar?" Theo's head swam as the rage flared within him. He took great care to keep it out of his voice.

"Of course not," said Christopher a touch too soothingly. "But you have a certain reputation for excitability, Archon. Maybe you were mistaken about the nature of the operation. I think there's no real need to get our baseball caps in a twist now, is there?"

"It is my belief," said Theo icily, "that the sale I disrupted last night was going to be to one of the kindred. Someone high-ranking, with considerable funds at his disposal. Someone, furthermore, who may have had a ritual purpose for purchasing red-haired virgin twins. If I find that such a person exists, he will surely be guilty of breaching the tradition of the masquerade, and I would of course have to seek that person's immediate execution. A rich, high-ranking ritualist, Christopher. I doubt there's many such in this city. Unfortunately, I'll only have time to conduct a truly thorough investigation into the matter if I'm prevented from investigating the root problem."

"Don't be a fool," said Christopher dismissively.

"If you have done nothing wrong, then you will have nothing to hide," said Theo flatly.

"This is puerile," snapped Christopher.

"Quite," said Theo calmly. "I seek leave to

investigate a threat that might just engulf us all. You have absolutely nothing to lose by getting in my way—unless you are somehow implicated. If you allow personal dislikes to overcome your common sense, you will only implicate yourself in the eyes of your colleagues. There is no reason to object."

Christopher gazed at him impassively.

Elizabeth spoke into the gap. "If the danger is real, then it is definitely worth pursuing further. Archon Bell is known to be both loyal and trustworthy, and there is nothing to be gained by stopping his investigations here. His testimony is significant. I trust that there are no further questions regarding its authenticity?" She looked expectantly at Christopher.

He scowled. "Oh, very well. Investigate your paranoid dreams, Bell. It makes no matter to me one way or the other."

After a moment's further silence, Elizabeth nodded. "Fine. Thank you, Christopher. Archon Bell, you are free to investigate this entire matter without hindrance throughout this domain."

Theo bowed graciously, ignoring the look the Tremere shot him. "Thank you. There is one further matter that I need to raise."

"The presentation of your mysterious guest," said Elizabeth.

There was a pause, and then Delphine suddenly remembered her cue and lurched forward a step, white as a sheet. She bowed deeply, noticeably shaking. "My... Um, I am Delphine of the Broo... Brujah, childe of Kristine, and I off... offer you my fealty, my prince."

Elizabeth's eyes flickered to Theo, clearly uncertain.

"Delphine was one of the slaves, ma'am. She was embraced by the rogue last night, so as to frustrate the plans of her would-be purchaser."

The primogen erupted. Christopher sprang to his feet, walked to the front of the table, and stared Theo straight in the eyes. "Tell me, *Archon*. What is the penalty for breaking the third tradition?"

"This is not the—" began Theo.

"I did not ask for commentary," interrupted Christopher loudly, "I asked you for the penalty for breaking the third tradition." The room quieted.

"Death," said Theo flatly. "For sire and childe. But…"

"What is an archon's role?"

Theo sighed. "To uphold the traditions, as directed by his Justicar."

Christopher smiled nastily. "So what are you waiting for? Kill the little bitch and get it done with." Delphine gasped. "Or are you going to turn your back on the traditions and your career, Archon?"

"She is a vital witness and may be the only link to locating the slave operation," said Theo furiously. "Stop playing games with me, warlock. If I'm going to stop this thing and save all our asses, I *need* her."

"I'm sure we don't need to go that far Christopher," said Angus uncertainly. "Don't you think you're overreacting?"

"Overreacting?" asked Christopher, furious. "Was it overreacting when Sandra and her childe were put out to burn? You didn't think so then, fop."

Theo could feel Delphine start to tremble beside him.

"There are circumstances…" began Angus.

"There are always circumstances," replied Christopher. "Always. One law for all, you said. One law for all. I invoke that law."

"Theo, I'm sorry," began Angus.

"Hang on a fucking moment," yelled Simon. "No one is executing any of my clansmen in here. Your bloody childe was a menace, Chris. She had it coming, and we all knew it. Her latest illegal neonate was so stupid, he could barely speak. Latest, remember? We were merciful before, and she had been warned." He turned to Delphine, ignoring the Tremere's outraged splutters. "Tell me, girl. Were you an unwilling and unknowing victim in this? More importantly, now that it's happened, will you obey our laws and codes faithfully, and support your clan, your primogen and your prince?"

"Yes, sir," stammered Delphine. "Yes and yes, of course. Please don't kill me now. Not after everything I've been through."

"More rebellious Brujah teens?" asked Gloria dismissively. "Don't you have enough, Simon? We're overpopulated as it is. She's an unwelcome burden. The course is clear. Eliminate her."

Simon turned to say something to her, while Christopher started in on Angus again. Elizabeth looked at the primogen and walked around the table to Theo. "Perhaps you and your companion would excuse us briefly, Archon Bell? I understand your plea. We shall discuss the matter and call you when we have reached a decision."

Theo nodded reluctantly, took Delphine by the arm, and led her out of the room. She followed numbly. As the doors closed behind them, she said, in a tiny voice, "Oh god. They're going to kill me."

"I won't let them do that," said Theo.

"You can't stop them." Delphine's voice was toneless.

"Wait and see," said Theo grimly. "This is more important than one prince and her council."

Suddenly, Theo's phone rang. His heart sank. Sure enough, it was Paschek.

"Justicar Paschek," said Theo pleasantly. "Good evening."

"What the howling hells do you think you're doing, you ludicrous idiot?" Paschek was screaming down the phone, on the verge of blind rage.

Theo blinked. "I'm not sure I…"

"We're supposed to uphold the traditions, Archon.

Uphold them. Not take in every pathetic waif and stray that crosses our paths. You are to kill the girl this instant. She is in breach of the third tradition, she is the product of our clan, and that is my judgment. Kill her. That is a direct order."

"How did… Look, wait a moment," said Theo.

"What?" His voice actually managed to increase in volume and pitch. "How dare you, you piece of excrement? I will most certainly not wait a moment. Not even an instant. Kill her right away, or I'll have you executed myself before sunrise as a collaborator in this ridiculous breach."

"I *need* her!" shouted Theo, furious. "Why is that so fucking difficult for everyone to understand?"

Suddenly, Paschek was icy calm, laced through with biting sarcasm. "Do enlighten me, Archon Bell, as to why this particular need is driving you to scream vulgarisms down the telephone at me. Tersely, please, for my patience is thin. Have you perhaps fallen passionately in love?"

"She is the victim of a slave-trading ring. A large, well-structured slave-trading ring, run by a collaboration of kindred with mortal criminals affiliated with the transnational criminal organizations. TCOs are not known to be under anything resembling secure influence from the sect. This could be immense, far larger than just Minneapolis."

There was a long silence on the end of the phone. Finally, Paschek spoke, sounding thoughtful and concerned. "That ties in with… No matter. Very well. I retract my prior judgment. Investigate as fully as you are able. In the matter of this humiliating fledgling, I will defer judgment in favor of the local prince. You are to obey her decision on this as if it came directly from me. Keep me informed regarding your progress with this operation."

"Yes, sir," Theo said, relieved.

Paschek severed the connection, and Theo put

the phone away. Delphine cowered away from him, terrified. Theo looked at her curiously.

Her voice was shaky, and quiet. "I heard him tell you to kill me. Order you. You have to obey orders, you said. Jesus, SWAT team, my ass. You are an assassin." Her voice got even smaller. "Don't hurt me. Please. Do it quick."

Theo shook his head. "I'm not going to kill you. He retracted the order."

Delphine collapsed onto the floor as her knees gave way. "Oh god. Oh god. I am *so* sick of this." She laughed, a little hysterically. "It's going to be the fucking death of me."

Theo helped her to her feet. "It's going to be okay."

The doors to the boardroom opened again. There was silence from the room. Elizabeth came out and sashayed over to Theo and Delphine, looking grave. "You've caused us quite a headache, Archon."

"But for the best of reasons," replied Theo.

Elizabeth shrugged lightly. "It doesn't matter. The council is deadlocked. I have decided to let them all cool off for a few days, and then we'll think about the issue again. As you've seen, it is an emotional one. In the meantime, the girl is to stay with you, under your protection, at all times. You will stand surety for her discretion and good behavior."

"Thank you, ma'am," said Theo with as much grace as he could muster. Elizabeth nodded thoughtfully and went back into the boardroom, closing the doors behind her.

"They're going to *fucking* kill me, you asshole," snarled Delphine.

"I'm not going to let that happen," Theo replied. "Come on. We've got work to do."

Delphine suddenly stopped dead in the middle of the corridor. Theo continued for a moment before noticing, then turned to face her.

"You really mean that, don't you?" She sounded a

bit calmer again, and a little curious.

Theo nodded. "Yes. I do."

"Why?"

"Because I gave my word."

She looked at him with a very direct stare. "Yeah, yeah, that old tune. That's not what I'm asking. You know what I'm asking."

"Because killing you is totally unjust. You didn't have any choice, and you have no idea what you're getting into. You were enslaved, then murdered and reanimated as a monster before you'd even had a chance to taste your life. The world owes you a break. Plus, as you heard me tell my boss, I need you on this."

Delphine continued looking at him. "Compassion? Don't worry, I won't spoil your reputation by telling anyone. It's great to hear, and I appreciate it, but you're still dodging the issue, Theo."

He scowled at her. "Where did you get so unwholesomely clever?"

"It's a gift. Well?"

Theo hesitated a moment, then shrugged, and smiled ruefully. "Because there has to be something. All those years, all that pain and death and loss and defeat, night after night… Longevity is not all it's cut out to be, kid. There has to be something, or else the hunger gets you. The risk is that one night, you just sink into it, and you never come out again because you no longer have anything to come out for. You have to have something. Well, I do. It kept me alive when I was alive, and it's kept me going since I've been dead. It's the only thing a slave can have. The only thing your master can't take from you. I have my self-respect."

chapter seven:
Bolt hole

The telephone rang, a shrill, intrusive noise. Matthew stared at it venomously for a few seconds, but finally acquiesced and answered the call.

"Yes?"

"Is this Matthew Flock?" The words were clear enough, but the voice was unrecognizable, altered into some electronic mishmash or other.

Matthew frowned. "Who is this?"

"We share certain common interests."

"Tell me who you are, or I shall terminate this conversation," said Matthew, extremely unimpressed.

"You have a problem. Actually, we both have a problem. Your lost merchandise has been embraced and is now in the hands of an archon."

Matthew grimaced nervously. "It *was* Bell, then. How do you know about that?"

"Call me a fly on the Elysian wall, if you must."

"Pathetic. I loathe traitors."

"That couldn't matter less," said the caller. "Bell has taken the fledgling under his wing. Persuaded the council to let her endure, for the moment at least. She threatens you, and, quite incidentally, she threatens me. That is not acceptable."

"No, it is not. What is Bell's involvement?"

"Accidental, it seems. He was after your other gatecrasher. But he may start prying."

Matthew shook his head in disbelief. "This is ridiculous. What do you want?"

"Bell is too high-profile to risk killing at this stage, but I plan to pull what strings I can to get him reassigned, and I plan to have the girl killed. There is room for cooperation in this regard—separate, simultaneous action may be more effective. Bell's reputation is well deserved. The man is a hellhound."

"I have no interest in your paranoia. Bell should simply be killed. He's only an archon."

"I would not be happy if Bell were eliminated."

"I really couldn't care less. Either way, I may consider taking some steps—if I knew any of this to be true," said Matthew suspiciously.

"Your own monitors in Elysium should confirm it soon enough."

"If that is so, then the girl's sister may be a useful bargaining tool."

"The danger is too great. I would urge you to kill her immediately."

"I am not in the habit of taking advice from anonymous callers," Matthew said coldly. "Still, your suggestions will be taken under advisement."

"I hope so," said the caller. The line went dead.

Matthew glared at the telephone, then clicked the cradle a few times and dialed. The phone was answered on its first ring. "Lucy? This is Matthew. I regret to inform you that a significant problem has arisen…"

***

It only took a couple of moments to gather up the few bits and pieces that Theo had left lying around the suite—cell-phone charger, maintenance kit for the shotgun, some spare rounds and so on. Delphine had even less, and Theo was impressed that she hadn't made a fuss about that yet. He was just stuffing the last bits into his bag when he heard the door open. Theo looked up, and saw Angus there, resplendent in a stylish Italian silk. He looked concerned.

"What's up, Angus?"

"Are you leaving us, Theo?"

"Don't worry, I'm not going far." Theo grinned.

Angus frowned, worried. "I'm really not sure that's a good idea. It's dangerous out there, and things are sensitive. I'd feel happier knowing you were well protected."

Theo shook his head. "That's the whole point. Here, everyone knows where I am."

"Surely you aren't suggesting…"

"I know you respect Elysium, Angus, but with something this big, chances are they have people here. They'll know about Delphine. They may decide that it's worth the risk trying something."

Angus looked a little affronted. "The security here is impeccable."

"I'm sure it is, old friend. I'm just being cautious."

"Well, I see it's no use trying to persuade you to change your mind. You'll need somewhere to stay. I have a place you could use."

Theo smiled. "Thank you, but no. I have something lined up. Something clean. If these slavers have been doing their research properly—watching the principals, and so on—they may know of the location."

"It's perfectly secret, I assure you."

"You've very generous, but I'm fine for a place to stay."

"Very well," said Angus with a sour smile. "I offered. You'll let me know where you are?"

"I'll be around," said Theo. "You have my cell number, too. I'll tell you what, though. If you do want to help, I could use some currency. We'll need a few things, and I haven't held a bank account for decades."

"Of course," nodded Angus. "I have a few hundred on me, or I can get a more substantial sum brought down in a matter of minutes."

"Whatever you have handy would be great," said Theo.

Angus rummaged around in his suit pockets and pulled out a wad of bills, which he handed over. "There you are."

"Thank you Angus," said Theo. "It's much appreciated."

"Least I can do, my friend."

"Hardly," said Theo. "Now, I'm afraid we have to get going. There's a number of things I have to take care of tonight."

"Of course," said Angus graciously. "Good luck, Theo."

"Thank you," said Theo. "I'll keep you informed."

As soon as he'd gone, Theo led Delphine out of the institute and around to his bike. She started to say something, but he put a finger to his lips and she subsided. They got on the bike and Theo took off, riding several blocks randomly before he found a handy parking lot to stop in. When he turned the engine off, Delphine tilted her head and looked at him curiously.

"What's the matter? Don't you trust Angus?"

Theo shook his head. "It's not that. I've known Angus for a long time, and I trust him as much as I trust anyone, although that's not much. There are ways of forcing information out of people if you're clever enough, though. Besides, I trust the rest of them about as far as I could throw the Institute. It's better this way."

"Okay, point taken. So where are we going to stay?" A flicker rippled over her features. "We're not going to be in that horrible safe with Kris, are we?"

Theo shook his head. "Not unless we have no other choice, no. Give me a moment, and I'll see what I can sort out." He picked up his phone and dialed a number.

A deep, husky-voiced man answered the call. "TBP, Lance Laker speaking."

"Lance, it's Theo Bell. How you doing, cuz?"

Delphine looked at him questioningly, but kept silent.

Lance sounded pleased to hear him. "Theo! Good to hear from you, m'man. Yeah, it's good. How about you? You still knocking around in New York?"

"Nope. In the Midwest, for the time being. Are Kirsty and the boys well?"

"Great, thank you. I'll tell K you asked after her. Are you keeping safe?"

"You know it," said Theo.

"Good news," said Lance. "So, Theo, what can I do for you?"

"Do you have anywhere empty on the books in Minneapolis that I could use for a week or two?"

"Maybe," replied Lance. "Hang on a sec, and I'll check for you." There was a loud clattering of computer keys. "Yeah, actually we've got a couple of places. There's a pretty nice three-bedroom down in a district called Tangletown. Good area, nice community spirit. And there's an economy apartment a couple of blocks outside downtown, but that's a bit rough. You're better off in Tangletown."

"Actually, cuz, being close to downtown would be a benefit, so if you don't mind blocking the apartment out to me for a week or two, that would be great."

"Okay m'man, whatever you want. It's yours."

"Fantastic. Thanks Lance. I take it the place is on the master ring still?"

"Of course," said Lance. "It's at Elliot and 15th East, just back behind a Bible college according to the notes. I'll page your phone with the full details."

"Thank you, man. You're a real lifesaver."

"De nada, cuz," Lance said. "Be seeing you."

"Yeah, you too," said Theo, and hung up. Before Delphine could say anything, he looked at her and said "No, obviously Lance isn't really my cousin. He is a descendant of mine, though."

"How does that work?" Delphine asked.

"The normal way, people have children who grow up and have their own children."

"Well, duh. You're being obtuse."

Theo shrugged. "It was an imprecise question."

"All right, Mr. Precision, how about you tell me

how you manage to retain social links to people you can never see on a normal basis?"

"Actually, it's not that hard. I used to do it with letters, and now I use email. I try to visit everyone once every few years, when I'm in the area and have time. I make myself useful, though, and people will forgive a lot of eccentricities for that."

"Hah, got you, what about the whole not aging thing?"

Theo grinned. "I leave off visiting for a decade every twenty years or so, then come back as my own son. I think the family has me down as Theo Bell Junior VI at the moment. The 'my dad knew your dad' routine works pretty well, especially backed up by a few letters from me as my own father."

Delphine frowned. "Hm. Pretty smart, I guess." She sounded vaguely grudging. "So is this place going to be safe?"

"Safe enough," said Theo, nodding.

"What about daylight? Will we have time to lightproof it?"

Theo shook his head. "There's no need."

"How do you know?"

"Trust me, will you?"

Delphine glared at him. "I'm already trusting you with my life in at least two ways, and I'm not happy about either of them. Don't expect a third any time soon."

Theo sighed. "The place will have a lightproof walk-in cupboard or closet, okay?"

Delphine looked suspicious. "How do you know?"

"They all do."

"Why?"

"This isn't twenty questions," said Theo, irritably.

Delphine looked at him flatly. "Why?"

"I persuaded Lance to make it a feature of the properties, as a unique selling point. He took some convincing, but I got him the job in the first place, so he agreed."

Delphine laughed, delighted. "I bet he thinks you're an absolute wacko."

"Thanks," said Theo sourly.

"You're welcome," she said brightly. "So he's okay with you breaking in too, is he?"

"We won't be breaking in. I have a key."

She looked at him curiously. "What, like you're psychic or something now?"

"All Lance's properties have locks from the same series and can be opened with the same master key. Another suggestion of mine that took some persuasion."

"Thorough," said Delphine, sounding reluctantly impressed. "Do all vampires do this sort of thing?"

Theo grinned. "Absolutely not. I'm unusual. Then again, most kindred are settled in one city, rather than on permanent roving assignment. I've been moving around almost constantly for over a hundred and twenty years. Speaking of which, we've got to get on with it."

They got back onto the bike and cruised the short distance to Elliot Avenue. The area looked grimy and downtrodden, a mess of cheap apartments and even cheaper businesses washed over with a light covering of old newspapers, cigarette ends and street trash. Theo nodded with satisfaction but didn't stop. He drove half a dozen more blocks into the heart of downtown, then parked the bike at a long-term lot and walked out onto the street.

Delphine followed him out onto the busy sidewalk, looking wild around the eyes. Of course—her first time out in the mortal world since her embrace. Silly of him. He put an arm around her shoulders and led her back to the entryway of the parking ramp.

"Do you want to tell me about it?"

She shuddered, but when she spoke, her voice was slow and distracted, with a hard, hungry edge. "It's…

different. Brighter. Louder. Harder. Faster. And the people… It's like I'm not actually seeing them as people. They're just… I can smell their blood, and… and it's making me so hungry… so hot… I… It's like I just want to launch into the middle of them and start ripping into them… This should feel *so* wrong. Theo, why doesn't it feel wrong?"

He answered her gently. "Try to keep a lid on it. You're not alive any more, remember?"

"I don't feel any different…"

Theo arched an eyebrow, amused. "Oh, really?"

"I… Um. No, I do feel different, but it's still me. I didn't think it would still be me. My god, is this what it's going to be like?"

"Every night. Except it gets stronger."

Delphine blinked. "Stronger? Don't you just want to drink it all down, *bathe* in all that gorgeous blood?"

Theo nodded. "Yes. Do you remember what I told you earlier, about sinking into the hunger one night and never coming out? That's exactly what it is like. You have to resist."

"It's impossible. You'd never be able…" She sounded awed.

"You'll find that your willpower is a lot stronger now that you're free of mortal distractions. You can resist anything, most of the time, if you put your mind to it. Don't let yourself get too hungry, though, or else you *will* lose it. Fire, sunlight, fury, those can do it, too."

"Is that it then? One strike and you're out?"

"No, you snap out of it sooner or later. There'll be times when you really wish you hadn't though, when you remember what you did. When it all goes red, you'll do absolutely anything. Those are the times when you need something to give you a reason to continue. Without it, you might not make it back at all."

"How do you face it?" Delphine sounded horrified. "Doesn't it scare you?"

"It terrifies me," said Theo. "But I face it, because I prefer it to the alternative—which is dying now, rather than later." He looked at Delphine's eyes darting hungrily around the crowd. "I think we need a cab."

There were a number of taxis roaming the street, and Theo quickly flagged one down. He bundled Delphine into the back and got in after her, noting with a certain amount of relief that she seemed to calm down a little once she was isolated again. Theo had the driver just head around the city aimlessly for a while, watching Delphine watch the night, then had him drop them off. They switched straight into another cab, which eventually took them back to Elliott Avenue.

The driver pulled up and Theo got out, went round to the man's window, and gazed deep into his eyes. The man's will was a tiny thing, undermined by years of sorrow and privation. At some level, his mind welcomed Theo's control, maybe even hoped for deliverance. "Come with us silently."

The driver nodded once, took the keys out of the ignition, and got out of the cab.

"What are you *doing?*" Delphine hissed. "He…" She trailed off.

"I'm laying on some dinner," said Theo, with the ghost of a grin.

"But… We can't just do this, can we?"

"Depends who you're asking. We all have to nourish ourselves somehow. You can't take too much— you don't want to hospitalize or kill him—but a bit won't have any lasting effects. Okay, legally, mortal society would be pretty hostile, but then you're not mortal any more. Don't you want to feed?"

"I… Oh. Oh, yes…"

"Not here," said Theo sharply. Delphine jerked back, looking a little guilty. "Let's get inside, eh?"

The apartment had a ground-floor entrance. The key worked perfectly, opening onto a claustrophobic little staircase. The first few steps were drowned in flyers, free newspapers and other junk mail, but the floorboards seemed relatively free of dust. Theo shooed Delphine up first and then the driver, before closing the door to the street and following on.

At the top of the stairs, another door led out into the main room. It was furnished cheaply, but everything appeared relatively tidy, and if the stuff had seen better days, at least it wasn't falling to pieces. Theo warmed to the place immediately. He turned to the cab driver, pointed to a patch of floor, and said "Lie down there and keep quiet."

The driver obeyed immediately.

Delphine was eyeing the man hungrily. Theo grinned at her and said, "Well, what are you waiting for?" She didn't even bother answering. She dropped to her knees, fell over him, and sank her fangs into the soft flesh where his neck met his shoulder. She drank slowly and sensuously, making little moans of pleasure through the mouthfuls of blood.

Theo watched her for several minutes. When he estimated she'd had as much as the man could spare, he put his hands on her shoulders and pulled her away. "That's enough."

She glanced at him, disappointed. "Can't I just…"

He cut her off. "No. Sorry. Any more and you'll damage him. You don't want to hurt the poor bastard, do you?"

Delphine shook her head vigorously, sending little spatters of blood left and right. "I only want to hurt the bastards who've got Nathalie."

"You have to make sure never to have more than a couple of pints at a time. For now, you have to lick the wounds you were feeding through."

She looked at him, confused.

"It stops the bleeding, and heals the puncture marks."

She raised her eyebrows, but bent back down and

licked the man's neck. Her eyes widened a little as the puncture marks healed over. "Wow! How cool is that!"

"Yeah, it's useful," said Theo laconically. "Now, if you'll excuse me a moment…"

Delphine got out of the way, and Theo locked eyes with the dazed-looking cab driver. "Get up." The man obeyed immediately. Theo then stepped forward and smashed his will into the driver's mind like a hammer, shattering the man's already confused thoughts and memories. "Listen to me. You picked us up downtown, where we had been shopping. You drove us here—the traffic was fairly light, and you were thinking about getting home when you finish work tonight—and when we arrived, you gave me a hand carrying some bags upstairs and putting them away. Nothing out of the ordinary happened. You suspect that we are students at the Bible school, rooming together to save money."

Theo released the cab driver's mind and stepped back. The man shook his head a little, clearly confused. Theo reached into his pocket and fished a twenty from the cash Angus had given him and handed it to the driver with a smile. "Thanks for the hand with the cases, friend. Keep the change."

"Yeah, it was a pleasure," said the driver uncertainly.

Theo put a friendly hand on his shoulder and nudged him gently toward the door. "God bless."

"Yeah." The driver was sounding more sure of himself. He nodded to them, then headed off down the stairs. Theo heard the front door slam.

"Hey! Isn't he just going to run straight to the cops and turn me in or something?" asked Delphine.

"He was weak-willed, and I overwhelmed him. He'll remember my version of events, not what really happened."

"You can do that?" Delphine sounded impressed.

"Yup," Theo said.

"Way cool! Can I?"

"You might be able to do it," said Theo. "It's pretty advanced though. I can show you how to feel some of what the blood inside you can do. Teach you a trick or two."

"Wow," breathed Delphine. "Really?"

"Really," said Theo.

"What can I do?"

"I don't know for sure. We're all different."

"Well, I want to be beautiful," said Delphine immediately. "You said that Kris was doing it somehow, didn't you? If I'm descended from her or whatever, it seems a fair bet that I should be able to do it too. I want people to do shit that I want them to."

"Think about it for a bit," said Theo. "It's pretty important."

"Damn right it's important," said Delphine. "If you're beautiful, you can get away with just about anything. Well, I guess being rich helps, too."

"You're still thinking mortal," said Theo. "Look, you may as well sit down and get comfy, because this might take a while…"

chapter Eight:
Dumb Blondes

Theo snapped awake, wrenching straight into full consciousness as usual. He lay there for a while, aware of Delphine beside him and of the rising darkness outside, thinking about the night's work.

"Th-Theo?" Delphine's voice—tense, quavering slightly—snapped him out of his contemplation.

"I'm right here," said Theo.

"What's wrong with me? I can't see. I can't move. Oh god." Her voice was getting steadily more panicky, the first ragged edges of frenzy starting to creep in.

"Shh, you're fine," he said soothingly. "Let go of the fear. Relax. You're perfectly safe. This closet is lightproof, remember? There's nothing to see by. Your arms and legs are fine too, they're just heavy. You aren't alive any more, so they don't work quite the same way. Take it easy, and it'll come back to you. There's no need to panic. It's…"

"If you tell me it's all perfectly natural again, I'm going to fucking smack you."

Theo grinned. That sounded better. "Okay, how about we settle on 'it's the same for all of us?'"

"Hmph. I guess that will do."

"Waking up can be a bit of a shock the first few times. You really do get used to it quickly, though."

"Why didn't I feel like this yesterday?"

"You would have, but you probably just didn't notice. If you have other things on your mind, your body just gets on with it."

"I was too stressed to notice being dead?" She paused, and Theo could just picture her eyebrows furrowing slightly as she thought it over. "I guess that makes a peculiarly sick kind of sense." She chuckled grimly. "So what's the score then?"

"You wait here while I take care of a few small chores, and then we'll go find you some fresh clothes."

"Shopping?" Delphine sounded delighted. "That's my kind of plan."

While Delphine stayed at the apartment, a quiet, late-night car rental outlet obligingly provided "Harry Bowman" with a boxy Ford that would do for getting around town. The eager young assistant totally forgot donating a couple of pints of blood, although Theo was unable to make her wipe the ecstatic grin from her face. He then left a message reassuring Angus that everything was under control, drove back to Elliot Avenue and picked up Delphine. He resisted the urge to check on his R1 and parked instead in a sprawling multi-level lot attached to some mall or other.

Twenty minutes later, Theo was getting extremely bored of waiting around. He shot another bemused glance at a tall stand holding various colorful bits of string that claimed, implausibly, to be female undergarments. There was a rustle of curtains.

"Well, what do you think? Come on, be honest." Delphine stepped out of the changing room, smiling brightly.

The shop's fashions catered largely for the alternative music scene, and Theo had been amused to see a couple of obviously mortal youths who seemed to be trying to look like vampires. Delphine, however, was another matter.

"You look like a whore."

To Theo's surprise, Delphine's smile just broadened. "You don't like it?"

"No," Theo said, shaking his head. "I don't."

"Perfect."

Theo sighed. "It's not exactly going to be subtle for trawling around bars in. It's not going to impress the primogen much, either."

"Whatever." Delphine shrugged, disinterested.

"Look, if we're going to get your sister back, you're going to have to concentrate on being practical."

She glared at him. "You're no fun. I'm trying really, really hard to come to terms with this and make the most of it. I've gotta find ways to hunt for myself, right?"

Theo nodded. "Yes, you do, and the styles you choose to wear when you are established will be entirely up to you, but until then, do as I say, and find an outfit that will attract less attention. A skirt that actually covers your panties would be a good start. You don't want a bare midriff, either—you don't feel the cold properly any more, and a lack of reaction to what would be uncomfortable for mortals can attract the wrong sort of attention."

Delphine pouted at him. "You're so out of touch, old man. I mean, please."

Theo growled. "We'll save the fashion debate for another time. Find something else to wear, child."

She huffed and flounced back into the changing rooms. She came out again a few minutes later, in tight matte PVC pants and a scuffed-leather biker's jacket, both black. "Better?"

Theo shrugged. "It will do."

"Don't let your enthusiasm run away with you," Delphine said, sounding a little hurt.

Theo shot her a stern glance. "I'm worried about your potential to attract hostile attention, not would-be sexual partners. My main concern is that you don't go setting alarm bells ringing when we have to talk to people. Don't worry about your appearance. You look pretty, child, and the clothes flatter you."

"Really?"

"Really," said Theo. He took the tags over to the counter and paid for the clothes that Delphine was wearing. By the time it had all been totaled up, there was little of Angus's money left. Theo shook his head and left the shop.

As Theo was heading out of the door, Delphine suddenly darted back inside. She was back less than a minute later with a hundred-dollar bill. She handed it to him with a broad smile. "There. Discount."

Theo looked at her narrowly. "Where did you get that?"

"From the clerk. I wanted to see if I could get that charm thing I was practicing last night to work. I told her she'd shortchanged us and gave her this big helpless smile. She looked kinda doubtful, so I was like all apologetic and told her how broke we were, and how losing a hundred would mean we didn't eat and… well… it was like reaching out to her with a big, warm fuzzy and making her feel all loved and special. Then she just smiled and apologized, and handed the cash over! It was really neat."

"That's excellent progress, and I'm impressed," said Theo. "But that money will probably come out of her wages—which, I'm sure, are pitiful. We don't really need it. She does."

"Oh," said Delphine, crestfallen. "I hadn't thought of that."

"Why don't you go give it back?"

"That doesn't seem very… well… monstrous of me."

"Do you *want* to degenerate into an inhuman animal?"

Delphine shuddered. "I'll take the money right back, then?"

Theo nodded.

She shrugged and vanished again for a few moments. When she returned, she was grinning broadly. "I told her it was my mistake. She was really grateful."

"Good girl," said Theo.

"I don't really care anyway. I just wanted to test out some of that stuff. Hey," said Delphine with a glint in her eye. "Would it work on you?"

Theo narrowed his eyes dangerously. "I don't recommend trying to find out. I have been known to react rather extremely to attempts to play with my mind."

"But you've got to look after me," said Delphine cheekily.

Theo whipped around and advanced steadily on Delphine. She backed into the wall, suddenly uncertain. He followed her retreat, bringing his stone-cold face very close to hers. "There are older and deeper promises that bind me harder, little girl. I am not your father, to play games with. I have not even been alive for a century and half. I am going to considerable personal trouble to keep you safe because you may be useful, and because I still remember what it felt like to be young and screwed over." He let the veil drop a little and felt the boiling rage and resentment flood up into his eyes and voice. "But fuck with me, even once, and I'll rip your heart out of your chest and eat it before you've had time to realize the mistake you just made." He pulled the usual mask of blandness back up over his features. "Do you understand me?"

Delphine nodded wordlessly, eyes wide and frightened.

"Good. Come on, then. We have work." He turned and walked away.

A moment later, he heard Delphine following along behind. "Jesus," she muttered to herself. "Talk about grouchy." She was clearly unaware of the sensitivity of his hearing. He grinned, and led them out of the mall.

It was a fairly pleasant night, and the sidewalk was relatively busy in this part of downtown. Theo was pleased to see that Delphine was coping much better with the crowds than she had been the night before.

He gave her a moment, then turned to her, careful to keep any hint of sympathy out of his voice. "We need to start trying to track down your former captors. Is there anything that you can think of that might be useful?"

She shook her head. "I've asked myself that a thousand times. That bitch used some kind of taser on us, and then I think they must have put us under, because when I came round, we were in a little padded white room. We stayed in there for a couple of days, I guess. It's difficult to be sure. There was some noise—scary stuff, screaming and things—but it was pretty muffled. Then they must have drugged the food again or something, because I blacked out, and when I came around, we were shackled and being led out of those vans. I don't know a fucking thing." She glared at him. "All that crap about how much you need me on this better just be bullshit, for both our sakes."

Theo shrugged. "You may find you know more than you think. You're the only source of information I have, and who knows what little snippet might tip the balance?"

She looked at him incredulously. "You're nuts."

"Maybe," agreed Theo. "But in my experience, you never can tell. Besides which, I have other uses for you too."

Delphine arched an eyebrow. "Oh, really?"

"Such as helping me find my way around this wretched city, for example. What do you know about the criminal structure here?"

Delphine glared at him. "What are you suggesting?"

"The only people who might know anything about these slavers are the scum that move in the same circles. That means we have to find some of them and see if we can persuade them to give us some information. Which are the bad bars, the ones you'd only go to in order to make a score?"

She snorted. "Are you trying to imply that I drink and do drugs?"

"I couldn't give a rat's ass if you had to have two trips and a hit of Special K before you could face Friday nights. I'm not asking for a personal history. I'm asking for some suggestions about where we can start looking to try to find the people who have your sister."

"Yeah, well, for the record, I don't touch that shit."

"Delphine…" said Theo warningly.

"Okay, okay. Jesus. Mr. Fucking Efficiency or what? You are *so* uptight. When was the last time you got laid?"

"Eighteen fifty six, as a matter of fact."

"Oh." Delphine blinked. "No wonder you're crabby."

Theo sighed. "This is like pulling teeth. Think, child. Bars."

Delphine pouted. "All right already. Um. Well, the 'Jack of Both Sides' has a pretty nasty rep. It's up near the U. Then there's one of those yucky pole dancer places on Forty-Third that a friend of mine always insisted was full of dealers and pimps, that's called something like 'Funky Monkeys.' Oh yeah, and there's a biker bar out west somewhere that's got a *really* heavy reputation. That's called 'Not-499.' I always thought that was a stupid name."

Theo shook his head. "It's almost witty, actually. It's just a matter of perspective."

"Oh yeah? What perspective is that? Stupid-Thug-Cam, perhaps?"

"Ignorance is so refreshing. Let me enlighten you, child. The criminal motorcycle gangs refer to themselves collectively as 1%ers, in mockery of the American Motorcycle Association's statistic that 99% of bikers are law-abiding. If the bar is called 'Not-499,' then it is declaring that it is not for that 99%—in other words, that it is for the 1%ers."

"So we're going to start there, then?"

"No."

Delphine blinked. "What? Why not?"

"For the same reason that I don't want to just take you into the middle of a Mexican crack house. Shotguns and automatics are *dangerous*. I'd rather not take the risk of inflaming an entire gang unless there's no choice."

She frowned at him. "I can take care of myself."

Theo shook his head. "No, you can't. Not like that. Not yet." She stuck her tongue out at him, which he ignored. "We'll start somewhere a bit mellower…"

***

The Jack of Both Sides was located in what looked like a demilitarized zone. The area claimed to be known as "Cemetery Junction," although there was no obvious reason why. Half the shops along the street were boarded up, and most of the rest had security grilles over the doors and windows. Stinking piles of trash dotted the sidewalk—some obviously just crap from the squalid shops or the vile apartments above them, others still breathing and muttering to themselves through alcoholic hazes.

Picking his way through the mess of litter, broken bottles, used syringes and dog shit, Theo made for the bar, Delphine close behind. It was every bit as unpleasant as Cemetery Junction itself. The building was large, an old, multi-level affair with several peaked roofs. Grimy gray windows peeked out from underneath rotting eaves that may, once, have been painted green. Lights shined out of all the ground floor windows, old neon signs boasting that the bar sold beer, hot food and cheap rooms. Theo was slightly surprised to find a bouncer just inside the door and was relieved that he'd left his weapons behind. The ape glowered down at him for a moment, adjusted his lapel unnecessarily, then grunted and waved the pair through.

The inside was just about as shitty as Theo expected. The bar was divided up into three or four different areas by the structure of the building, which was obviously a converted house. The restrooms were immediately in front of them, but through wide openings in the walls, Theo could see cheap, flimsy wooden tables and chairs dotted around the place. Centerfolds had been tacked up in places around the walls as a form of decoration, their faded charms glinting greasily across the rooms. Off in the distance, a pool table had been boarded over and was being used as a makeshift drink stand. Tinny rock music floated out from somewhere at a surprisingly low volume. Theo turned to Delphine.

"I thought you said this was a place kids came to score?"

Delphine shot him a withering glance. "No. If you remember, I told you that I didn't know jack shit about the drug scene, and that this bar had a bad reputation. I don't know anyone who comes here."

"Oh. All right. Well, be careful. It could be rough. Stay close, keep quiet and don't make eye contact with anyone. In fact, it's best if you ignore everyone except me. Just look at the floor or at me, okay?"

"Whatever." She sighed.

Theo headed left, more or less at random, and walked into the bar. He glanced around at the patrons, a predictable selection of the poor, desperate and criminal. He was pleased to see there were no obvious signs of the bar being a gang stronghold, and only one patron was displaying significant colors. He made his way straight to the counter at the back of the room, ignoring one muttered racist slur leveled at the pair of them. He could feel Delphine stiffening slightly, but the girl had the self-control to let the comment pass.

He walked up to the deserted bar, pulled up a stool and sat down. Delphine came up and stood close behind him, draping herself over him lethargically in an impressive display of quick thinking. The woman serving turned and looked at them with an open sneer, then turned away again, pretending to be doing something else. Theo fished out a twenty and slapped it down on the counter. After a short while, she came over.

"What'll it be… sir?" The woman had a whiny voice, with the rough grate of a hardened smoker. She delayed the honorific to the point of mockery, following it up with a hard, challenging look. Her voice got even more sarcastic. "I'm afraid we don't serve liquor to children."

Delphine managed to remain relaxed and just gazed at Theo, apparently bored out of her mind. "I wasn't after liquor," said Theo. "I was hoping you'd be able to get me something a little more exotic."

The woman's face turned to stone, and she looked dismissively at Delphine before turning back to him. "I think you're doing just fine for exotic tonight. Officer."

"I'm not a fucking cop," said Theo menacingly.

"Sure you're not," said the woman. "You just stumbled in here coincidentally to get a glass of milk for your little piece of ass, right? Well, officer, let me reassure you we're *real* worried about safety here. You're full-square on candid camera right this very instant. You and the jailbait both."

Theo shook his head and reached out to her, probing his mind past the years of bitterness and loss that swathed her personality, drilling down to the woman underneath, letting her become aware that he could see her and accepted her without judgment. Her rock-hard patina of resentment crumbled. He then made eye contact and didn't even have to push past her willpower—she invited him in. He spoke quietly to her, the words burying deep. "You trust me completely and want to help me."

She nodded, her face immediately relaxing into an almost pretty smile.

"I'm really not a cop," said Theo. "I promise."

"I can see that," said the woman. "Sorry about that. We have to be sure, and you were being so obvious… I hope you understand."

Theo nodded pleasantly, ignoring Delphine's little shakes of silent laughter. "Of course. Who's the person to talk to round here? I need a few favors done."

"Speak to Ben. He's over by the pool table with his, uh, 'droogs.' Tell him I said you're okay. I'm Alison."

"Thanks, Alison."

"No problems, big guy. See you again soon, maybe?"

Theo forced a smile. "Yeah, maybe. Keep the twenty." He stood up, pulling Delphine upright with him, and sauntered back out of the room and across the hall to the other half of the bar. She poked him once in the ribs but otherwise kept quiet. The guy holding court by the pool table certainly looked the type, scruffy but strongly muscled, with patchy stubble and a grimy T-shirt. He looked up as Theo and Delphine approached, dumb aggression his instinctive response. Before he could speak, Theo held his hands up placatingly and said "Ben? Alison said you might be able to help me with a little problem I've got." Delphine slipped under one arm, keeping up her bored junkie impression.

His expression didn't waver, and his voice was thick and ugly with anger. "Yeah?"

"Yeah. She said to tell you she thinks I'm okay."

"Yeah?" The thug sounded doubtful.

"Yeah," replied Theo, starting to wonder if the man was actually capable of conversation.

"Oh."

Theo sighed to himself and realized that Delphine was fighting down giggles again. "So, can you help?"

Ben laughed, a nasty, brutal sound, and immediately the rest of the pack joined in on cue, sniggering away. Eventually they ground to a halt, and

Ben looked at Theo expectantly.

Theo looked back.

Finally, Ben shrugged. "Yeah."

"Good," said Theo, trying not to grind his teeth in frustration. The idiot and his pals were starting to look a lot like an early evening snack. "I need to find some people."

"I know people," said Ben.

Theo felt a sudden, wild urge to rip the man's throat out. "I need to find some *specific* people." Delphine started shaking again, although there was no sign of her amusement on her face. He made a mental note to talk to her about taking things seriously.

"Yeah?"

"Yeah," said Theo sourly.

There was another long pause, and then Ben collapsed giggling helplessly across the pool table, to the great amusement of his companions.

Theo blinked.

"Oh brother, I wish you could see your fucking face right now. '*I wad the poor, th'gift he gi'us…*' Man, you're a picture! Talk about patronizing and leaping to assumptions. What is it with you fucking wannabes? You always assume that we're all so fucking stupid that we're hardly capable of rational thought, let alone of holding critical opinions. Jesus, do you really think that it's that easy to gain some influence that any monosyllabic cretin can make the grades? Well, who's the idiot now, hey?"

Theo felt the fury boiling inside him. The pathetic little piece of shit was actually laughing at him. Some disgusting, insignificant street punk. It would be the work of a moment to lash out and rip his fucking head off, gorge on the hot blood as it spurted out of his corpse, tear his moronic cronies to splinters… Red mists started to descend, and Theo welcomed them. He tensed himself to spring, feeling Delphine's silent giggles again as he moved. Delphine? If he lost it now, there'd be no telling what happened to her. That couldn't be allowed to happen. He fought the frenzy for several moments before he finally regained a measure of control.

In fact, to be fair, the punk was right—Theo *had* made a fool out of himself. He relaxed again, silently thanking Delphine and her amusement.

"I guess I am," said Theo wryly.

Ben grinned, his voice light with mirth. "I like a man who's not ashamed to stand up and say he's made a significant misjudgment. Well, just so happens I know pretty much everyone worth knowing in this place, one way or another. Who do you want to find, friend of Alison?"

"The Minneapolis Triangle."

Ben stepped back immediately, his face icy, and his pack closed in around him protectively. "Time you left."

"I…" began Theo, stopping when he saw several of the men reaching for poorly concealed weapons. This could become a problem. "Wait." He took another step toward Ben and the group all pulled large-caliber pistols from jackets and belts, and pointed them straight at him.

"Not interested," said Ben flatly. "No such thing. Go away. Now."

There was too much determination hammering against him to just overwhelm the pack. Theo focused inward, to the burning core of his spirit, and called to it, cajoling, teasing it into full bloom. His blood sang as his spirit infused it, a siren song of intoxicating power and beautiful danger, and then his aura ignited, washing out over the pack in a tide of love and respect. Their expressions immediately cleared, and the guns came down. Delphine sighed a little, still gazing up at him, and clung tighter to him, rubbing her cheek against him where she was nestled on his chest. He fought down a sigh of his own. He'd have to deal with that later. He glanced down at her, surprised to find himself noticing how beautiful she was. He fought his mind back on topic.

"Where can I find the Triangle, Ben?"

Surprisingly, Ben shook his head. "I'm really sorry, but I can't tell you that man. It'd be killing you. Listen, trust me. Just forget it, give it up, go home."

"I need to know, Ben."

"No way. I wouldn't tell you how to find them, even if I knew how. I respect you far too much to do that to you, and anyway, as soon as they'd killed you, I'd be dead."

"Tell me," said Theo, locking eyes with Ben and throwing the full force of his mind against the burning conviction of the man's will.

Ben shook his head sympathetically. "I'm sorry man. I know how much you want this, and it kills me, but I can't help you on this."

Theo sighed, defeated. "Okay. We'll find them some other way."

"Don't, man. Really. Don't."

Theo ignored him, disentangled himself from Delphine a little. She immediately stretched her arm around his waist and rested her head on his shoulder. He sighed again and headed out of the bar. As they got outside, Delphine pulled him to a stop and turned to him, pressing up against him.

"Theo, I…"

Unsurprised, Theo put a finger to her soft lips, silencing her immediately. "Shh. Do you trust me?"

She nodded, silently, eyes wide with adoration.

"Follow me, then." He led her quickly back to the car, relieved that it had remained unmolested, and they got in. "First of all, I want you to close your eyes."

Delphine obeyed immediately, happy anticipation lighting her lovely face.

The sudden, overpowering urge to have the girl drink from him welled up, so strong that he could hardly think. It would be so much easier if she were devoted. Theo tried to shake it off, reminding himself it was just another set of shackles, but the memory of her soft curves nestled against him ate away at his self-control like acid.

"Open your mouth." She did so, lips parting softly, expectantly. She flicked her tongue over them, moistening them. He shook his head again, stubbornly. What was he thinking? Heh. That it would be so good to have her, that's what. So sweet to be loved without reservation. It would certainly make the primogen go easier on her too, if she were bound. It might even save her. In fact, it might be the only way to keep her from the chopping block. If he didn't take the opportunity to do so now, he might actually be killing her. He reached his arm toward her, hypnotized by the horrifying image of her paralyzed body burning as the sun hit it.

Then, reluctantly, a sour note intruded. He remembered her silent amusement at the mess he'd made in the bar, and the way it had pulled him back from frenzy. That irreverent humor would be gone forever if he bound her. Along with most of the rest of what made her herself. Vile indeed. He shuddered and pulled his arm back, and a nasty thought hit him. He disentangled himself from the last shreds of the magnetism he had activated in the bar, noting wearily that Delphine still looked beautifully awestruck. He looked away from her and gave his head a moment to start clearing.

"Delphine, did you turn the charm on me?"

"I wanted you to love me the way I love you," she said dreamily. "Don't be angry, baby."

"I'm not angry," said Theo. "But you have to stop it. Right now."

"Okay." The desperate need to bond her faded completely, and Theo sat there for several seconds, shuddering at how close it had come.

"Good. Now, I want you think back to your first night as a vampire. Do you remember when we were in the car? When you told me that I was treating you like a charity case?"

"Yes…" said Delphine, sounding troubled.

"I want you to think about that really hard. You said I was an asshole."

"Yeah," she said, her voice getting a bit stronger. "You were."

"I was going to abandon you with your father, if he'd still been alive."

"I'd never have lasted a week. Jesus." Her eyes flicked open, angry. "I was right. You are an asshole." She paused a second, and confusion flooded her face. "Oh my *god*. What the hell was that? You were like the second coming or something!"

"And now?" asked Theo.

"Now you're an asshole again," said Delphine flatly.

Theo sagged back, suddenly exhausted. "I'm really sorry. You got caught in the backwash of me turning the charm on to those thugs. You then responded in kind, and I didn't notice. You've *got* to make sure that doesn't happen again. I almost made you drink my blood, and you'd have done it joyfully."

She shuddered. "Yeah, I would have two minutes ago." She frowned again, pissed off. "Hey, no fair. I can't *believe* I told you I loved you. It's totally not true, okay? You're a jerk, and you're like totally ancient, and you're a weird monster thing. I mean, eww."

Theo snorted, amused despite himself. "It's okay, I know that."

"Oh, it's okay is it? You *are* a jerk." She giggled suddenly. "You're a really crappy undercover agent too. Tell you what, Mr. SWAT Team—next time, why don't you leave it to me?"

Theo arched an eyebrow. "Oh yeah? What would you have done?"

"I'd have bought a few drinks, to start with. I'd have sounded that girl out a lot more gently, too."

"Why bother?" asked Theo pointedly. "We don't have all that much time. It makes more sense to cut corners."

Delphine shuddered delicately. "Would you use a sledgehammer to open a can of beans? Trust me. We could have kept a much lower profile and probably gotten more information."

Theo shook his head wryly. "We'll see. In the mean time, we're going to have to try somewhere else, and *not* the biker bar."

Delphine grinned at him. "Lead on, oh mighty secret agent."

The car pulled away and out of Cemetery Junction, leaving several extremely doubtful people in its wake. A pair of them retreated back behind the cover of the bar door as the tail lights faded.

"He's gonna get himself killed," Ben said. "I can't just let that happen, for fuck's sake. He doesn't understand."

"It's the only thing you can do," said Alison. "They'll just warn him off. It's not betraying him. It's saving him."

"Yeah," said Ben, sounding troubled. "It *is* the only thing I can do."

The door swung shut.

chapter nine:
fugue

The villa nestled in a small, lushly forested valley, high up in the hills overlooking the sprawl of Sao Paolo. It was a warm, clear night, and with the moon on the wane, the stars were brilliant. This far up, the city was a silent whimsy, a beautiful, glittering map of endeavor and possibility—as above, so below. Only Scops owls, cicadas and crickets intruded. The couple that sat on the lush stone balcony looking out over the landscape could possibly have been mistaken for mortal lovers. Even a half-hearted scrutiny would have warned an observer that these creatures were something very different, however.

The woman turned away from her lazy examination of the city and looked her companion over. "You seem to be keeping well."

The man bared his teeth in a gesture that might have been a distant memory of a smile. "As do you."

"Well enough, thank you."

"I'm afraid I might have to correct that."

The woman arched a perfect eyebrow, amused. "Surely that can't be a threat?"

"Good gracious, no. Although I do apologize for my sloppy phrasing. There have been some troubling developments in the design."

She nodded, graciously. "I see."

"We seem to have attracted a little attention in Minnesota."

"It was inevitable," said the woman, shrugging. "I've heard the rumors. Sooner or later, someone was going to start sniffing around."

The man grimaced. "Unfortunately, our bloodhound is Theophilus Bell."

"The anarch-slaughterer?"

"Yes."

The woman shrugged. "Does he pose a significant threat?"

"Possibly. He has a reputation for combining competence, ruthlessness and a pathologically stubborn streak."

"There's some reason why you can't just have him killed, I assume," said the woman.

"It would be simple enough, but there is an issue. The Justicar, Paschek, is even worse. If Bell were eliminated, Paschek might just take it upon himself to get involved. They dislike each other, but the Justicar reacts badly to the loss of his agents. If he did take an interest, he'd be able bring a lot more pressure to bear than Bell can."

"Yes," said the woman. "I can see that might cause some inconvenience, and it's too soon to have the Justicar murdered. Perhaps he can be purchased, however?"

"We've already tried that," said the man, scowling. "If it hadn't been the Brujah, then perhaps…"

"There is a certain poetic symmetry there."

"That is by the by."

The woman steepled her fingers together pensively. "Perhaps *Bell* can be purchased?"

"I don't see how. He disdains wealth and property, and has little personal vanity. He was a slave in life and still retains many of the prejudices associated with that role."

"He's a crusader. Trying to do his bit. He might respond well to a challenge."

The man looked doubtful. "What did you have in mind?"

"A principality with a weak council would give him enough to do to keep him out of our hair."

The man shook his head. "He has no interest in politics. He was offered New York on a plate."

"I was thinking of something different," said the woman. "A purely administrative role would not appeal to that type of soldier."

"Pray tell," the man said with a sweeping gesture.

The woman smiled, a much better attempt than her companion's had been. "Give him a territory where he can make a difference. We have a few places sufficiently under our thumb. Somewhere beleaguered by the Sabbat. We could instruct the locals to invite Bell in, and then have the attackers fall back in response to his forays. It would be simple to mire him in the situation."

The man nodded thoughtfully. "Yes, that might work. If the prince were killed, the primogen could be instructed to plead for his help in taking over and helping them to repel the new offensive. His reputation is good enough. Where were you considering?"

"Fresno?"

"That's no good. It's not blue collar enough to stir Bell's sympathies. He identifies with the downtrodden."

"Flint, then, in Michigan. That should be downtrodden enough for anyone."

"Ideal," said the man enthusiastically. "Just his sort of territory."

"I'll have the prince of Flint eliminated and instruct the primogen to start screaming for Bell's assistance."

"Perfect. I'll speak to the Archbishop of Detroit later and have him start a program of attacks immediately."

"Do so. In the meantime, can we rely on the Minneapolis team to keep Bell occupied without revealing the scope of the operation?"

"I think so," the man said.

"Good. I take it his lair is known?"

"Of course."

"Fine. If Bell doesn't go for the bait, make arrangements to have him killed, and we'll deal with Paschek later. Are there any other issues?"

The man frowned. "Rumors are starting to circulate about San Diego, and we've had to eliminate a missing persons taskforce in Miami, but Seattle, San Antonio and Detroit are running smoothly."

"Very well," said the woman, rising smoothly to her feet. "If anything changes, inform me."

"And vice-versa," replied the man. "Be seeing you."

"Yes," the woman said, "You will." She stepped into the night and vanished, leaving the man to the cicadas, the owls and his thoughts.

***

Saxon's was a cruddy little dive on the wrong side of the river, a cheap, nasty place with plastic furniture and shabby customers. It was the fifth bar that Theo had visited since leaving the Jack of Both Sides, and it had only two useful virtues—it was still open at 2 a.m., and it was the favored late-night drinking hole of a local fence named John Torrance. Someone earlier in the evening had recommended him, so they'd come to this place and given it a good try.

Despite Delphine's best efforts, Torrance wasn't going to provide anything useful. The girl was good, he had to admit it; people went to more effort to be creative with their help and make intuitive leaps when they weren't being browbeaten, and she was such a good liar even he found himself half-believing her. No wonder she'd been so amused earlier in the evening. Still, half an hour of very subtle probing later, Torrance still hadn't said anything useful. Either he didn't know, or he genuinely considered passing information on to be suicide.

Now they were back down the deserted block, where they'd parked the car, and Theo was trying hard to come up with some alternatives. A whole night wasted. He thought longingly about hitting something.

Delphine must have noticed his expression, because she kept her voice relatively serious. "Where do we try next, Theo? I'm out of suggestions for late-night places."

He shrugged. "I'm surprised we haven't been able to turn anything up. We'll just have to head back to the apartment and start again tomorrow night."

"Don't you want to try that biker bar?"

Theo shook his head stubbornly. "No. No way. Not with you in tow."

"It might be closed by now," Delphine said.

"That doesn't mean it'll be unguarded," said Theo. "Places like that are always scared that the cops are going to raid them, so they have all sorts of security going on."

Delphine grinned. "Hey, c'mon, it sounds like fun!"

Theo looked at her for a moment then shook his head. "You know, maybe we're going about this the wrong way."

"I'm afraid that's an accurate assessment, Mr. Bell," said a man crossing the road toward them. He was fairly tall and powerfully built, with short, tidy black hair. He was wearing a black Italian suit over a white T-shirt, and moved with a grace that suggested he was kindred.

Theo stared at him, motioned Delphine to move behind him. "Who the fuck are you?"

"You've been making a lot of noise tonight," said the vampire pleasantly. "My associates have been watching you on and off since the Cheeky Monkey.

They have a rather impressive array of high-caliber weapons trained on us all right now, in fact. We could have destroyed you both a dozen times over tonight. The fact that we have not harmed either of you should tell you something."

Theo snorted. "It tells me you're full of shit."

The vampire smiled politely. "As you say, Mr. Bell."

"Who are you?"

The smile stayed locked in place. "A friend."

Theo looked at the vampire steadily. "I don't have any friends."

"That may be both more and less true than you realize."

"Look, I've had a long night, and you're really starting to piss me off. What the fuck do you want?"

"I want to give you something to think about," said the vampire, still smiling. "For the future. Our interests do not have to clash. There's no reason why we can't be good neighbors. My associates and I on one side of the yard, and you, your friend and her sister on the other. There's no reason for relations to deteriorate."

"My sister?" screeched Delphine. "Where is she, you fuck?"

Theo grabbed her as she tried to charge past him wildly. "Stop it. Delphine! Stop!" He turned her around to look in her eyes as he spoke the last word, summoning up a thick blanket of caution and reserve, and smothering her outrage with it. She subsided, muttering angrily.

The vampire shot her a patronizing look. "Don't worry, your sister is alive and well. She is being treated with all the respect and consideration she so richly deserves. Concentrate on other matters, forget about my associates, and she will be released."

"What do you mean, 'other matters'?" asked Theo suspiciously.

The smile broadened a little further. "There are certain consolations that my associates can provide, assuming that you decide to stop working against us."

Theo's expression darkened. "I'm not for sale."

"Be that as it may, Mr. Bell, I would advise you strongly not to interfere. The consequences would be regrettably dire—for you, your companion and her twin. This is a lot larger than you suspect."

"I'm not easily scared off," said Theo.

"As you wish, Mr. Bell," said the vampire, smiling and bowing slightly. "Good evening to you."

The vampire turned to walk away, apparently unconcerned to be presenting his back. Theo thought about snapping his neck, but regretfully decided against it, just to be safe. Delphine glanced past Theo at something behind him, and her eyes widened. Without even hesitating, Theo dropped to the ground, pulling Delphine down with him. There was a loud blast, and gunfire, passing over the space that Delphine had just occupied. Someone shrieked, briefly.

"Run," growled Theo, then rolled forward toward the place that the shots had come from. The blood ignited within him, hot and furious, his muscles burning with its power. He leaped forward, the world seemingly stuttering around him, and was rewarded with a muffled curse. A male vampire with a shock of long, floppy blond hair leaped back so swiftly he almost blurred, neatly avoiding getting tangled in his calf-length overcoat. As he did so, he threw a shotgun at Theo's face. Theo ducked under the gun and jumped after the vampire, and the newcomer dove forward underneath him. Theo landed heavily, surprised to see that the vampire was continuing to move forward at high speed. It took him a moment to understand, but then it twigged— he was heading for Delphine's retreating form.

Theo lashed out swiftly with a boot, catching the vampire in the calf. His opponent staggered, and Theo took advantage of the pause to whip round and grab the vampire's heel. He pulled, and the vampire came crashing to the ground.

"Delphine, go!" yelled Theo. "Run!" He tried to keep hold of the vampire's leg, but the man jerked his leg away before Theo could get a proper grip and wormed his way out from the hold. Theo leaped to his feet, pleased to hear Delphine's footsteps fading, and caught the vampire in a huge football tackle as soon he was standing. The pair of them crashed back to the ground again, rolling around. At first, the vampire was only really trying to get out of Theo's hold, twisting and slipping around to try to make it out, but Theo was able to keep up with his wriggling, and the hold was a good one.

As soon as he realized that he wasn't going to slide out of Theo's grapple, the vampire changed his tactic and scissored a ferocious openhanded jab at Theo's eyes. Theo swayed aside and smashed his forehead into the side of vampire's skull, knocking him backward against the road. The vampire responded with a brutal knee to the pit of Theo's stomach, simultaneously trying to push him away. Theo held on tight and sunk his fangs into the ball of the vampire's shoulder, straight through the skin and into bone—almost bloodless, but agonizing. The vampire screamed and punched Theo hard in the side of the face, once, twice, a third time, until Theo was forced to release the bite. His grip weakened as he did so, and the vampire grabbed one of Theo's thumbs in both hands and wrenched at it. Theo cursed, but the vampire tore free and sprang to his feet. Theo shook his head to clear it as he got up.

The vampire took a cautious step backward, crouching low, hands spread wide. Theo advanced a step to keep close, not wanting to give the vampire a chance to chase after Delphine.

"Police! Freeze!" The voices came from back up the road toward the bar, the direction that Delphine had fled in. The blond vampire shot Theo a disgusted glance, and then tore off, blurring away.

Theo sighed, and decided that it was going to be easier to play along. He raised his arms slowly and called out "Thank God you arrived, officers. He was crazy. I thought he was going to kill me."

"Stay right there sir," called one cop, clearly nervous.

"Of course," said Theo.

"Are you injured?" asked another cop.

"I don't think so," said Theo, trying to sound as if he might be shaken by the whole thing. There were four cops, obviously attracted by the shotgun blast a few minutes earlier. All of them had their guns out, and they were advancing cautiously, ready to open fire if he proved a threat. Less disruptive if they could be dealt with peacefully. He focused and dug deep within his mind, down to his rock-hard conviction, and pulled it up over himself like a cloak. The blood inside him absorbed it and smashed it back out into his aura, infusing him with it. He slumped slightly, pulled his face into a mask of subservience and waited for the police to approach. As they closed, one of the stories that Delphine had used earlier in the evening came back to him. "Hey, did you guys see if my assistant was okay? Tall girl, red hair?"

"She's fine, sir," said a dumpy cop. "She took shelter in Saxon's, a bar just up the road. She was the one who alerted us to your location. Are you okay?"

"I'm fine, thank you," said Theo, forcing a smile. "You guys scared him off."

"Do you have any idea why he would have wanted to attack *you*, sir?"

Theo shook his head slowly. "No, officer. I really don't. We didn't do anything to provoke him in any way, and he didn't say anything. Maybe he was on drugs."

"Possibly," said the older one. "This is a pretty rough part of town. What are you doing here, anyway?"

"Dropping another colleague off. We had a going-away party tonight, and as it went on a little later than planned, I wanted to make sure that everyone got home okay."

"That's very Christian of you, sir," said the dumpy one.

"We should probably get some names and addresses from you, sir," said a third cop, a tall, burly guy.

"Is that really necessary?" Theo made his voice sound tired, the conviction still beating off him in waves. "It's late, and I have to get my assistant home to Tangletown. You scared that creep off, and no harm has been done. Surely it's easier to just let things lie?"

The cops looked at each other, exchanging troubled glances.

"He was just some junkie," said Theo, encouragingly. "I didn't even really get a good look at him, just enough to see he had long blonde hair and a long coat. Why waste the time and effort on it?"

The dumpy cop nodded, slowly. "I think you're right, sir. To be honest, we would be very lucky to even catch sight of him. I don't think there's any need to detain this gentleman further."

His colleagues nodded in agreement.

"That's great, thank you officer…" he glanced at the man's name badge "Barnes. I know my assistant will appreciate it, too."

"You're welcome, sir." They turned to leave, seemingly satisfied.

"Could I just have a quiet word with you, Officer Barnes? You seem like a wise man, and I'd like your advice on a rather sensitive personal matter."

"Of course, sir," said the dumpy cop, natural suspicion tranquilized by Theo's aura. He turned to his colleagues. "I'll catch up in a moment."

"Sure thing," said the burly one. "We'll be by the cars, keeping an eye on the girl."

Theo backed up to a shop window and beckoned the cop to approach. As the others retreated, he smiled encouragingly, looked the cop deep in the eyes and lashed out mentally, crashing straight into the man's unsuspecting mind. "Stay motionless and silent until I tell you otherwise."

The cop froze instantly. Theo double-checked that his companions were out of easy sight, and then bit deep into the man's neck, feeling the hot gush of blood spurt into his mouth. He fed until it got dangerous to continue, feeling considerably better for it.

He licked the wound shut, then waited until the cop was capable of focusing again, and gazed into his eyes, smashing into the hot, churning ball of his memory with enough force to throw him into total confusion.

"Once your friends were out of earshot, I called you over and told you I was an undercover agent for the DEA. I said I'd recognized you from a joint training seminar a few years back and you remember that pretty clearly now, too. You agree that calling all this in might compromise an investigation and your discretion tonight is going to help put some bad people away for a long time. You feel good about yourself. When you next get a chance to eat, you'll discover that you feel a powerful craving for a large, rare steak served with plenty of green vegetables. Do you understand?"

The cop nodded dreamily, started slightly, then beamed at Theo. "Keep your head down, okay?"

"Sure thing, Barnes," said Theo, smiling. "I owe you one."

They strolled back in the direction of the bar. About halfway, Delphine came up to meet them, self-possessed despite her obvious nervousness. The cop nodded to her. "Good evening, miss. I hope you're feeling a little better." He then turned to Theo. "I'll leave you here now, sir. Have a safe night." He strolled off, whistling tunelessly to himself.

"Are you okay?" asked Delphine, worried.

"Yes," said Theo. "We didn't really have time to do much damage to each other."

"He was after me, wasn't he?"

Theo thought about saying something comforting, but decided against it. "I'm afraid so."

She sagged against him a little. "I knew it. First your fucking prince, and now mysterious shotgun maniacs. Who the hell was he?"

"I don't know. There could be a connection between the two, you know. We'll find out though, one way or another."

They started walking back toward the car. Delphine shuddered. "I absolutely *hate* this. God. Did that creepy weirdo just run for it?"

"Which…" Theo suddenly remembered the messenger who had been trying to warn him off. "I'm not sure, actually." They were getting close to the site of the fight. Theo peered around carefully, trying to see any sign of the vampire he had been speaking to. Some crumpled, dusty clothes lay piled carelessly between two cars. Theo's heart sank. He crossed over to the pile, and looked closely, then picked up the clothing, shaking the dust off a little. It was the remains of the messenger. "As it happens, no, he didn't make a run for it. Someone got to him while the gunplay was going on. Whoever sent him is going to think that we did it." He wadded the suit into a roll, and tucked it under an arm.

Delphine blanched slightly. "That dust… is him?"

"Most likely. Once we go, we crumble pretty quick."

"But he said we were being watched…"

Theo shrugged. "Maybe. We'll see, I guess."

"Is it going to be a problem?"

"I don't know," said Theo. "I hope not."

"You don't know? There's a hell of a lot you don't fucking know, asshole."

Theo nodded. "That's what this is all about, remember? Getting information?"

Delphine frowned at him. "It's not going very fucking well so far, is it?"

"No," said Theo thoughtfully. "It isn't. I'm actually surprised. They're either extremely secretive, or they have people very scared."

She arched an eyebrow. "Masterful. Did they train you to think like that?"

Theo grinned at her. "No. It comes naturally."

"I bet it does," she said, sounding faintly disgusted.

"I have another idea though."

"Let me guess. You get the boys, I get the van, we've got three minutes to be in and out?"

"I thought I'd try recruiting a bit of expert assistance," Theo said. He unlocked the car and got in, tossing the wadded ball of dusty clothes onto the back seat. Delphine joined him, taking the passenger seat. "We'll have to dump this car somewhere out of the way now, and then switch to a new one. I'll sort it out first thing tomorrow night. We've been too obvious tonight."

Delphine sniggered nastily. "You think?"

"I was talking more about the whole approach of trying to get information from strangers. I don't know who did it, but obviously someone sold us out."

"Yeah, but to who?"

Theo looked over at her. "What do you mean?"

"The blond guy who attacked us was obviously not working for the same people as Mr. Smiling-And-Creepy rolled up on the back seat there. I assume that neither your screaming superior on the phone nor Elizabeth the Elegant would have sent assassins out after me, so that means someone else is involved."

Theo pursed his lips thoughtfully. "That's a good point, but you can't assume much about the prince or her council. Kindred society subsists on a few rules and a balance of fear. If one of the primogen thought the council was going to go against him, he might decide to settle the matter directly before anything formal could happen. Or if your sire was in the right at all about this whole conspiracy thing, it could be that they are involved, whoever they are, and that the people we're after don't know about it. I'm not sure she's sane, but I suppose it's worth talking to her when we have a chance."

"Now *you're* making assumptions—that the guy who warned us off was working for the slavers."

"Well, he did say he had your sister."

"Actually, he only said that Nathalie was alive and well, and being treated okay, and he made some vague threats. He didn't say that it was his 'associates' who had her."

"I suppose not," said Theo. "You've got a devious mind, girl."

Delphine grinned. "I go to high school, remember? I don't care how savage your Camarilla is, they're nothing compared to the kind of shit the Bitch Squad can pull."

"Don't underestimate the kindred," said Theo seriously.

"I don't," said Delphine. "I promise. But don't underestimate teenage girls, either. The battles might be over boys or coolness, but they can be genuinely ruthless, particularly at the top of the heap. It's a hard game."

"I suppose you were a good player?"

She smiled wryly. "One of the best. I've always hated that scene, but Nat and I make a lot of them jealous. It's the whole twins thing. After the first few times, you learn that your only choices are to get screwed over constantly—and trust me, that's not an option—or to make sure that the bad ones respect you."

He sighed. "I've no doubt that will be put to the test, child. Hush now a moment, please. I need to make a call." Ignoring Delphine's pout, Theo pulled out his mobile phone, flicked through the stored names and selected one. The call was answered within a few rings.

"I see you, Theophilus Bell." The voice was cultured and elegant, with a faint hint of an oriental accent lying underneath smooth, generically East Coast tones.

"Hello, Itio. I hope you are well."

"Thank you for asking. I am rather troubled, actually. I fed earlier off a Dutch woman whom I have been observing for several days, but I did not accurately judge the strength of her spirit, and the shards of her soul have been plaguing me for hours. Worse still, she seems to be stirring up the old remnants of other victims, and they are making a terrible noise within me. It is most distressing."

"I'm sorry to hear that," said Theo, careful to keep the amusement from his voice. "Don't they usually subside with the dawn, though?"

"Mostly, yes," said Itio, sounding mournful. "But not always. I heard of a fellow whose stolen souls were so strong that one morning they overwhelmed him, and dragged his body out into the sun, where he was consumed."

"I'm sure you'll be fine," Theo said reassuringly. "Besides which, it is probably an apocryphal tale. How would anyone know what had happened?"

"There are ways, Theophilus. There are ways."

"I'll take your word for it."

"You are a wise man. Now, to happier things. It is

good to hear from you. I assume that you are not contacting me about the situation here in Milwaukee."

"Correct as usual," said Theo, grinning. "I've been forced to set that incident aside for the moment."

"That is unfortunate. I have obtained the material that I needed—thank you once again for your assistance—but it was a peculiar matter. I still do not understand it fully."

"Me neither, which is why it's still making me nervous."

"I share your unease, my friend. It will comfort you little, I am sure, to know that two of the survivors are now dead."

Theo frowned, worried. "How?"

"Street violence, it would appear."

"You don't sound convinced."

"It seems rather convenient."

"Yes," said Theo, nodding to himself. "It does. Do you suspect that someone is cleaning house?"

"It is possible," said Itio.

"Unfortunately, there are more pressing matters on my plate. I need to find some rather evasive people in Minneapolis, and I'd greatly appreciate some assistance."

Itio thought for a while. "There is someone I know of in Minneapolis who deals in timely information, and it has been my intention for some weeks to visit the Twin Cities when opportunity presented itself, so that I may take care of some business. This is a good reason to come. I shall meet you by the Target tomorrow night, at midnight."

"The target?" asked Theo, confused.

"Indeed," said Itio. "You are welcome, Theophilus."

Theo grinned. "Sorry. Thank you, Itio. I…"

Itio cut him off again. "Good night."

"Good night. See you tomorrow."

"Most certainly." The line went dead.

Theo put the phone back in his pocket, and looked doubtfully at Delphine. "What the hell did he mean that he'd meet us by the target?"

Delphine looked at his expression and started giggling.

***

The cell was surprisingly warm and comfortable, all things considered. The walls and floor had been padded, like in an asylum, and they provided plenty of insulation. There was a mattress with no sheets or blankets, and a stinking latrine hole in the corner by the door. Food was pushed in through a small slot regularly, mostly large hunks of bread and cheese, with a big paper cup full of water. It was difficult to tell what the day was, because the lights were always bright, even though there was nothing to look at. Most of the time, she was simply left to sit there on her own, going mad with fear and loneliness. Sometimes, however, someone would come, and that was when being alone seemed like heaven.

The first time, it had been a small, dumpy man with a suitcase of medicines. He'd given her a series of injections while a second man had held her down, and then they'd left. Twenty minutes later, it suddenly started feeling as if insects were crawling around under her skin, scurrying and biting their way along her veins and muscles. Then it became a burning, white-hot, and even the slightest pressure on her skin was like being branded, even standing on the padded floor. She remembered rolling around screaming and screaming, trying to make the pain stop, but there was nothing she could do. Even running headfirst into the door and walls hadn't helped; the padding was too thick.

There had been other visits after that. A man who had made all sorts of really shallow, fine cuts all over her with a sharp knife while she screamed and begged for mercy. He kept each one as slow and painful as he possibly could and then poured alcohol and other stuff into the slashes. Another time, a grinning maniac had come into the room and beaten her, punching her in the stomach, slapping her face, twisting her arms up too far behind her back, and ripping at her hair. She still had the bruises. Then there were the men who had… but there was no need to remember that particular visit. She half-regretted not taking the risk and biting the one in her mouth, but fear, pain and humiliation had stopped her.

A rattle at the door stopped the endless, whirling repetition of her thoughts and memories. Her mind froze, and her stomach locked up into a tight knot. She immediately scurried as far away as she could, back onto the mattress and up into the corner, and sat there curled up defensively with her arms locked around her knees. A man walked in, tall and strongly built, with an impassive face. He was familiar, and it bothered her that she couldn't remember exactly who he was. She noted details— a thick scar across one knuckle, the way the short hair spiked back at the temple, the curve of the jaw—but seemed unable to actually process the whole person. She realized he was carrying a big, thick stick. It was a bit like a baseball bat, only black with silver strips, humming with power.

She tried to shrink back further, her mouth like parchment, but there was nowhere left to go.

He didn't even hit her with the rod. Somehow, that made it worse, as if he couldn't even be bothered to do that little. He just walked up to the edge of the mattress, and pushed the end of the rod against her arms. The pain wasn't immediate, but it came on quickly, rising like a tide. She suddenly lost control of her body, which went into wild spasms, but she couldn't get away from the current. She couldn't even scream to let the agony out because her throat wouldn't work. Finally, the pain overwhelmed her, and she blacked out.

When she came around again, she discovered that she had been stretched out on the mattress, on her back, but apart from that nothing had changed. She was still naked, still untied, and the man was still there, standing over her. As soon as she opened her eyes and looked around, he leaned forward and brushed the rod over her, an electric caress of pain running across her skin. He pulled it away before she started convulsing, leaving her panting for breath, too terrified to even whimper.

Staying expressionless and silent, he brushed her again and again with the baton, each time a stroke of fire—along one arm, down her neck, over her cheek and lips, circling one nipple, then the other, and on, and on, and on. She screamed from time to time, but more often she was just fighting for breath, fighting to remember some shred of identity, fighting to make some sense of it. In fact, just fighting, because it was that or die.

Finally, after a long time, the man looked her straight in the eyes, brought the baton up high, and then crunched it down between her legs . The agony was unbelievable, worse than anything she had experienced so far, and he kept the rod jammed against her. It was like nothing she had ever imagined. The pain mounted and mounted, and despite her wild shrieks and frenzied writhing, the man just calmly held the rod in place, his face expressionless. She finally passed out, with a tiny, brief feeling of triumph at her temporary escape.

When she awoke from her nightmares back into dull pain, a long time later, she was alone again, and there was a new portion of bread and cheese under the door.

chapter ten:
codes (London, 1888)

The stone platform jutted out from the London Embankment and into the Thames. It was a slight dip below the level of the promenade itself, but chest-high walls provided a safety barrier and a degree of shelter when the river was high. Stone staircases led down from the left and right and vanished into the murky river itself, possibly to provide access to the physical shore of the Thames at low tide. The area was relatively small, but nevertheless it could probably fit a hundred people, if they all crammed together.

The platform was dominated by a towering sandstone obelisk that apparently commemorated the Egyptian Pharaoh Tuthmosis III. According to the instructional bronze plaques that the British had covered the obelisk's pedestal with, it had been carved almost 3,500 years earlier. It had finally made it to London ten years ago, a present from an Egyptian viceroy to the British nation. The English, with typical perversity, called it Cleopatra's Needle, presumably either because Cleopatra was the only Egyptian most of them had heard of, or because "Tuthmosis' Column" was too complicated for them.

The Needle was undeniably impressive, though. It had a significant physical and spiritual presence, one than demanded respect. Because of the way that it was placed—where the platform met the promenade, at the top of a flight of steps—it seemed to present a barrier between the platform and the rest of the city, a great stone guardian carving a little tranquil spot out of the bustle and chaos of Westminster. The Londoners had added a large pair of homebrewed bronze sphinxes facing the Needle, one on either side at the top of the steps, and they further reinforced the sense that the platform was being held apart.

If anything, in fact, the platform felt like it belonged to the river. The Thames was high tonight, the dark waters rushing past angrily. The river looked as if it disliked its containment, resenting the stone channel that had been built around it. The platform seemed almost like an offering to the water, a little space where city and river could coexist. The effect was strangely compelling—considerably more so than the assorted kindred clustered around, anyway.

Theo recognized maybe four or five from previous gatherings over the last few months, including Angus Abranson, the Toreador who had been trying to talk to him at Lady Merritt's disastrous party, and a seemingly diffident Tremere named Bainbridge, who had developed the odd habit of cornering Theo wherever possible and asking him extremely surreal questions about Mississippi. There were about twelve of them in total, all listening more or less politely to Don Cerro, who was—as usual— taking center stage. His sire was telling the gathered group about some of their exploits in Prague, with particular reference to the time they had spent in the glassblowing workshops there. Theo shuffled uncomfortably, continued gazing out over the Thames, and tried to ignore his sire as much as possible.

Fortunately, Don Cerro seemed to be winding down. "The end product was that Venetian-style perfume bottle you were so delighted to receive last month, Lady Archer. All the work of Theophilus here." Cerro clapped him companionably on the shoulder.

The crowd turned to stare at Theo thoughtfully. He did his best not to scowl back at them all, keeping his face impassive.

"Yes, it's all very impressive Don Cerro, and I'm perfectly happy to admit that your fellow here has a deft touch, but I don't really see what you're getting at." Theo dimly recognized the speaker, a heavy-set kindred with long, waxed mustaches. Thomson, perhaps?

"It's a matter of spirit, Mr. Tomkinson."

"Nonsense," replied Tomkinson. "Early scribes were perfectly able to copy intricate volumes letter by letter without being able to read one bally word of them. Any dog can be taught a few tricks."

Theo fought to keep calm and stay impassively silent. After a brief battle, he succeeded, and the urge to attack the patronizing fool faded.

"There's more to it than that," said Angus. "Cerro is right, Tomkinson. Art is not a trick, nor a matter of copying existing form."

"Oh really?" A slight woman that Theo hadn't seen before stepped forward, looking bored. "Tell me Abranson, how many masterpieces have you created in the seventy years since your embrace? I remember your work when you were alive, and there is no comparison."

"That is a different matter entirely," said Angus stiffly.

She shrugged. "Keep telling yourself that if you wish."

"It's daft either way," said Tomkinson crossly. "Most of this whole art business is sheer balderdash perpetrated by people who ought to know better. The point, Cerro, is that the European is clearly superior in every respect to the African. You have only to look at our achievements, our cities, our technology, our victories on the field of battle. I don't care how much you've managed to train your pet up to speak nicely and whittle trinkets, he's still a savage underneath that veneer." Theo gritted his teeth and started concentrating on a slow count from one to ten. "Look at him. Vicious brute. Probably thinking about sinking his teeth into my throat right at this very moment."

"That would hardly be a surprise," said Don Cerro. "I suspect that you would be feeling quite violently aggrieved were I to stand here and pompously insult you, your mental acuity, your heritage and your queen, all without giving you a chance to respond." One or two heads nodded. "If you goad a man to the point of fury, you cannot then criticize him when he snaps and bites at you."

"Then how do you excuse the revolting display of animalistic lust that your fellow provided at Lady Merritt's back in April? That was simply inexcusable."

Don Cerro glared at the old fool. "You were somehow there to witness events then, I take it?"

"Of course not. But I've heard a full report regarding the events of the evening, and I have to say that it's very grim stuff. Abducting and attempting to rape one of her girls. What else can you expect from someone like that?"

"That's not how it happened," said Theo, unable to keep silent.

Tomkinson turned to him, looking surprised.

"Oh, so you do have a tongue in your head after all, eh? I was starting to wonder if you spoke any civil tongue other than a few mouthed greetings."

"I did nothing wrong. The girl was inflamed with lust by utterly spurious gossip she had heard. She demanded sexual intercourse with me in the most offensive manner possible. I had to slap her, once, to calm her down, and when I refused to oblige her, she concocted a rape fantasy to avenge herself."

"That's not what some of the people there thought, I hear," said Tomkinson.

"Which is why your sheriff, Miss Parr, felt the need to take action."

"Oh yes, of course." Tomkinson sneered. "Such a stable and well-adjusted individual, Juliet Parr."

"She's hardly exhibited any fondness for me," said Cerro with a wry grin. "If her version of the story corroborates mine, then that is despite her bias rather than because of it."

"Who knows what someone like that is thinking?" said Tomkinson.

Angus shot Tomkinson a mischievous grin. "In my experience, ignorant, self-important bigots can rarely tell what anyone else is thinking, because they're so wrapped up in themselves. To the rest of us however, it is eminently clear that Miss Parr has a strong sense of her own duty, and that her paramount desire is to discharge that duty effectively, regardless of her personal inclinations."

"Ah yes, the ludicrous popinjay," said Tomkinson coldly. "Nothing wrong with you that twenty years in the army wouldn't have put right."

Angus bowed sarcastically. "But of course. After all, we can't have people running around, thinking for themselves and even, god help us, daring to create anything, can we? You're quite right, round us all up and hammer every inch of spirit and personality out of us until we're just good little slaves for the Imperial Machine."

"I'd do it in a second," said Tomkinson with some feeling. "Bloody menace, your sort. The Empire has made this country great, and given you the leisure to come up with all your subversive nonsense."

"The Empire is a bigger parasite than I or even you could ever be. It feeds off the populace, eating them whole by the thousands every day, turning every day of their lives into a misery. We'd all be better off without it."

"Come off it, Angus," said the slight woman. "Are you seriously suggesting that you'd do away with all your fancy toys and beautiful outfits and luxurious suites just to give the kine something they don't want? They're not interested in freedom. They want direction."

"You might be surprised on that score milady," said Theo as politely as he could.

She looked at him, impassive. "I'm not doubting your resolve, Mr. Bell. Most people, however, are content enough with their lot. Even Negroes."

"Content or hopelessly resigned?" asked Angus pointedly.

"Oh, for the love of God," snapped Tomkinson, clearly exasperated. "Give it up man. We've all heard your ridiculous arguments before."

Three different people started talking at once, and the focus shifted away from Theo. He used the opportunity to go and stand away from them all over by the platform wall, and gazed down at the dark, roiling surface of the river. The waters reflected his mood perfectly. London was becoming extremely tiresome.

"Being in a foreign culture is never easy," said Angus quietly, coming up to stand next to him. "It's considerably worse when you stand out and are looked down on for your differences. We have given you small welcome, Mr. Bell."

Theo shrugged, slightly uncomfortable. "It's not really any worse here than it would be in New York or Paris."

Angus just looked at him.

"Well, not much anyway," said Theo. "It's just…"

"Just sometimes you want to rip it all apart and stuff it down their smug, arrogant throats?"

Theo nodded. "All the time."

Angus sighed. "Me too, Mr. Bell. Me too."

"I'm not sure I understand," said Theo.

"Then I shall explain a little of my history. I came from a poor family. Nowhere near as disadvantaged as yours, of course, but my father had little in the way of freedom. He died on his acreage, broken by it before his years. I had some talent at whittling wood, so when my mother died shortly after, a crafter took me in. To pass over some tedious details, I eventually became a talented sculptor and started using my gift to express myself. My works were an attempt to make people see the controls that burdened them. To make them see their chains.

"Oh, eventually I became quite renowned, but not for the right reasons. Nobody seemed to *see*. 'Pretty,' they said. 'Vivid.' When my sire found me, the prospect of death seemed quite a blessed relief. Alas… All those years, and nothing changes. I would rip it all down in an instant, stop this insane greed that the rich seem to have for the few remaining possessions of the poor, and then maybe no one's father would have to work himself into an early grave, and no one's mother would starve to death six months later. I wanted to know how it might be done, so I have spent many years now talking with the best philosophers and humanists to come through London. I have been very lucky to be in the position to learn at their feet."

Theo watched the dark waters churn for a long moment. "So why are they like that, then? They already have so much. Why do they need more?"

"The wealthy?"

Theo nodded.

"They're scared."

Theo shot a glance at Angus, confused. "Scared? What of?"

"Most everything, actually. Scared of losing what they have. Scared of not being able to get what they want by merit alone. Scared of seeming to have less than those around them. Scared of somehow failing. Scared of things they don't understand. Scared of changes that might threaten what they have. Scared that one day the poor will see these parasites for what they are and rise up to consume them. Most of all though, they are scared to die, so they are scared to live, and they hope that having more and more will make the fear and the emptiness go away. But it doesn't.

It just makes it worse, and all they know how to do is to clutch at more and more to try to fill the void. The more they grab, the more hollow and frightened they feel, and the greater becomes their need. It will drive them to any excess or cruelty. It consumes them."

"I thought it was about power," said Theo doubtfully.

"Power and money are interchangeable crutches in this particular regard. In fact, there could be some truth to the suggestion that they are interchangeable at all levels, but the aristocracy persists in pretending that their breeding is important, which blinds them to the realities of the situation. Why do you think that people long for power? It is because they are scared to face their own inadequacies."

"How about desire, then?"

"Another escape route, another way of distracting yourself from reality and your own shortcomings. 'I would be a whole man,' you say, 'if I only had that woman, or that house, or control over that person.' Nothing more than another trap."

Theo mulled a thought over. "So it is fear that makes them so unpleasant?"

"For the most part," said Angus. "Bigotry is primarily a combination of ignorance and fear of the unknown. You are something new, and the implications of your presence disturb them, remind them that there are things outside of their control. That is unbearable for them, so they seek to belittle you in order to make themselves feel better about the situation."

"Which 'them' are we talking about now? The rich?"

"Partly. People as a whole, actually, kindred and kine. There are other issues involved as well, though. Jealousy, for one. You are tall, powerful and clean-limbed, with a strong jaw and clear brow, and a skin tone that makes the whites look somewhat pasty. The English and European nobility is rather inbred, and their physical stature is diminished, so they will naturally resent you for your physique. But there is guilt in there as well."

Theo raised an eyebrow.

"Our Empire is built on the exploitation and discomfort of the rest of the world, and deep down, we all know it. They lie to themselves and pretend that it doesn't matter, because otherwise the guilt would eat them all alive. That lie is justified by pretending to themselves that a darker skin is somehow an indicator of sub-humanity. By reducing your people to the level of beasts, in their own minds, they justify the atrocities that they heap upon you, in the name of your greater interests. They tell themselves that they rule your countries because you, poor savages, are unable to do so—heedless of the fact that our own nation is younger than most of yours. If they admit that you are as human as anyone else, then their carefully constructed justifications fall apart, and they would have to face the immense guilt for the evils that they have done. No, my friend, it is far easier to talk down to you, and pretend that you are inferior."

"That's no excuse for their behavior," said Theo angrily. "We're all scared of something, we all have things to feel guilty about…" *Like Daisy*, said a nasty voice in his mind. "But we get on with it, bear the burden, learn by our mistakes. Why the hell can't they?"

"They've poured too much of themselves into not seeing it. The mental investment it represents is too great to ever reclaim. There's no way back for them."

"I don't care. I'd like to find a way to make them see. Rip it all down around them, so they've nothing to hide in. Maybe then they'll be able to face up to their own shortcomings."

Angus nodded, sadly. "I feel as you do, Mr. Bell, but you must be careful about indulging in such emotion too freely. Revenge is a cold, dark thing. It will eat away at you like cancer, stripping sympathy and understanding and emotion from you, until there is nothing left to stand between you and the beast that you have become, and in that instant, you have lost— not just your revenge, but everything else too."

"Perhaps," Theo said, reluctantly. "But what does that matter? In war, soldiers die or get maimed and mutilated. There's no difference. What does it matter if I lose certain parts of myself, if I fall and am lost?"

"It doesn't," said Angus bluntly. "But I'm no fonder than you are of the structures that bind both mortal and kindred society, and slipping into darkness is not the most effective way of working against them. You have to work within a society to bring about change inside it, unless you have the power to force that change from on high. We, sadly, do not have that power. Therefore it is always going to be more effective for us to work within the structures that exist."

"I don't agree," said Theo. "When I slew my former master and freed his slaves, that was direct, effective and well outside the accepted social structure."

"Yes, of course, but with all due respect, that was only the tiniest prick in the overall fabric of slavery, even in the erstwhile Confederacy. Society is geared to respond to external threats. If you had continued long enough, turned into a full-scale crusader against plantation owners, what do you think would have happened? Do you think you would eventually have killed them all?"

Theo shook his head reluctantly. "Unlikely. It wouldn't have been for lack of trying, though."

"Assuredly, but all societies have defenses against attack. Sooner or later, the survivors would have banded together, got the army involved, hunted you down and killed you. The plantations you had destroyed would have been rebuilt, and the people you freed replaced with other Africans who had, until then, been at liberty. The net result is that some individuals are fortunate, others unfortunate, but the balance stays the same. Nothing changes. That is how society deals with external pressure. Some rise, others fall, and the sum total is unchanged."

"So what is the answer?"

"Work within the system. Society expects a degree of change from inside, following the lawful structures. It is called progress, and it is encouraged, not defended against. It is the only way to effectively bring about change."

"But the poor, weak and downtrodden have little or no recourse to influence through lawful structure," said Theo. "Not within the Camarilla, and most certainly not in mortal society. Aggressive action is the only option that remains open."

"That plays into the hands of the people in power. Open rebellion justifies ever greater repression and control, excuses brutalities, and even causes bad feeling within the masses—every solider or policeman is someone's son, every commercial building is a place of work for people who need their wage desperately. All those human tragedies can be turned against a rebel. Besides which, most rebels think that they desire an anarchy, a place without lords and laws."

"Why not? That sounds pleasant enough," said Theo.

"Only while you envision it as *your* personal ideal," said Angus. "Anarchy is a self-gratification. However you envision it, others will envision it differently. There would be no structure you could rely on, no decency built into the species to fall back on… the result would be destructive chaos, and that benefits no one. Nasty, brutal and short, as it were."

"I see what you're getting at, I think," said Theo slowly. "But the implication appears to be that the only way to change the system is let the system tell you what to do, and that doesn't make any sense."

"You're quite right, it doesn't. The most effective

tactic is to work the system to your advantage, seeking to gain greater and greater influence. So long as you keep strongly mindful of the fact that you are accumulating power solely to unleash at a propitious time, then you should be able to avoid personal corruption. The danger, of course, is that when you are finally in a position to make a difference, you will no longer want to."

"I don't think I'm going to be too concerned about that risk," said Theo wryly. "It's as much as I can do to forget some of the things I've seen—done—for even an instant."

Angus shrugged. "You might be surprised, but anyway, there are ways to make sure that you resist the enticements that the system has to offer—wealth, power, status and so on. To start with, you have to have a strong sense of your own personal objectives. They will keep you from going astray. Then you need to ensure that you gain your self-respect from internal sources, rather than from external validation. If you like yourself, you will not feel the need to prove how strong you are by suppressing others. It is also important to let go of personal ambitions, and just accept each day as it comes. By living in the moment, you defeat greed."

"So you resist everything and try to build power in the hope of being able to use it one day?"

"Well, there will be occasions when you find yourself in a position to shake things up a little, cause a little chaos. A blind eye here, a neglected fault there, a bit of confusion stirred into orders… you'd be amazed at the difference a little creative mayhem can make. If you can lure an institution into looking foolish, you weaken it. But for the most part, yes, stay within the structure, try to win allies, groom promising new recruits to the cause, and apply whatever pressure you can."

Theo frowned. "How many people ever manage

to gain influence with their good intentions still intact?"

"No one said it was an easy or quick path, Mr. Bell. But it can make a difference, and in your current position, you have to follow the rules anyway. Did you have anything better to do?"

"Not really." Theo grinned.

"Excellent," said Angus with a broad smile. "If I might make a suggestion then…"

"Of course," said Theo wryly.

"The first thing to do is to put some thought into setting a personal code of moral and ethical conduct from which you will not ever voluntarily deviate. One you believe in utterly. That is the bedrock that you will need in order to resist temptation, keep a strong sense of yourself and maintain your fight against the inner darkness."

"Do you have a personal code?"

"Of course," said Angus, smiling. "The exact ramifications can get a little complex in practice, but the core of it is to treat all people fairly regardless of accidents of status or appearance, to bring no harm to the undeserving, to cherish and nurture things of beauty as treasures that enrich all, to attempt to enlighten those who genuinely seek understanding, to respect those individuals and institutions that are worthy of it—no more, no less—and to seek ways to make society more equitable."

"That's impressive," said Theo thoughtfully.

"What things do you think you might incorporate into your code, if you were to have one?"

"That's an excellent question. I'll give it some thought," Theo said.

Don Cerro breezed up, smiling grimly in greeting. "Good, Theophilus. I approve of thought. It is a shame that these idiots do not do more of it. No disrespect, Mr. Abranson. I do not include you."

"None taken, Don Cerro."

"Thank you. Now, I am afraid I must steal my protégé away."

"Of course," said Angus pleasantly. "We shall have to talk again soon, Mr. Bell."

Theo nodded, thoughtfully. "I'll look forward to that."

"That would be nice," said Don Cerro. "Come Theophilus, it is high time that we moved on."

"Yes," said Theo. "It is."

Cerro led him up the steps and out onto the Embankment, waving to his driver to come over and collect them. "There is someone we need to see. A very interesting oriental gentleman by the name of Itio Shima, who deals primarily in the acquisition and dissemination of information. He has a fascinating mind, particularly for one of the kindred. I rather think you're going to enjoy his company."

chapter Eleven:
smart cookies

Even turning on the charm, it took Theo the best part of ten minutes to persuade the fussy clerks at the rental franchise that ditching the car across town was okay, and that they could give him a replacement while sending someone to retrieve the first one. The assistant who'd been there the night before was off sick with a mild flu, unsurprisingly. Delphine didn't say anything, but Theo could see that she was amused. He had to bite down on his anger several times, and had started seriously considering incapacitating one and mesmerizing the other before they gave in apologetically, and told the garage to bring another machine up. He was just signing the paperwork when the phone rang.

"Hi Angus. What's up?"

"You're going to have to come back to the Institute right away. The council has been in discussion, and they have a proposal to put to you that would safeguard your fledgling."

"Very well, I'm listening."

"You'll have to come here, my friend. The prince herself wants to discuss it with both you and the council."

Theo frowned. "It's not exactly the most convenient night for it."

"That's as may be, I'm afraid," said Angus. "If you don't turn up, I fear that the ruling will go against you."

"I understand," said Theo, resigned. "When do you need us there?"

"We are reconvening at nine o'clock, so you have a small amount of time."

"All right. Thanks."

"You're welcome. See you later."

"Yeah, later. Bye." He hung up, turned back to the clerks and pushed the signed form over. "Sorry about that, gentlemen. I trust everything is in order?"

"Yes, Mr. Bowman," said one, with a hint of hesitation.

Theo smiled smoothly. "Thank you. I really appreciate it."

"We understand," said the other, also sounding a little doubtful.

Theo nodded, then moved over to Delphine and started making quiet conversation to avoid any further questions. The clerks talked quietly to each other for a few moments, looking concerned, but then another client arrived to provide a timely distraction. A few minutes later, Theo was relieved to take charge of the new car.

Delphine didn't say anything about the trouble that the clerks had given him, mainly because she was preoccupied thinking about the call from Angus. As soon as the car doors closed, she turned to him, looking concerned. "I take it that we've been summoned back to see the council?"

Theo nodded. "Yeah. They want us there in forty-five minutes. It sounds good though—he said they had a proposal that would secure your position."

"With chains probably," Delphine said bitterly.

"It really didn't sound that way," said Theo reassuringly.

"Didn't he go into details?"

"No. We have to be there in person."

"Great. So if Blond Goon last night was sent by one of that lot, he'll know exactly where I am."

Theo frowned. "That's a good point, actually. We're going to have to stash this car somewhere, and get there by cab."

Delphine sighed. "More mad taxi swapping? Isn't that a little old?"

"What else would you suggest?"

"If it was me, I'd have slipped a bug into your pocket during last night's little promenade around town."

Theo looked horrified.

Delphine couldn't help grinning at him. "Relax. If they'd done that, they'd probably have killed us during the day today. Well, me anyway. Look, how about we park up in one of the hotels, skywalk to another exit, and get a cab from there? It's a shit-load easier than screwing around in the middle of the road. We've got time."

Theo nodded. "All right. I'm not very happy about any of this, though."

Delphine shrugged. "I'm hardly wild about it myself, but I don't seem to have much choice about any of it. I *will* find Nat, and that just means you're going to have to keep me alive long enough to do it, whatever it takes. So if we can at least get your damn prince off my back, it's worth the exposure. It's better than sitting around waiting to be killed."

They left the car at the Hilton and strolled briskly through the crowds, following the skyway around to the Energy Center. By the time they'd come back out onto the streets and leaped into a cab, Theo was confident that any possible pursuer would have been thrown off. The chances of anyone having been present to follow from the car dealership were small of course, but they had the time to spare. To be on the safe side, Theo had the cab drop them off half a block down from the Institute. Theo and Delphine headed down the side of the building and then around the back, rather than going up to the main doors or through the staff parking lot. Delphine had gone quiet again, which suited him well enough.

As they came round toward the door, Theo pushed Delphine in front of him, shielding her as best he could from behind. The gatekeeper, Gary, opened the door almost before Theo had time to ring the bell and ushered them in swiftly. "We've been expecting you, Archon. Please, come in. The council is in session."

Theo followed Delphine in, relaxing just a little once they were safely inside. He didn't drop his guard, however. Violence was strictly forbidden in an area defined as Elysium, but "accidents" did happen from time to time. Gary escorted them swiftly through the building and up to the doors of the boardroom that they had visited before. He knocked politely. To Theo's surprise, the doors opened immediately, without so much as a second's delay.

Theo strode in confidently, Delphine following nervously at his heels. He approached the table where the council sat, in approximately the same positions as before.

Elizabeth stood as Theo walked up and regarded him gravely. He bowed respectfully, aware of Delphine attempting a curtsey next to him.

"I'm a little surprised by your lack of interest in these proceedings, Archon Bell." Elizabeth sounded pissed off.

Theo looked at her uncertainly. "I don't understand, ma'am. This matter is extremely important to me."

"You choose a strange way of demonstrating that, Archon. Or perhaps there was some unusually significant problem with the traffic system in the city tonight that accounts for your tardiness?"

A slow pressure began building behind Theo's forehead. "Please forgive me, ma'am. We had no intention of being disrespectful or causing disruption. I was informed that the meeting was to begin at nine."

"Theo, I'm really sorry," said Angus contritely. "You're absolutely right. I did tell you nine; I'd completely forgotten. I was rather distracted. The fault is all mine. Please forgive me."

Elizabeth looked at Angus doubtfully. "I'm surprised that you did not think to mention this earlier, Mr. Abranson."

"I offer my most humble apologies, milady. As I said, it had totally slipped my mind until Theo here reminded me."

Christopher chuckled nastily. "Who to blame? The boorish archon or the flighty harpy?"

"Enough," said Elizabeth icily. "I dislike the implication, Mr. Houghton."

"A thousand apologies, madam," said Christopher smoothly. "No insult intended."

Elizabeth visibly reined in her temper, and when she next spoke, she sounded as serene as usual. "Archon Bell, as we hope Mr. Abranson remembered to inform you, the council has reached a compromise regarding your companion's unusual status. If it is acceptable to you, then we shall proceed on that basis forthwith."

"Yes, Angus mentioned that there was a suggestion, ma'am. I will of course give full consideration to any possible solution."

"Good," said Elizabeth. "We would like you to blood-bond the girl."

"Out of the question," said Theo instantaneously, before Delphine even had a chance to start stiffening in outrage. The pressure surged, as if his head were going to explode.

Elizabeth arched an eyebrow quizzically. "Your full consideration would appear to be a disappointingly brief process, Archon."

"Forget it," said Theo flatly. "It's not going to happen." Delphine elbowed him in the ribs urgently. "Ma'am."

"May I inquire as to the justification for your vehemence?" Elizabeth sounded slightly sarcastic.

Theo thought quickly. "I would not be able to accept that responsibility in line with my other duties, ma'am."

Christopher smiled smugly. "I believe that Archon Bell is being somewhat economical with the truth," he said. "While what he says may be accurate, I cannot believe that it is his primary motivation. It is well known that he finds the concept abhorrent."

Theo tried to stop himself, but he couldn't. The words started pouring out, coldly furious, pushed on by the pressure between his eyes. "It *is* fucking abhorrent. And disgusting. It's mental slavery that strips the victim of the very core of his personality and leaves nothing but a cotton candy shell. That any kindred could be party to that revolts me on all levels. If I were in a position to break all blood bonds and render the process useless, I'd cheerfully give my existence to do so. I'm astonished that you would be so crass as to even entertain the notion. I will not be party to the wholesale rape of the girl's personality and freedom. I'll kill her with my own two hands before that."

Delphine gasped, looking stunned. The collected primogen seemed almost as shocked. Theo trailed off, horrified at himself for his outburst.

Elizabeth was the first to recover herself. "Well, I can certainly see that it is a matter about which you feel passionately," she said wryly.

"I rather think that we should take the archon up on his kind offer," said Gloria nastily. Christopher nodded.

Elizabeth ignored them. "Would you perhaps consider having the fledgling bound to a third party, someone of your own clan nominated by Mr. Crieff?"

Theo shook his head firmly, back in charge of himself. "No, your highness. The danger of working that closely with someone of external loyalty is too great."

She nodded thoughtfully. "Yes, I can see the sense in that. Very well. In that case, you leave me no option."

Delphine started trembling, but stayed silent.

Elizabeth smiled grimly. "We are mindful of the reasons why you would have us spare this fledgling, Archon Bell. This council is adjourned. I will speak with my councilors individually and attempt to find another solution. I will warn you now though, if that solution is not forthcoming, execution may be the only remaining path."

"Thank you, ma'am," Theo said, putting a hand on Delphine's back to help steady her a little.

"You are excused, Archon."

Theo bowed and led Delphine from the room.

Once they were clear of the doors and had got a short way down the hall, Delphine turned to Theo and slapped him across the face, hard.

"How *dare* you," she said, shaking with rage and delayed shock. "You total fucking asshole. How dare you make that decision for me?" She drew her hand back to slap him again.

Theo caught her arm and pushed her back against the wall of the corridor, holding her hands above her head. She tried to fight free, writhing and spitting curses, but he kept hold of her easily. "I will not let them turn you into some sort of mindless drone," he said softly. "I will not compromise myself like that, and I will not have you reduced to that state. I will *not* enslave you."

Delphine sagged suddenly, fighting for breath she didn't need, tears streaking red down her cheeks. Theo released his grip, folded his arms around her, and let her cry herself out.

A few minutes later, Delphine had recovered enough to go in search of a restroom, leaving Theo waiting in the hall. He heard footsteps from the direction of the stateroom and turned to see Angus approaching.

"Hi Theo. I'm glad I caught you. How goes the search?"

"I'm looking into a few different possible leads," Theo said. "Nothing firm yet, though. This bunch are pretty elusive, and no one is talking. You could be right about a traitor in Elysium, too."

Angus looked worried. "What makes you say that?"

"Just one or two hints from what some people have said."

"Do you have any leads on who it could be?"

Theo shook his head. "No, nothing. It might even be a false alarm."

"Well, keep me informed. Is the girl proving useful?"

"Fairly, but so far she hasn't remembered anything directly relevant that I can use."

"Are you sure she's worth this hassle?"

Theo just looked at Angus impassively.

"I don't want this unfortunate situation doing you any damage." Angus smiled. "You are my primary concern, old friend."

"Then you should be concerned for her too. I gave my word. Maybe I shouldn't have, but I did.

If the sister is still alive then I'll do what I can, but I will not allow Delphine to be compromised or destroyed just because that Tremere's nose is out of joint."

"I understand," said Angus. "There are things I have to see to, but I'll talk to you soon. Take care."

"I will," Theo said grimly.

Angus headed down the hall, exchanging pleasantries with Delphine, who was coming back from freshening up. As she approached, Theo nodded to her. "How you holding up?"

She smiled wanly. "Oh, okay, I guess. I'm not sure how much more I can take, though. Jesus. My nerves are absolutely fucked."

"I hope Itio will be able to get us a decent lead tonight." He started making his way to the entrance.

"Yeah, who is this guy?" asked Delphine, following.

"Who, Itio? He's a, well, a scholar of sorts. He specializes in information gathering."

"Huh?"

"He spends his time hunting down lost or hidden information, from ancient legends and rumors through to current business plans. He's got a lot of contacts, and he's good at sneaking into places."

Delphine shrugged. "So spends his immortality reading other people's mail and shit?"

"Among other things, yeah."

"Is he crazy or something?"

"Yeah," said Theo, nodding as he made his way out into the public galleries and started hunting for the route down.

"Peachy. Where did you find him?"

"I first met him in London more than a century ago, and then I saved his ass down in Baja maybe 80 years ago now, and helped him recover some scroll or other. He then decided he owed me big—for the scroll, mind, not for pulling his nuts out of the fire—and we help each other out when we can."

"Do you trust him?"

Theo shrugged. "I try not to make a habit of trusting people."

Delphine grinned. "I take it that's a no, then? Great."

"Oh, you don't have to worry about him. It's everyone else you need to be careful of."

Gloria was standing in an open office doorway, looking relaxed and comparatively unthreatening. "Sound advice, Archon."

Theo stepped forward, unobtrusively putting Delphine behind him. "Words I make a point of acting upon."

Gloria didn't deign to acknowledge the movement. "Excellent. I admire caution in a man. Which actually leads in rather nicely to the crux of the problem. There's a matter that I think perhaps you should be aware of. One of my colleagues has been, well, less cautious than is admirable."

"I see," said Theo guardedly.

"Indeed. There is a notable breach of tradition involved. Unfortunately, he is not without support in the clan, and has used his influence within the principality to ensure that the matter is overlooked internally. It could endanger the masquerade, and that is your remit, Archon, is it not?"

"I'm just a little busy at the moment," Theo said.

"But presumably you would have more free time if your pretty little playmate's status were not in question."

Theo smiled humorlessly. "That's fairly unlikely."

Gloria's eyes narrowed. "Are you certain?"

"Almost entirely," said Theo.

"Let me know if you change your mind," Gloria said acidly. "Good night." She turned on an expensive heel and stalked off down an aisle of ornately woven rugs.

Delphine frowned at her departing back and then up at Theo. "She was offering me her vote, and now she's going to make extra sure she votes against me just out of spite," she said accusingly.

"Yes, I know," said Theo.

"Well?"

Theo shook his head. "The price is too high. Do someone like that a favor you're not supposed to, and the next thing you know, they own you."

"How about the fact that she'd be using you when she shouldn't? Wouldn't that even things out?"

"Not really. The rest of them would applaud her for being sneaky and devious, whereas I'd just get into really deep shit with my boss. That's a very bad position to be in. Plus you'd be in her debt too. I don't fancy being subject to the whims of anyone, particularly a viper like that."

Delphine sighed. "Oh well. I suppose at least she left things open."

Theo nodded. "I'll bear it in mind."

"You promise?" Delphine grinned cheekily.

"To bear it in mind? Yes. To act on it? No."

"It's a start."

When they got down to the ground floor, Theo made his way around to the staff entrance. Gary was sitting at the security desk looking bored, his face seeming even longer than usual. He looked up as Theo and Delphine approached and nodded politely to them.

"Good evening, Archon. Leaving already?"

Theo nodded. "Can you let us out of the main doors?"

Gary frowned. "Those doors are supposed to remain sealed after the Institute closes, Archon. I'm sure you can appreciate the reasons."

"Oh, I'm sorry. Allow me to rephrase that. Open the main doors and let us out right away."

The frown turned into a grimace. "Look, with all due…" began Gary apologetically.

"Just do it. I wouldn't ask if it wasn't genuinely important."

Gary looked at Theo's expression and nodded in resignation. "Very well, Archon Bell. As you wish."

"Thank you," said Theo, with a tight smile.

Gary led them back through the Institute to the luxurious, marble-clad entry hall and spent a couple of minutes fiddling around with alarm pads and locks, before opening a normal-sized door set within one of the towering main doors. Through it, Theo could see the green grass of the ornamental lawns, with the road glittering damply in the background.

"There you go, Archon," said Gary.

"I greatly appreciate it," said Theo. They headed out of the Institute and angled away from it across the lawns, making for the sidewalk at the far corner of the grounds. He grinned evilly. "Maybe I could get to like that man after all."

"We've still got a couple of hours before we're supposed to be meeting your friend," said Delphine. "Why don't we get a bite to eat?"

Theo looked at her disapprovingly. "You'd be surprised how old that joke gets over the course of a hundred and fifty years. I should tell you to go and find someone on your own."

"But you can do all that shit that makes it so much easier," protested Delphine.

"Exactly," said Theo grimly. "What are you going to do if something happens to me and you haven't learned how to hunt for yourself?"

"I..."

"Precisely. Still, at the moment I don't want you blundering around town on your own, and we don't have time to teach you a load of lessons, so I think that in this instance, you're probably right. You have to make sure you don't get into the habit of expecting to be fed, though. That can cut your existence real short." They headed down the block away from the institute, looking out for a cab. A short distance down the sidewalk, a couple of teenage girls were approaching, chatting animatedly. Theo pointed at them subtly. "They look convenient."

"You can't!" Delphine sounded outraged.

Theo looked at her, amused. "Why on earth not?"

"That would be..." she struggled for the right word. "Creepy. Yucky. I don't know. Just not them, okay? They could be friends of mine, or anything. Jesus, they could be Nat one night. I really don't like the idea of it."

Theo shrugged. "That's a nasty mental block to develop. The only way to break it is to face up to it, make your way past it. If it becomes a habit, you might get into trouble some time."

"What, like if I find myself stranded in the mountains with nothing but a busload of cheerleaders for company? You watch too many horror movies, Theo. It's fucking tough being a teenage girl, and I'm not going to make it any harder than I have to. It's not as if they're after my boyfriend or anything."

Theo watched as the two friends walked past, ignoring them completely. "All right. If we go hungry though, don't say I didn't warn you." He spotted an approaching cab and flagged it down.

***

By midnight they were well fed and standing on First Avenue, outside the main entrance to the Target Center. The warehouse district was still fairly busy given the time of night, with a steady stream of passers-by. No one paid them the slightest attention. Even so, Delphine seemed tense. She was standing with her back to the doors, watching the street carefully. Theo kept an eye on her, making sure that he was in a position to restrain her if she suddenly lost it.

"Are you okay, Delphine?"

She forced a smile. "I'm feeling a bit ground down, to be honest. I keep expecting that blond guy to just appear out of nowhere, and I'm really worried about Nat too. The longer we leave her... Ah, shit, I could do with a break."

"I know what it's like to lose a sister. To feel responsible. We'll find her in time, Delphine."

"I didn't know you'd had a sister," Delphine said. "What happened?"

He shuddered involuntarily. "I don't want to talk about it."

"That bad, eh? No worries. Maybe some other time."

"Maybe," said Theo doubtfully. Suddenly, Delphine looked shocked and alarmed. "What is it? Is someone sneaking up?"

"Really, Theophilus. You should know better than that." Theo looked around to see Itio standing behind them. He was wearing a burnt-orange turtleneck, with nut-brown slacks and a long honey-colored overcoat, and he carried an ebony cane topped with a brass handle. The outfit really didn't suit him.

"Ah, hello Itio. Thank you for coming all this way. This is Delphine. Uh, are you trying to look Eurotrash tonight or something?"

Itio waved Theo's comments away grandly. "Tell me what you see."

"I see you, dressed like some kind of fruit salad."

Itio shook his head, his straight black hair so unresponsive that it almost looked glued in place. "Try again."

"Uh, okay. How about a fashionable street full of late-night people on their way home from the restaurant and theater?"

Itio frowned disapprovingly. "That is merely the wrapper. A street like this, a time like this— what you see is raw possibility, the flow of information, the tide of synchronicity.... Everyone has stories, and one of them will be the one you need to hear."

Theo raised his eyebrows a little. "I'll bear that in mind."

"Since you asked, it is a favor," said Itio.

"Excuse me?"

"You asked about my outfit. I apologize if it seems garish, but it was the only way that I could persuade the woman I drank yesterday to stop plaguing me. She wanted me to dress in the outfit her father used to wear when he went into the village."

"I see," said Theo. "Where in hell did you find clothes like that on short notice?"

Itio smiled indulgently. "They were waiting for me, of course." He turned to Delphine and bowed his head to her respectfully. "It is a pleasure to meet someone so beautiful."

"It is a pleasure to meet you too, Mr...."

"You may call me just Itio," he said.

"Thank you, Itio."

"Good. Now, Theophilus, who do you need to find?"

Theo shared a glance with Delphine. "There's a well-connected criminal organization in the city abducting victims and selling them as slaves. They are holding Delphine's sister. I intend to get her back. Unfortunately, they seem to have terrorized the underside of the entire city into silence."

"There is someone I know of who may be able to help you."

"Yes, you mentioned that on the phone last night. One of yours?"

Itio looked amused. "No, Theophilus, he is not one of 'mine.' He is not even one of 'ours.'" He waved absently at Theo and Delphine, then pointed out at the street. "He is one of 'theirs.' But he knows many people and many things, and he is to be treated with respect."

"Of course," said Theo reassuringly.

"I take it that you have some cheap, cumbersome, white-painted rental vehicle waiting somewhere close-by?"

Delphine burst out laughing. "He knows you well, doesn't he?"

"It's a Ford," said Theo, a little defensively. "They're good cars."

"It will serve," said Itio, grinning impishly.

They were just approaching the car when Theo's cell phone rang. It was Paschek. He answered it with an apologetic smile at Delphine and Itio.

"Good evening, sir."

"How are you investigations proceeding, Archon?"

"I have a reasonably solid lead to follow up," said Theo cautiously.

"Will it take long?"

Theo's eyes narrowed. "A few nights at least."

"Unacceptable," said Paschek flatly. "You have tonight. After that, your services are required elsewhere. To deal with a tangible threat, Archon."

"With all due respect, sir, this is a tangible threat."

"Not a pressing one, however. It has quite possibly been going on for some time already without causing any significant problems, and seems likely to be able to continue doing so for the foreseeable future. It is not an immediate concern."

"Except for the people who are enslaved," said Theo crossly.

"Archon Bell, I am well aware of your emotive stance on this issue. Do I need to remind you that your duty requires you to sacrifice some of your more tender feelings?"

"No sir," said Theo.

"Good. If it is any consolation, the assignment I have for you may quite plausibly further your standing among our fellows."

Alarm bells started ringing in Theo's mind. "I don't follow you," he said warily.

"Sabbat packs are pressing out of their cages in Detroit and have begun an incursion into the nearby city of Flint, in central Michigan. They are targeting our sect's interests and have already succeeded in having the prince assassinated. The council of primogen has asked for urgent assistance. It seems your good work along the East Coast has been noticed, because they want you to lead the defense, and step in as acting prince for the duration of the conflict. They feel that you are the best person to assist them, and I don't see any reason to disappoint them. It would be valuable experience."

Theo thought back to his conversation with the messenger outside Saxon's the night before. What was it the vampire had said? *There are certain consolations.* He frowned, mind whirling. "Sir, I formally request permission to conclude my current investigations. What is your judgment?" Before Paschek had a chance to answer, he tightened his grip, crushing the telephone into little fragments. Delphine looked at him wonderingly.

He smiled at her. "Oh dear. I seem to have lost the signal. I guess I'll have to consider the question unresolved and just proceed as I was until I can get an answer from him."

"Won't it take a while for Paschek to track you down?"

Theo nodded. "Several nights, I'd imagine, particularly if I don't spend much time around Elysium."

"Isn't that a shame," she said, grinning savagely.

"Tragic."

chapter twelve:
no fool like an old fool

Itio sat up front with Theo so that he could give directions, bumping Delphine to the back of the car. She sprawled across the back seats, making the most of the extra space. After ten minutes, Theo was starting to get a little concerned.

"Do you know where you're going, Itio?"

"Yes, Theophilus. We are going to meet with Sayeed."

"It's just that I could swear we've been through this junction before."

To Theo's astonishment, Itio nodded. "Indeed we have, Theophilus. More than once, in fact."

Delphine tried to hold back a laugh.

"Uh, am I missing something here?"

Itio nodded. "Yes. But that is not unusual."

Delphine started giggling, and it took her a moment to regain control. "Is it the jackets, Itio?"

Itio turned to look at her approvingly, clearly surprised. "Very good indeed, pretty lady. Yes, it is."

Theo growled, irritated. "What the fuck are you two talking about?"

"Can I give it a shot, Itio?"

Itio smiled. "Please do, pretty lady."

"Itio is getting directions from some guys on the street. I've seen three of them clock us and give some sort of signal, and they're all wearing identical bright red jackets. The first two passed us to a third guy at the junction back there, but he's had us circling for the last five minutes—checking us out, maybe. Now we're off somewhere else. One of a number of possible locations, I'd guess." She grinned at Itio. "So how did I do?"

"Almost exactly correct," said Itio, clearly pleased. "We were circling so that they could check that we were not being followed. We have now been told on which road the fourth man will be found, and he will inform me regarding our final destination."

"You could have told me," said Theo.

"Yes," Itio said. "I could have. My apologies if you feel slighted." He didn't sound particularly contrite.

Theo sighed. "It's fine. We all have our secrets."

Itio grinned. "Thankfully, yes. I owe a lot to other people's secrets."

A few minutes later, Theo spotted the fourth guy, a tall, muscular man in a bright red team jacket standing outside a dingy Laundromat on a rundown street. He nodded shallowly to them as the car approached and made a strange flicking gesture with three fingers. Itio nodded back at him.

"That was the guy, right?"

Itio nodded. "Yes. I now have our destination."

"Which is?"

"Not far."

Theo shrugged. "Be like that. This guy we're going to visit seems to be well organized."

"Take the next left. He is a cautious man. Yes, here. Many people would like to see him removed from the scene. One of the hazards of the business, sadly."

Theo nodded. "I suppose it's reassuring that someone who deals in local information has people on the street, too."

"Indeed."

Several minutes later, Itio directed Theo into a filthy alley between a seedy diner and an equally rundown hair salon.

"It's going to be difficult to get out of here in a hurry if we need to," Theo said. The alley barely had room for the car, and he felt unpleasantly boxed in.

"That will not be a problem," said Itio confidently. "Proceed to the end. All will be well."

Fifty feet in, a large heap of crates and other trash blocked the alley. Theo stopped the engine. Itio opened his door as far as it would go and squeezed out, gesturing to Theo and Delphine to do the same. Theo—far broader than either of the other two—scraped his way out of the vehicle, muttering under his breath, and joined the others at the back of the car. Apart from the muck and two fire escapes near the road, there was nothing to see.

Another vehicle pulled into the alley, boxing them in, and advanced on them, lights dazzling. Theo pushed Delphine back down alongside the car and stood in front of her, getting ready in case anything touched off. Itio shot him an amused look but said nothing.

The other vehicle slowed and stopped about five feet away, just as Theo was starting to get ready to spring into action. The doors opened and several people got out, but thanks to the glare off the headlights, it was hard to see how many, or whether they had weapons. One stepped forward into the light, while the others remained obscured. Theo wished he'd brought his shotgun.

The man who stepped forward was short and shabby, with a wary, haunted expression. Despite a shock of jet-black hair over piercing green eyes, he looked like a harassed shopkeeper. The man looked at Itio and nodded thoughtfully. "All right then Mr. S., we're sorted from April." His voice was rough, thickened with a heavy Jersey accent. "I might be able to find out that other thing you wanted, if I work at it, but you can't afford it, so you're going to have to look somewhere else." Surprisingly, Itio just nodded. The man turned to Theo. "You probably know to call me Sayeed. What do I call you?"

Theo shrugged. "If you call him S., you can call me B."

Sayeed shrugged. "I don't know. You look dangerous to me. A bit of a killer. How about I call you Killer B?"

Theo flinched and felt his muscles tense.

"Yeah, you can be my African Killer Bee. A real one-man swarm." Sayeed chuckled—a wet, phlegmy noise.

Theo studied the man narrowly, trying to make out whether it was just a lucky guess. Sayeed's expression wasn't giving anything away.

"And what do I call you, sweet thing?"

Theo shook his head, cutting Delphine off before she'd even finished drawing breath. "You don't call her."

"Feeling protective, huh? Don't worry, big man, I'm not going to do anything unpleasant to her." Sayeed leered suggestively.

"Let's just get on with it," Theo said.

"What my friend means," said Itio, his voice surprisingly conciliatory, "is that we are grateful for you taking the time to meet us, and we are in need of your services."

"Is that what he means?" Sayeed was clearly

enjoying himself. "If you say so, I guess it must be true."

Theo tried to rise above his irritation, forced his face into a pleasant expression. "Yeah. Thanks."

"Always a pleasure, Bee. Never a chore. So what's up?"

Theo braced himself, ready to burst into top speed and throw Delphine back into cover if anything went wrong. "I'm looking for the Minneapolis Triangle."

There was a long silence.

Finally, Sayeed nodded, and Theo relaxed just a fraction. "Tricky. Very tricky. They keep themselves well hidden. Don't deal with any locals. Get twitchy about security breaches."

"But can you help?"

"Well, that's the question, ain't it. There was this dumb biker guy from way out west. Had an East Coast pal who wanted to sell some broads. Westy had been to the Triangle once, ignored his boss, and told Easty how to contact them. Not where, mind. Just how. They whacked 'em both, no surprise there. But they also killed their old ladies, Westy's gray-haired mother and both of Easty's brothers. One of the brothers was out in Thailand, too. They took Westy's kids after that, got them hooked real good and sold them on. Made sure people knew all about it. Folks learned their lesson after that. No one asks, knows or says nothing about them anymore. Damn thing is, not a word of it is true, but the past is a funny place—it's all about belief, and people believe. Like I said, very tricky."

"Very expensive?" asked Theo archly.

"But within your means, Bee. Always within your means." Sayeed chuckled again and out of the corner of his eye, Theo could see that Itio was nodding.

"All right," said Theo. "Do you know anything?"

"Well, I don't know where they are. Oh, I've got a rough idea, could probably narrow it down to four or five districts, but you could go looking for a month and never find them. But I do know of a man who has just put in an order for a specific individual."

"Would he know where to find them, then?"

Sayeed shook his head. "Of course not. It'll be done through drops and contacts."

Theo shook his head wearily. "So it's not much use then, is it?"

Delphine tapped him on the shoulder. "Actually, if we could find out who the victim is, we might be able to surprise the snatch team. I'd really like to have a few words with that bitch myself."

"It does sound like a viable lead," said Itio.

Theo looked from Delphine to Itio, then back to Sayeed. "It's not exactly the most useful tip I could have imagined. What's the price?"

Sayeed looked him squarely in the eyes. "Your binding promise that you will do me one favor of my asking, at a time that I choose."

Theo squinted suspiciously at Sayeed, then shook his head. "No freaking way. You have to be out of your mind."

"I can guarantee that it will not inevitably harm or compromise you or those you care about."

"That's very generous of you," said Theo sarcastically. "There's a whole world of pain lurking between 'safe' and 'inevitable harm.'"

"Every day that passes brings you closer to the end." Was the man's accent fading? "Every step that you take has the potential to start a chain of events that could lead to your destruction. Every voice you hear could be the tolling of your personal bell. Causality is as complicated as hell itself. There is no 'safe.' Just the illusion of comfort that hides acceptable risks."

"Yeah? Well, this sounds like an unacceptable risk to me. The price is too high."

Sayeed's voice dropped, suddenly hard as rock, and the Jersey accent vanished completely. It sounded like a death knell. "Then the Day Child will die in torment and the Night Child will be lost to darkness, and the deep waters will rise up to consume you, Wave Man."

Theo blinked, ignoring Delphine's strangled gasp. "What the *fuck*?"

Sayeed shrugged. "That's the deal. Take it or leave it." His voice had lightened again, and his accent was back in place. "It's all the same to me, Bee."

Theo hesitated, suddenly unsure. The man's mind was a steel trap. "What if this guy of yours is a dead end?"

"Then the deal is off. You won't owe me."

"And your favor won't involve me doing any obviously self-destructive stuff?"

"Not in and of itself, no."

Theo sighed wearily. "All right." Behind him, Delphine let out a long, relieved breath. "I swear by my sister's name that if the information you provide tonight leads me to the location of the group known as the Minneapolis Triangle, then I will do one task of your choice when you call upon me to do so, providing that you do not ask me to do anything that will inevitably harm me or mine."

"Done, and done. The man's name is Paul Coglin. He's a fine-art dealer, philanthropist and heroin smuggler with apartments over a gallery on Sixth Avenue North. The place is named after him, of course."

"Do you know anything about his victim?"

"Only that she is an archivist named Milly, and she is going to be taken as she leaves work, late tomorrow evening. I think that covers everything."

"Actually, I had—" began Theo.

Itio took a step forward, cutting him off. "Our most grateful thanks for your assistance, Sayeed."

The man nodded. "Not at all. In fact, I should be thanking you, Mr. S. Solid work. It was good doing business with you too, Bee. I'll be in touch through your friend here."

Itio shot Theo a meaningful glance. He nodded, resigned. "Yeah, thanks. I'll look forward to hearing from you."

"When you least expect it, Bee. When you least expect it." Sayeed grinned and made a curious gesture. "Be seeing you." He stepped back behind the glaring lights of his vehicle. A few moments later, several doors slammed, and then the car was reversing out of the alley.

"Can I say something now?" Delphine sounded indignant.

"Of course, pretty lady," said Itio pleasantly.

"What in god's name was all that shit about Nat and I? What happened to his accent?"

"Yeah," said Theo. "I was wondering that myself."

Itio shrugged. "I cannot say."

Delphine's eyes narrowed. "O-kay. Well, can you tell me why you kept shooting me 'shut up' looks?"

Itio smiled. "My most sincere apologies for my rudeness. I merely wished to ensure that you did not end up incurring debt. Sayeed is not someone to converse casually with."

"Hm. All right." She still didn't sound particularly happy.

Theo sighed. "If we're going to get value for money from this deal, we ought to go see what information we can shake out of Coglin."

Delphine nodded. "Yeah. Let's get on with it. I'm sick of this dump."

They all piled back into the Ford. Theo reversed carefully out of the alley, escaping with just a few scratches. Delphine sat in the front, and once she'd got her bearings, it took her only ten minutes to direct Theo to Sixth Avenue. Five minutes more, and they'd found Coglin Fine Arts, nestled between a small deli and an upscale boutique.

Theo parked up several doors away, on the other side of the street, and took a long look at the gallery. It was glass-fronted, with large classical oil paintings on stands at either side of the door. More canvases were visible deeper in. The layout was tastefully chic. There were bars over the windows, and a large alarm box on the wall above the glass. The apartment entrance was nestled next to the gallery, and it also had an alarm system.

He looked at the gallery thoughtfully. "I may be able to disable the alarm—or at least rip the box off the wall—but this is the sort of thing you're good at, Itio. Would you mind checking the place out?"

"It would be a pleasure," said Itio.

"Thank you. Can I help at all?"

Itio grinned mischievously. "I appreciate the thought, Theophilus, but you would merely be an impediment." He hopped out of the car and started crossing the road.

Theo looked at Delphine, grinning. "You'll want to see this." She shot him a glance, and the pair of them watched Itio as he walked toward the gallery. A taxi went past, attracting Theo's attention for an instant, and Itio was gone.

Delphine gasped. "What the fuck? Where'd he go? I only took my eyes off him for a moment."

"Impressive, isn't it?"

"I don't get it." She sounded a bit stunned.

"He's still there, really. He's just sort of faded into the background."

"In that outfit? Jesus."

"Yeah, well, he should be able to case the place and find out the score."

"How's he going to get in?"

Theo smiled wryly. "He'll find a way. He specializes in information retrieval, remember? He's good at alarms."

Delphine nodded thoughtfully.

Five minutes later, Theo was still scanning the street for some sign of Itio's approach when he knocked on the driver's side window. Theo jumped despite himself, then wound the window down. "How did it go?"

Itio smiled. "It was easy enough. The security arrangements were of a type familiar to me. We should proceed swiftly and search the man's apartments."

"What about Coglin?"

"Elsewhere, it would seem."

Theo frowned. "That's inconvenient."

"There might be something in there to tell us where he is," said Delphine optimistically.

"Yeah, I suppose. Okay, let's do it."

They walked back to the gallery, and Itio let them into the apartment. There was a short stretch of hallway lined with expensive-looking prints, and then a gleaming chrome elevator took them up to the second floor. The apartment itself was designer decorated, lots of empty space punctuated by simple rugs and pieces of low, strangely shaped furniture. It all looked extremely expensive.

The cavernous kitchen could have been straight out of any five-star restaurant and looked like it had never even been entered, let alone used to cook anything. The lounge area was bracketed by a fifty-inch plasma screen television and entertainment center on one side, and a floor-to-ceiling tank of tropical fish on the other. Down past the kitchen, there was a room that clearly served as an office. It had several filing cabinets, a slim computer, a big desk with assorted notes and papers, and a number of bookcases. Theo started with the desk. Itio took on the filing cabinets, while Delphine examined the bedroom.

About twenty minutes later, Delphine stuck her head round the door. "Found anything yet?"

Theo shook his head. Itio looked around and said, "One or two fascinating documents that I shall look at more closely before leaving, but nothing relevant to our current situation, I'm afraid."

"I've been through his bedroom, and I'm about to start on the lounge. I don't have any leads yet, but I did find this Itio, and I thought maybe you'd like a look at it." She tossed a slim, leather-bound black book to him. "It's an address book. Doesn't look like there's any personal stuff in there, no obvious Milly or a second home or anything, but a bunch of names I know from the papers."

"Thank you, pretty lady," said Itio, beaming. "I am indebted to you."

"It's a pleasure. Have either of you come across his receipts yet?"

Theo nodded. "There wasn't anything in there."

"Did you spot any delivery invoices from gift places—florists, candy shops, wine merchants, that sort of thing?"

"Maybe. Why?"

"Having had a look through this guy's bedroom cabinets, I'd say he's a class-A creep. He's got some pretty exotic toys hidden away in there, and a lot of them look like they'd be fucking uncomfortable for any poor girl on the receiving end. That says power freak to me. If you think a woman scorned is dangerous, try pissing off a rich, sadistic egomaniac."

"Hm. So you think this woman might have turned him down or something?"

"Could be," said Delphine. "If he just wanted an archivist or librarian or whatever, it would have to be safer to have these assholes just pick someone he didn't know by name. Anyway, would he really want a slave to do filing?"

Theo nodded. "Yeah, makes sense. Maybe he's got some other grudge against her, though."

"True enough. She could be a customer of his who didn't pay her bills or something. She could have some kind of special talent, too. I reckon the romantic angle is worth a double check though."

Theo shrugged doubtfully. "I suppose it can't hurt to go through the receipts again, just in case."

Delphine nodded. "I'll get on with searching the lounge. I'm assuming we're trying to hide the fact we've been through the place, right?"

"Ideally," said Theo.

"It is never possible to be entirely invisible about these things," said Itio. "A small amount of disruption usually goes unnoticed however."

Delphine looked slightly hurt. "Please. Like I've never been through someone's room with a fine-toothed comb before?"

"My apologies, pretty lady. No slight intended."

She smiled. "Oh, there's no bad, Itio. I'm being careful. I just thought I'd check. If we wanted to go for a break-in instead—like if you boys were swiping some paperwork—then Creepy has a few goodies I'd really love for an early Christmas present. A really top-line portable minidisk, for instance."

"We'll save the larceny for another time, I think," Theo said.

Delphine grinned and headed back toward the lounge. Theo rifled through the paperwork again until he found the sheaf of receipts, then started going through them again more slowly. Itio, meanwhile, was having a quick read through the address book Delphine had brought in. Theo could hear him making noises that might have been words as he committed details to memory.

Toward the bottom of the pile, Theo found a receipt he didn't remember noticing the time before. He wasn't surprised; it was a small, handwritten thing torn from a little pad, and it had gotten caught up in the folds of a larger, more formal piece. The company stamp was barely legible, one of those ink pad things, and the delivery address—Sumner, on Emerson—didn't mean anything to him either, but the recipient was listed as "M Redfield," so he set it aside just in case. He then continued going through the rest of the assorted documents.

Some time later, Delphine came back, looking a bit flat. "The lounge was a bust. He's got a good collection of DVDs, but that's about it. I don't hold out much hope for the kitchen or bathroom. Anything here?"

"Not much," said Theo. "Just this." He waved the note at her. "We've got a bit more paper to get through, but I'm starting to think we might have to have a shot at the computer."

Delphine frowned as she approached the desk. "Not really my forte. I prefer dealing with people."

"Fear not," Itio said. "I have developed a few skills in that regard. If we need to work with the machine, we can take it with us." Delphine took the paper from Theo.

"If possible, I'd like to avoid anything that would have Coglin calling the police," said Theo.

Delphine grinned broadly. "Have I ever told you what a gorgeous darling you are?" Theo peered at her suspiciously, and she laughed, and waved the paper at him. "This is it. This is what we're looking for."

"Are you sure?"

"Judy's is a flower shop a couple of blocks from here. I've used them once or twice because they have a great range of exotic singles. Even better though, Sumner is a library. It's got to be her."

"How confident are you?" Delphine paused, suddenly uncertain.

"Tell you what," Theo said. "First thing tomorrow, we can phone the library and ask to speak to Milly Redfield. If they don't recognize her name, we can come straight back here. We have until late evening, and we might find Coglin at home."

She nodded, and passed the receipt back to Theo. "All right."

"Itio, are you ready to get going?"

"Nearly, Theophilus. Pretty lady, would you be so kind as to replace this book of addresses?"

Delphine nodded and caught the address book deftly, then headed out of the room. Theo put the slip of paper back in the stack of receipts and rearranged the desk to more or less how it had been.

"Theophilus, it would be best if you two exited the building before me. Once you are clear, I shall reactivate the security systems."

"How long will you need?"

"No more than five minutes."

"Okay, we'll get out." Theo left Itio scanning a small pile of papers, collected Delphine as she left the bedroom and cautiously led the way out onto the street. The sidewalks were as empty as the road. He waved Delphine out. They walked swiftly back to the car in silence. When they were in safely, she looked over at Theo and smiled.

"We've got the right location, Theo. I'm sure of it. That guy seems to have come through."

He nodded, keeping his reservations to himself.

"Oh, I know that the plan to snatch this poor cow might change, or he might just have been flat wrong about that part, but finally it's something solid to work on. God, I hope Nat is okay." Her face crumpled a little, and her voice shrank. "Hang in there, babe. I'm coming."

Theo shifted uncomfortably. "I'm sure she's fine."

Delphine nodded mechanically. "Yeah." She picked up a little. "Yeah, I'm sure she is too."

A short time later, Itio got into the car. "I am pleased to say that all is as it was. Our host will have no reason to suspect our visit."

Theo nodded, satisfied. "Great."

"Thank you Itio," said Delphine.

Theo shot her a glance. "Yeah, thanks."

The drive back to the Target Center took about five minutes. Theo pulled up outside the closed parking lot and dropped Itio off. Itio walked around to the driver-side window and bowed cheerfully to him. "There are some matters I must attend to—I must give the dog a bone, so to speak. If I can be of assistance to you tomorrow, I would be happy to meet you here again, say sixty minutes after sundown?"

"Thank you, Itio. Yes, that would be great. I'd appreciate your help tomorrow. I'm really grateful for everything tonight, too. I bet that meeting took some setting up, and it would have been hell trying to get into Coglin's place without you. I owe you one."

Itio shook his head, looking amused. "There is no debt, but I appreciate your thanks. As well as being a good chance to help an old comrade, tonight's little adventure has also been rather lucrative. Everyone wins. I shall see you tomorrow. Theophilus, pretty lady, may your rest be ever peaceful." He turned abruptly, crossed the road and walked off.

By the time that Theo and Delphine had driven back to the apartment on Elliott, it was getting close to 5:30 a.m. Theo parked a block down the road and put his arm out to stop Delphine from leaping out of the car. "Hold it a minute."

Delphine immediately looked wary. "What is it?"

"Nothing concrete. I just don't feel entirely right. I want to be careful." He examined the road carefully, looking for any hint of anything out of place—observers, an ambush, whatever. After a couple of minutes, Delphine sighed theatrically, and Theo was forced to admit that nothing seemed out of place. "Okay then, let's do it."

They got out of the car and walked swiftly to the building. Theo kept in front of Delphine, varying his pace and weaving back and forth erratically on the pavement to make a clear shot a little trickier. Delphine rolled her eyes but joined in anyway, sticking behind him. When he got to the door, he unlocked it quickly then crouched down and pushed it open as quickly as possible, catching it before it hit the wall. There was no one on the stairs. He stood up, shooed Delphine in, and then pulled the door closed behind him.

Delphine waited at the bottom of the stairs, looking at him archly.

"Wait here," he whispered. "I'll check the apartment."

She shrugged but kept her voice down. "Paranoid much? Whatever. Give me a yell when you're done."

Theo nodded, and ghosted up the stairs silently. He paused at the top, the conviction that something was wrong getting stronger and stronger. If anyone were waiting, the door would be watched carefully, particularly now that dawn was drawing close. Sneaking in was going to be impossible either way. Speed, then. He crouched down slowly and concentrated on the blood pounding through his muscles. He was aware of it surging within him, and the energy within it ripped out like wildfire. It felt like he might be about to burst. He leaped up, blurring, his boot smashing heavily into the door. He rolled even as it flew open, barreling into the room and springing to his feet, a piece of debris clicking underfoot. He looked around quickly, feeling unusually nervous.

Nothing.

He stayed put for a moment, trying to assess the possible danger. There was no sound of any intruder, no assailants rushing to charge. He braced himself to lash out suddenly in any direction, listening hard in case an enemy was approaching undetected. No attack came, despite the strong sense of wrongness. Theo was about to write it off as imagination and do a sweep of the rest of the apartment when a very nasty thought occurred to him. He looked down at the rug he was standing on.

There was a small bump under the rug and, off to one side, a pair of thin wires snaked between a pair of floorboards, running toward the wall.

"Delphine, there's a problem," he called calmly. "Get outside and away from the building now."

"What's wrong?"

"Don't ask questions. Head back to the car and try to find some cover."

"Why? What's up?"

"Just do it, please."

"Tell me what's going on," she called. "I'm not very keen on going out there," she added in a far less stubborn tone. "I can feel the day. It's less than an hour away."

He sighed. "I think I've stepped on a detonator of some sort. There's a lump under the carpet, and there are wires. There was a click when I stepped on it."

"Oh shit. Are you telling me someone's put a bomb in our apartment?"

"I think so."

"Jesus Christ!" She sounded ragged. "I've got to go out into the early morning with nowhere to shelter, while you get blown to bits? What kind of a fucking plan is that?"

"Calm down, Delphine. You'll be safe, and I've been in tight spots before."

"Yeah? This fucking tight?"

"Just get out. If I don't make it, take the car back to where we left your sire, spend the night in there with her. Or just huddle up in the trunk, but somewhere away from here. Meet up with Itio tomorrow as planned, and tell him I asked him to help you 'for Santa Ana.' He'll do whatever it takes to make sure you're okay. Hell, you can even release your sire if you want, though I'm not sure I'd advise it. Don't worry about me. You think

I'm an asshole anyway, remember? Get ready. Here come the car keys." He fished the keys out of his jacket pocket and threw them through the ruined doorway. They landed down the stairs somewhere with a loud clank.

"Uh, I guess." She sounded worse, approaching hysteria. There was a long pause. "Please don't leave me, Theo. I don't think I can do it without you."

He kept any hint of sympathy out of his voice. "You'll cope, because you don't have any fucking choice, and your sister is relying on you. Now quit whining and get ready to move. You listening?"

She drew a sharp breath. "Okay, asshole. What's the big plan?"

"The plan is you listen for a moment," he said grimly. "Kindred are really freaked by fire. All of us. It's an instinctive thing. So, first of all, get to cover and don't fucking look, no matter how damn curious you are. Second, and even more important, keep the hell away from me if I do make it out, because I might lose it, and if I do, I won't recognize you as anything other than a threat. You understand? You get away from this place, go up past the car, hide, close your eyes, and stay fucking hidden until I call for you by name."

"Yeah, all right," said Delphine nervously. "Don't take too long though. I don't want a sun tan."

"You've got ninety seconds," said Theo.

"I'm gone," she said. Theo heard the door open and close, and started counting. He gave her two minutes, then very slowly dropped down into a crouch, keeping his feet still and not letting his weight shift. He reached down and braced his hands against the floor for a bit of extra momentum. The blood boiled within him, and he drew on all its power, forcing it deeper and deeper into his screaming muscles, as much of it as he could stand. He could almost feel his skin writhing as it tried to contain the force. He leaned forward, then leaped for the window, streaking through the room like a missile, already imagining the crawling feel of torn flesh reknitting.

A vast, scorching hammer smashed him in the back, and waves of fire washed over him. His mind fled in a red haze of panic.

...heat, pain, impact... blood forcing his shattered body back together... white agony of broken bone grinding, lasting an eternity... terrible flame, maddening, horrifying... voices, noises, a rising babble... the rush of speed... prey cowering in a doorway... startled screams... a delicious, salty flood of hot blood... a small irritation, like a gnat bite... another shrieking body to tear into... sudden weight... pain erupting along his already-tortured back... tearing the enemy off and pinning it down... its helpless, thrashing body delightfully cold and hard...

Cold... cold? ...kindred.

Theo clawed back some shreds of his self-control, forced the wild urge to rip and tear aside with sheer stubborn willpower, and reality flooded back.

He was in a hallway that looked like a slaughterhouse. Delphine was crushed beneath him in a pool of hot gore, arms and legs pinned under his. Not hers then, hopefully. She was shrieking and clawing wildly, her eyes totally blank. He managed to angle a forearm around and clamp a hand over her mouth. She bit at it savagely, but he snatched it out of the way and tried again, silencing her successfully this time. He held her like that, immobile, calling her name softly, until finally she relaxed, and some intelligence returned to her eyes.

He eased the pressure on her, and helped her up into a crouch. "Hey, it's okay. We're back."

She tested her arms and then slapped him, hard. "It's not okay, you piece of shit." She was almost crying.

"Are you all right?" he asked, concerned.

"Oh, *I'm* fine," she sneered. "It's the girls you just slaughtered that have some problems."

Theo went cold and looked around. The ripped remains of a pair of corpses were strewn around the hallway behind him, both young women. He was drenched in blood and knew immediately it was theirs.

"Oh, fuck. I'm sorry…." He trailed off.

"What good is sorry? I saw you charge them back into their house, and I tried to stop you, get your attention, but you just tore them to shreds, draining them, first one then the other. Then I freaked, and everything went red, and all that mattered was stopping you from ever doing it again. I really tried to kill you. I've never tried to kill anything. Fuck, you deserved it, though. The way you had me pinned, I'm lucky you didn't slaughter me as well. You're a fucking monster."

"You were cold."

"What?" Delphine looked confused.

"That's what brought me around, stopped me doing the same to you. You were cold to the touch. It reminded me of who you were."

"You should have fucking started with me, then. They just came out to see if they could help. They never even made it out the door. Jesus. They're still in their damn pajamas, for Christ's sake. Students, probably. Good kids."

"I'm sorry," he said miserably.

"Is that going to help their parents? Their friends? Their teachers? Is you being sorry going to help their sister, when she wakes up in the darkness screaming…" The tears finally came.

Theo put an arm around her, wincing inwardly as she flinched away at first, but a moment or two later she let herself be pulled into an embrace. He held her, trying to ignore the accusing stare of the girls' dead eyes on the back of his neck.

After a minute or two, she stopped shaking and looked up at him, her eyes wide with horror. "What have I become?"

"It's not about what we are," said Theo softly. "We don't have any choice in that. It's about what we do with it. Can you walk? We have to get out of here before someone finds time to investigate, and get ourselves to shelter."

"God!" Delphine looked frightened. "Yeah, quick."

"Take it slow," said Theo reassuringly. "We've got enough time." He stood up and pulled her with him gently, turning her away from the ruined students, opening the door and steering her out. The apartment was the center of a circle of confusion, sirens and panic a block up the street. He ignored it and pulled Delphine along toward the car.

***

With the sky an angry orange and about ten minutes to spare, they made it back to the unit where Kristine was stored. Delphine was already getting sleepy. After Theo had made sure the handle on the inside worked, they squeezed into the vault. He pulled the door closed. It was a tight fit, but no light was getting in.

"Just for the record, asshole," said Delphine, worn voice muffled by the way that she was squashed up between Kristine's arms, "This isn't funny."

"Yeah?" Theo grinned into the blackness even as sleep rose up to claim him. "Could have fooled me."

chapter thirteen:
case in point

The warehouse was sheer chaos. A pack of slope-browed, greasy, dark-haired Europeans had brought in a cargo—economic migrants, apparently—but had neglected to pacify them properly. They were proving extremely difficult to unload. Several were screaming blue murder, which they might just be obliged with if it went on much longer. Liam was jabbering away at the gang leader in a tongue-cracking language, and the man was howling back while his men muttered and rumbled and made themselves considerably less than useful. Worse still, the noise was upsetting some of the other prisoners, and an assortment of voices had started shouting for help. The last straw came when one of the migrants managed to break out of the back of the truck and started running across the warehouse floor, yelling incoherently and dodging pursuers.

Matthew watched as the fool darted toward him, a beseeching expression on his face. As soon as the yammering ape was close enough, Matthew stepped forward, seized the man by the throat and snapped his neck. The bone broke with a loud cracking noise, and everyone turned to look.

"Liam, tell your *friends* that this one's value will be extracted from their cut," said Matthew coldly. "If they are dissatisfied with that arrangement, I suggest you have them added to the consignment."

Liam looked unhappy but turned back to the Europeans and started talking away rapidly in what was presumably their language. The jabbering started back up, rapidly becoming as loud as before. Matthew moved away toward the back of the warehouse, feeling martyred, and tried to put it all out of his mind.

"Sir?" The nervous voice was familiar, one of Liam's assistants or some such.

Matthew turned around to look at the man, displeased at the interruption. "Be swift."

"There's a phone call for you, sir. In your office." The lackey at least had the grace to look scared.

"And?"

The man looked at him blankly. "And what, sir?"

"Who is this communication from, imbecile? What is it about?"

"She said her name was Lucy, sir. I don't know what it's about."

Matthew grimaced. "Good for you that you do not. Very well, go away." He waved the little man off and walked swiftly to his office, lowering himself into his chair and taking a moment to compose himself before picking up the telephone handset. "This is Matthew."

"Matthew. I trust I'm not calling at an inconvenient time." Lucy sounded irritated. It would be an unpleasant conversation, then.

"Of course not," he said. "I am sorry for the delay in getting to the telephone. I was some distance across the warehouse."

She ignored his gracious apology. "I want you to acquire a particular individual for me. Tonight."

He frowned. "A specific person? Tonight?"

"Is your hearing becoming faulty? Yes,

tonight. I want her ready for collection by 1:00 a.m."

The frown deepened, becoming a grimace. "That is extremely short notice. Rapid procurements are unsafe and may cause difficulties. It is the type of situation that can lead to the entire operation being compromised."

"I don't care," said Lucy flatly. "You and your operation are ultimately replaceable. My personal standing is not. I have accepted a challenge, and if I am embarrassed, it will be considerably more than *unsafe* for you."

"Yes, ma'am," said Matthew, furious.

"Good. Her name is Millicent Redfield, and she works at a library called 'Sumner.' I will send someone to collect the goods. On the subject of difficulties, our lords and masters are concerned about the involvement of the archon, Bell. Do you know where he is laired?"

"Of course. He has an apartment on Ellio—"

"I don't care where he is," said Lucy bluntly, interrupting him. "I just want to be sure that you know where to find him if need be."

Matthew sneered at the telephone handset. "I know where he is, ma'am."

"Good. He has been given a warning to leave us alone, but no more, yes?"

"Yes," said Matthew shortly. "He killed the messenger that we sent."

"Then the fool should have been more careful. Bell is competent. Still, it is of no moment. We may need to have him destroyed on short notice. I want you to draw up a number of plans and be ready to put any one of them in operation if I so instruct you."

"Very well, I shall do so."

"Good. I suggest you start right away." Lucy hung up, leaving Matthew glaring at the telephone. He replaced the handset and went to find Liam. The mortal was not going to be particularly pleased either.

***

Theo awoke disoriented from dreams of the two girls he'd killed the night before. He was briefly confused about the bodies pressed against him until Delphine muttered something, and he remembered where they were. "Sorry, I missed that."

"I said, get a move on waking up so we can disentangle ourselves from Kris and get on with it."

"Yeah, just give me a moment." He reached around for the door handle and opened the vault, stepping out into the dim room. Delphine piled out after him, rubbing her wrist, looking slightly flushed and a bit guilty. He smiled at her encouragingly. "You still feeling attracted to her?"

She shrugged reluctantly. "Something like that. I'm okay, though."

"Good," he said. "I want to bring her around for a minute."

Delphine goggled at him. "What?"

"She might know something useful. I've been putting it off, but we need to talk to her."

"Isn't that dangerous?"

He nodded. "Some. But we'll take precautions. Wait here a second." He went and fetched his shotgun from the trunk of the car, checked that it was loaded and brought it back in. "Do you know how to shoot this?"

She nodded reluctantly. "Yeah. After... Well, whatever. I can shoot some."

"We should be fine then."

While Delphine had a look at the gun, he went back into the vault, pulled Kristine out and laid her out on her back on the floor. Then he folded himself over and around her, one arm locked around her neck, with his torso pinning her hips and thighs to the ground. He looked up at Delphine. "Right. Get a few feet past the top of her head, and get a bead on her crown. Be ready when I pull the stake. If she throws me off, or does something odd, or she vanishes, or even if I start acting all chummy toward her, open fire. Don't worry about me. Got it?"

She nodded and got into position. "Cover her, and shoot her if she tries anything. Yeah, I got it." Theo had long ago done away with the gun's stock, so Delphine did her best to brace her arm against her chest. She aimed the barrel at her sire's head.

"The safety."

"Oh yeah." She flicked it off.

Theo nodded, satisfied. "Here goes." He took hold of the stake and pulled it out, stopping with the point still at the opening of the wound he had made.

Kristine shuddered, and her face relaxed a little. She tensed, but didn't try moving.

Theo looked at her gravely. "Your new fledgling is standing over you with a shotgun pointed squarely at the top of your head."

Kristine smiled warily at him. "Good evening, Archon. I trust you are well." Her eyes flicked upward, and her smile wavered. "And good evening to you too, daughter."

"My name is Delphine."

"You have a beautiful name," said Kristine. "It suits you well, Delphine. You're very pretty. I really am sorry about what I had to do to you. I promise it was nothing personal."

"Death never is," she replied coldly.

"I'd like to make it up to you, daughter. If you'll let me."

Delphine licked her lips nervously, then pouted. "What, you mean make up for murdering me and turning me into some kind of fucking undead monster?"

Kristine shrugged microscopically. "I did what I had to, and it's too late to feel guilty about it. The offer remains."

"Hey," said Theo, getting irritated. "Sorry to break up the knitting circle here ladies, but we're not doing this for a damn social event."

Kristine nodded. "So to what do I owe the pleasure, Archon Bell? I rather expected to be destroyed, to be honest."

"Those slavers. What do you know about them?"

"Ah, I'm useful, am I? Goody. Will you let me survive a while longer if I cooperate?"

"I don't see why not," said Theo warily.

"Not good enough, Mr. Bell. Do you promise?"

"I could just do what I've already let everyone think I've done and kill you now," he pointed out.

Kristine grimaced. "Go on then. I'm lost either way."

Theo sighed bitterly. "Does *every* fucker... Oh, all right. I promise not to kill you unnecessarily if you cooperate."

"Define 'necessary,'" said Kristine.

"No." Theo shook his head. "It's the best you get."

She grinned. "Worth a try. All right, big boy, I'm all yours. The slavers are part of a conspiracy led by an ancient vampire named Meonia. Their goal is domination of all the kindred resources in the Midwest, maybe even more than that."

Theo grimaced. "Doesn't that seem a rather impossibly tall order?"

"I never said that they were sane. Just dangerous."

Theo shook his head wearily. "Look, I'm much more interested in the local picture at the moment."

Kristine grinned. "Meaning you think I'm paranoid? Maybe. Well, the local slave ring is a branch. They have a high-security operation somewhere quiet. They're into the Camarilla here in a big way, and they've got a lot of eyes and ears out, so they know where everyone is. That's why the locals are so scared, and why the Whistler was feeding me info—they know everyone's lairs, and they have enough human manpower to take out the whole lot in one busy lunchtime. I don't know where they are, but I know that they screen all incoming vehicles, and that the operation is in a place where no one else ends up going—an old cul-de-sac, I guess."

"Hang on," said Theo. "What do you mean Whistler was feeding you information? Who the hell is Whistler?"

"An artist from around the turn of the last century. I said *the* Whistler. It's just how I think of him. Or her. A whistleblower in the local Camarilla. Digitally altered voice. He or she was providing me with info about targets in this area associated with Meonia. I don't know anything about him or her, though."

"How the hell did you find this person if you don't know anything about him?"

"Actually, he found me," said Kristine, looking slightly perturbed. "I didn't really question how."

"Did it occur to you to question why?"

"He or she claimed to want to work against Meonia. That was enough." She didn't sound convinced, though.

"Okay," said Theo, unsettled. "Next question: Do you know anything more about the slave ring's security arrangements, or their specific operations?"

"Sorry, no. No more than I already told you."

"All right," said Theo. "That's all for the moment."

"So what happens now? It's not necessary to kill me."

Theo slammed the stake back down through her heart, and she immediately froze again. "True. But I can't really afford to have you running around loose at the moment either. Things are just a little bit busy. I'll bring you something to eat in a day or two." He disentangled himself from her, picked her up and stashed her back in the vault, bolting and locking the door. Delphine handed him back his shotgun, safety on. He nodded his thanks.

"Hey, Theo, was that any use?"

"I don't know," he replied. "We know a little about their defenses, which is good. I'm not very happy about this whistleblower of hers, though." He headed out of the warehouse, around the back to where they'd hidden the car the night before. "We're going to have to do something about this car again," he said, unlocking it, stowing the shotgun back in the trunk, and getting in.

"How about using Dad's car?"

Theo frowned thoughtfully. "They might have the plates."

"So switch them," said Delphine.

"All right. It's as good an idea as any."

When they got to the long-term parking lot at the Amtrak station, Theo left the rental car in one of the bays. While Delphine got into her father's car, he quickly switched plates with another sedan of the same make and transferred his stuff over. He then left her in the car while he went over to a bank of payphones a short distance away. The call was answered on the third ring.

"Hello?"

"Angus, it's Theo."

"Theo! My god!" Angus sounded concerned. "I was really worried about you, old friend. After that bomb, I feared the worst. Is…"

"We're both fine," said Theo reassuringly. "It was a close call, but we managed to make it out all right."

"I'm very glad to hear it," said Angus, troubled. "Do you have any idea who was behind it?"

"Not yet. I'm starting to suspect that it may be one of your colleagues, though."

"The traitor?"

"Yes. It's just a feeling at the moment. I've got a lead on the slave ring, too."

"That's fantastic," said Angus. "What is it?"

"A possible sighting that might provide a location."

"Great news."

"I'll let you know how it pans out," said Theo. "Any word on Delphine's situation?"

"There might be a compromise coming up," said Angus, sounding very drained all of a sudden. "To ratify her creation and to give her visiting rights, but not to allow her to settle here. Simon seems to have managed to win Gloria over under those terms, though I can't imagine how. I'd think that the prince will be contacting you herself to ask you to come in for a final meeting."

"That may prove a little tricky," said Theo. "My phone is on the fritz. Could you pass her my thanks, and maybe relay messages to me?"

"Of course," said Angus. "Actually, that reminds me. I have an urgent message for you from Ju—"

"Sorry Angus," said Theo quickly, cutting him off before he could complete the word. "Gotta run." He slammed the phone down and made his way back to the new car.

Delphine looked at him expectantly. "Well? Was she there?"

"Oh. Um, I didn't phone the library. I thought I'd wait for Itio, since we'll need him either way. I was just checking in with Angus."

"Oh," she said nervously. "Any word?"

"Actually, they might be coming round to a deal that would clear you, although you wouldn't be able to stay in this area permanently."

"So where would I go?"

"We'll sort something out. You can't hang around with me forever."

"Thank Christ for that. I don't know how much more of you I can put up with." She grinned impishly and pretended to shudder.

Theo shook his head wryly, started the car and pulled away. By the time they got back downtown, it was almost time to meet Itio.

They parked the car and waited for Itio by the center's main entrance again. It was still open this time, and a steady stream of people went in and out. Delphine eyed one or two of them hungrily but seemed in control. When Itio approached from up the street, Theo was relieved to see that he was wearing nondescript black clothing. He saw them and raised his hand in greeting. Theo and Delphine went to join him.

"Good evening Itio," said Theo.

"To you too, Theophilus, and you, pretty lady."

"Did you manage to take care of the business you wanted to attend to last night?"

"Yes, thank you," said Itio. "She was most appreciative and had all manner of interesting gossip to trade. How was your night?"

"Unpleasant," said Theo. "Someone blew up my apartment. We managed to get out of it unharmed, but it must have drawn a lot of attention."

"Ah, that must have been the Elliott Street incident, yes?"

Theo nodded.

"The rumor from the daylight hours is that some rogue extremist had deluded himself into thinking that enemies of the people were plotting evil deeds within the rooms. I understand that two different groups have already claimed responsibility, although with little credibility."

"It was definitely an assassination attempt," said Theo.

"Of course," said Itio. "But do not worry. I shall not pass on any word that you were the intended target. None shall know of it."

"Thank you," said Theo. "I appreciate that."

"It is the least I can do," said Itio breezily. "Now come, tell me. What have you discovered regarding our mysterious librarian?"

"We've been taking it easy on that score," said Delphine sarcastically.

Itio looked at her curiously.

"What she means," said Theo, "is that we haven't telephoned them yet. I thought I'd wait for you."

"You are very generous," said Itio smoothly.

"My cell's broken, and I'd rather use a neutral land line in any case. Have you noticed any phone booths in the area?"

"There are some at the other end of the center," Itio said.

"I've got a better idea," said Delphine. "A way of killing two birds with one stone." She gestured toward the center's management office, where a man was just visible at reception. "Come on." She started off toward the door. Theo and Itio shared an amused glance, and followed on behind her. As they got close, she turned around to them and said "Leave this to me, eh? Oh, and you'd better not look."

Seeing Itio's puzzled expression, Theo said, "I think she's feeling peckish."

"Ah, I see. Thank you, Theophilus."

Delphine went up to the desk while the others hung back by the seats. She waited there patiently, smiling brightly. After a moment, the man looked up at her impatiently, his frown melting into a smile as he caught her eye.

"How can I help you, miss?"

"I'm really sorry to bother you," said Delphine, putting on a girlish voice and leaning forward. "Our car broke down up the street, and we need to find a twenty-four-hour mechanic. Do you think we could have a quick look at a phone book and then maybe make a local call?"

"I can't let anyone use the phone," said the guard reluctantly.

"Please?" Delphine actually fluttered her eyelashes a little, and peered at him hopefully. "I'd really appreciate it if you could help me. We won't be any bother, I promise."

"Well…"

Delphine beamed at him. "Oh, you're my hero. Thank you *so* much."

The man smiled back at her, then rummaged around behind his desk. A moment later, he handed a set of Yellow Pages over.

She thanked him effusively and brought it over to Theo and Itio with an evil grin. "He says dial 9 for an outside line. Give me a couple of minutes though." She went back to talk to the man, who had put a telephone out on the desk. She leaned over even more, close to him, and started chatting away conspiratorially.

Theo flipped through the directory, looking for the library. It took less than a minute to get the number. He looked up to see that Delphine was following the man toward a small room behind the desk.

Itio grinned. "My hearing may not be perfect, but I believe she offered to show her gratitude for the receptionist's help by photocopying her rear for him in that room over there."

Theo shook his head as the door closed.

"They will be discreet in that room," said Itio. "She has a quick mind."

Theo nodded. "Yeah, that she has." He closed the directory then went up to the counter and dialed the library. Eventually, a briskly polite woman answered.

"Sumner Library. Good evening."

"Good evening. Could you tell me whether Milly Redfield is working tonight, please?"

"Just one moment, please." Theo was put on hold. A few seconds later, a younger woman came on the line.

"Catalogues, Milly speaking."

"Sorry," said Theo. "Wrong extension."

"No problem," said Milly brightly. "Would you like me to put you back to the main desk?"

"That's okay," said Theo. "Actually, maybe you can help me quickly. Could you tell me what time the library closes tonight?"

"We're open until 9:00 p.m., sir."

"Great. Thanks for your time."

"You're welcome."

Theo hung up then crossed back to Itio, nodding. "She's there, all right."

Itio smiled. "Excellent. We should get ourselves into position swiftly." The door behind the counter opened, and through it Theo could make out the receptionist, sitting on the floor against the photocopier with a big grin on his face.

Delphine was kneeling next to him. "I've got to go, baby. Have a great night." The man mumbled something in return, and she laughed.

"You too. You're sweet. Maybe I'll see you around. Bye-bye." She leaped to her feet, grinning like the Cheshire Cat, and sauntered over to Theo and Itio. "Come on, guys." She opened the door, and they filed out. As soon as it was closed and they were heading away, she turned to Theo, looking tense. "Tell me."

He smiled. "She's there."

Delphine sagged a little as some of the tension drained out of her. "Thank God! So what are we waiting for?" Theo looked at her flatly and she poked her tongue out at him, then started off toward the car.

***

Half an hour later, they were in the northwestern part of the city, parked opposite the library. It was a large, red-brick building that looked like it had been based on an old English castle, set in modest grounds. There was still more than an hour to closing time, and the building was brightly lit. Plenty of people were moving around inside.

"We have to in there go find Milly," said Delphine. "We have to warn her of the danger she's in."

Theo looked round at her, surprised. "Are you nuts?"

"We can't just let them jump her." She sounded outraged.

"We have no choice. How else did you think we were going to do this?"

"She…" Delphine faltered, and her eyes widened. "Oh my god. You're just going to let the team have her, aren't you? You not going to interfere."

"We need to follow them back to their facility. It's the only way."

"But you can interrogate the team, get the information from…"

Theo shook his head, cutting her weakening protest off. "Too dangerous. There's no way to guarantee they'd ever tell us the truth. In fact, they might even have been conditioned against it. The only way we can be sure is if everything goes smoothly for them, and they feel safe."

Delphine looked horrified. "But we're going to warn her, and then rescue her before anything bad happens to her, right?"

"We'll try to get her out, if it is feasible."

"Promise me we'll get her out."

Theo shook his head. "No."

"But…"

"No, child. We have to find the slave ring, work out how to get in, investigate their operation and find your sister. Then, if it's safe to do so, we'll free this mortal. Or do you think she's more important than your sister?"

"Oh God." Delphine's voice was a whisper, and her cheeks ran red with tears. "Is it always like this? How do you do it? How do you keep from going mad?"

Itio placed a sympathetic hand on her shoulder. "Theophilus is right, child. This is the only way. When the guilt becomes too great, think of all the lives that will remain unblighted because of the woman's sacrifice. Believe in the necessity and virtue of your cause."

Theo nodded. "Besides which, she's not lost yet."

Delphine closed her eyes and took several deep breaths. The tears eased, and when she opened her eyes again and looked around at him, her voice was steady. "We still need to get a look at her. If we pretend to deliver something, insist on a signature… We must be able to mock up a clipboard somehow, and I'm sure I can find something to deliver. It shouldn't be too hard."

Theo looked at her flatly.

"What?"

"No, child. There's no time for elaborate games. I'll take care of it the direct way. You wait here."

He got out of the car while she was still spluttering, crossed the road and walked into the library. Inside, it was institutionally neat and tidy, a strong contrast to the outside of the building. A large information board covered with assorted notes and posters hung just inside the door, and a few plants stood against walls, doing their best to liven up the thin gray carpet tiles. A large circulation desk stood directly ahead, flanked midway by entry and exit turnstiles. Past them, the stacks stretched away into the distance. People milled about everywhere, but even so the library didn't seem overcrowded, just well lived in.

Theo walked up to the counter and knocked on it. A clerk looked round from the man she was serving and waved irritably at him to wait a moment. A couple of minutes later, she came over, her disapproval obvious.

Theo looked into her eyes, reached out to her and grabbed hold of her mind. Her will folded immediately, crumpling like an eggshell, and she gazed at him passively. There was no one else in immediate earshot, but he kept his voice pleasant and reasonable anyway. "I need to speak to Milly Redfield about a personal matter. Please show me to a room where I can talk to her privately, and then have her sent in at once. It's very important."

The woman nodded obediently. "Of course, sir. Follow me." She buzzed Theo through the turnstile and then came out from behind the counter. She led him a short distance to a small, windowless partitioned office. "If you'll wait in here sir, I'll have Miss Redfield sent up to you." She ushered Theo in, then closed the door.

The room contained nothing more than a desk, a couple of chairs, and a cheap print on one wall. Theo pulled out a chair and sat down to wait. A few minutes later, there was a knock on the door. A young woman came in, all golden hair and smiles.

"Hi, I'm Milly Redfield. Did you want to talk to me?" Even looking uncertain, she was still sweetly beautiful. It was easy to see why she had attracted Coglin's interest.

"Yes, that's right. It won't take a moment. Close the door please, Miss Redfield."

Milly shut the door. "Do I know you? Your voice sounds…"

She trailed off as Theo made eye contact and crashed into her mind, shattering her playful will and breaking her consciousness into a cloud of shards. "Stay motionless and silent." He could feel her obedience, a soft yielding.

He got up, took hold of her, lifted her wrist to his mouth, and sank his teeth into the soft flesh. Her blood gushed into his mouth, beyond delicious, and for a short time there was nothing else. Eventually, he licked the wound closed with a sigh, released her, and stepped back. She was trembling a little, her face ecstatic, her mind totally given over to his will.

"You may speak, but only to answer my questions. When do you finish work tonight?"

"Quarter to ten." Her voice was slow and distant.

"When you leave work tonight, you will stretch both your arms above your head briefly as you step outside. If someone approaches you on your way home, you will do as you are told, without trying to fight or escape. You will not consciously recall these instructions, but you will act upon them without fail. You came to this room to meet me as requested. I explained to you that I was a researcher at the University of Minnesota, and one of your friends had told me you might be able to help me track down an obscure academic textbook—" Theo cast around for a suitable subject "—about slavery in the South. You explained that you were unable to help me because of the age of the work. Nothing unusual or untoward happened. Do you understand?"

"Yes."

Theo withdrew from her and felt her mind slowly piece itself back together. She shook her head once, gathering her thoughts.

"Sorry for wasting your time," said Theo.

She smiled at him uncertainly. "Not at all. I'm just sorry I couldn't be more help. If I can track down anything else for you, just let me know."

"Thanks again."

She turned round, and opened the door. "Good luck." She walked off.

"You too," murmured Theo sadly. "You too."

He left the library quietly, ignoring a puzzled look from the woman at the desk and crossed back to the car. Delphine waited until he closed the door, and then turned to him expectantly.

"So how did it go then?"

"No problems. She's there, and she's finishing at 9:45, so she should be out soon after that. She's fairly easy to spot—young, blond hair, pretty— but she'll lift her arms up as she leaves, so that we can identify her quickly."

Itio nodded thoughtfully. "Most satisfactory."

"Does that mean you let her in on it?" Delphine sounded hopeful.

"No."

She sighed. "I thought not. I suppose you just reamed her. So now what?"

"We wait."

"Peachy."

* * *

About five minutes before Milly was due to leave, a strange sense of isolation started to creep over Theo. He could still clearly see Delphine next to him and Itio in the rearview mirror, but it was as if they weren't really there. If Delphine's expression was anything to go by, she was feeling it too.

Itio smiled. "Do not be alarmed, pretty lady. I have merely taken the liberty of obscuring our presence a little." He kept his voice quiet.

"Um, neat." She sounded distracted.

"I'm impressed, Itio," said Theo. It had taken him years of study to be able to blend himself into the background, and it still required substantial concentration. To casually obscure two others was well beyond his abilities. "Thank you."

"A pleasure, Theophilus."

Theo looked at Delphine. "Are you okay?"

She nodded. "Yeah, I'm fine." Her voice took on a hard edge. "I'm not going to do anything to screw your little plan up, so don't worry."

Theo swallowed his retort and just nodded.

The minutes slipped by in silence. Just before ten, the door to the library opened and Milly came out, yawning mightily and stretching her arms over her head. Delphine tensed beside him. Milly locked the door behind her and started down the path. A smartly dressed man walked up from the road toward her. He said something as she drew close. She stopped, smiled at him and replied.

Suddenly, the man grabbed her and pushed her

off the path into the shadow of a tree, one hand clamped over her mouth. Theo could hear her muffled scream. A moment later, the man came back out onto the path, his arm around Milly's shoulders. A long knife was in his other hand, pressed against her ribs. As instructed, she was doing what she was told. He led her toward the quiet sidewalk.

"No," said Delphine, sounding strangled.

Theo laid a finger across her lips. "I'm sorry, Delphine. Truly I am. But you have to think of Nathalie."

A high-sided white panel van pulled out from a parking spot half a block down the road and drove up to the couple. As soon as it stopped, the man led Milly over to the van and pushed her back against it. A moment later, she went limp and was dragged out of sight. There was a clunk as the door closed.

As soon as the van started to move, Theo started the engine. He waited for another couple of cars to pass him, and then pulled out, keeping the van well within sight. He flashed a quick look at the others, ignoring Delphine's sick expression. "Keep your eyes on them."

"Count on it," said Delphine.

chapter fourteen:
squaring the circle

Theo followed the van through the city for the better part of half an hour, keeping his distance, letting a few other vehicles come and go between them. There were a couple of times driving through some of the one-way streets downtown when he was able to take a different route for a block or so, because the two roads led back to the same point. During one particularly long, straight stretch, he even parked up at the curb and let an extra car or two through before pulling out again and rejoining the traffic.

By the time the van pulled into a rundown commercial district far out toward the southeastern edge of the city, Theo was fairly confident that they had remained undetected. Traffic was light, so he took his time turning into the road, waiting as the van approached another side street.

"How old is this car, Delphine?"

"Pretty old. We got it used, a few years back. Why?"

"Do you know if it has running lights?"

"Uh, god, I don't know. I don't remember any. It's not exactly the first thing I look for in a vehicle though, you know?"

Theo shook his head and flicked the light switch. The road in front of the car looked dark. "I guess we're okay." He turned the lights back on.

The van headed onto the side street, and he went after it, speeding down to the junction it had taken before killing the lights and sidling out again to look down the road. It was a depressed street, many businesses vacant or crumbling. The van turned again and Theo did the same, playing catch-up carefully. There were no other cars around, so he left the lights off entirely. The new street was even worse than the last and looked almost completely abandoned.

"I think we're close," he said quietly.

Delphine nodded fiercely. "Good."

The van turned again, and Theo tagged along softly. It drove a short distance and pulled into a large, apparently derelict unit. He immediately pulled back up the street a little, getting out of sight and parked. "Got them."

Delphine immediately whipped her seatbelt off and reached for the door handle. Theo put a restraining hand on her shoulder. "Where the hell do you think you're going?"

"Come on," she said. "Let's get on with it. I'm sick of all this fucking around."

"We need to watch the place," said Theo, trying to be patient. "Make a plan."

"I've got a plan," said Delphine. "We go in there, we get Nathalie, and you kill all those fuckers."

Theo arched an eyebrow quizzically. "How do you expect to get through their defenses?"

She sighed, deflated. "Sneak?"

"We can do better than that," said Itio.

Theo looked back at him. "You don't have to come in, Itio. You've done more than enough already. It could get messy."

Itio shook his head. "I'm afraid I do, Theophilus."

"Not on my behalf."

"No," said Itio. "Not on your behalf."

When it became obvious that Itio wasn't going to explain further, Theo nodded. "Okay, great. Thank you. Glad to have you on board."

"I owe you a huge favor Itio," said Delphine impulsively.

Itio grinned. "The time may come when I collect on that, pretty lady. In the meantime, I suggest that we approach cautiously. If we remain quiet and unobtrusive, I will ensure that we are not easily seen."

"We need to watch them for a while, see if we can work out anything about their security arrangements," Theo said.

"That will not present any difficulties."

"Let's go then," Delphine said.

Theo nodded, and they got out of the car quietly. He went round to the trunk and fished out his shotgun and a pocket of spare shells. He stowed the firearm uncomfortably under his jacket then rejoined Delphine. Itio stood between them, and the feeling of inexplicable solitude welled back up, a strangely unpleasant sensation. It reminded Theo of the isolation he'd felt walking a London street, a proverbial stranger in a strange land, some hundred and ten years ago. Itio then gestured down the road. Theo set off at a fairly slow pace, keeping his footsteps quiet and picking his way carefully to avoid litter.

When they got to the corner, he could clearly see the building that the van had pulled into, but there was no sign of the vehicle itself, and nothing much to distinguish that particular abandoned factory from any of the others. It was a sprawling unit with a shabby corrugated roof set in several acres of concreted space. Four or five smaller substructures wormed their way out from the main building, including a bunkerlike section and a low tunnel that faced out toward the road, its entryway hung with long, thick strips of shabby plastic.

"I think we should wait here for a bit," said Theo softly.

"Why here?" Delphine sounded unconvinced.

"We can see almost as much from here as we can from that alley down there opposite the drive, and we're a lot better hidden here. No disrespect to your talents Itio, but if I were using that factory, I'd have surveillance equipment along the road down there. Maybe even pressure sensors."

"You are right to be cautious," Itio said. "There is no disrespect in prudence."

"I guess," said Delphine. "How long do we have to hang around on this lonely fucking street corner then?"

"As long as it takes," said Theo. "At least half an hour."

"Jesus," said Delphine disgustedly. "I'd better get comfy then." She sat down on the sidewalk, crossed her legs and looked out around the corner. "What am I trying to find?"

"Movement, any signs of cameras or electronic equipment, noises, anything that might give us some sort of clue as to what we're up against."

She nodded. "Okay then. But we go in tonight at some point."

About forty minutes later, Theo realized that there was a faint glow just visible underneath the plastic strips that covered the tunnel mouth. "There's a light," he said quietly. "By the entrance." The others nodded, Delphine looking excited. The light intensified a bit, and Theo distinctly heard the muffled rumble of a large engine. It paused for several seconds, and then the van that they had followed pulled slowly out through the plastic strips. As it cleared the passage, Theo caught a glimpse of a mechanical barrier folding back into place. The van came out of the grounds and pulled toward them.

Theo crouched behind Delphine, motioning Itio to do the same. The shotgun jabbed him uncomfortably in the ribs. The van pulled up to the junction and turned past them without hesitation. The driver, a heavyset man with short dark hair, didn't even glance toward them. The van accelerated up the road.

Theo looked at the others. "What did you see?"

"There were traffic bumps on the floor just inside the plastic," said Delphine. "I think they had spikes facing out."

"That's good," said Theo. "I saw a barrier coming down."

Itio's face was transcendent, and when he spoke, his voice was hollow. "There is a small, ugly checkerboard of tarnish above the entrance. Dark and light war in deadly step. Rivets gleam from around it, pitiless metal eyes scanning every direction. They are ever vigilant. On that slope, there is a blemish like a panther springing, all teeth and claws and hunger, and next to it, a small outlet that reminds me of a memorial stone I saw in London once, remembering victims of terror. A discarded newspaper, caught within the wire fencing, is yesterday's news. Lost forever. Most importantly, I have watched the wind stirring against the plastic. The strips are a nest of vipers, intertwined, deadly. They stroked against each other as the van emerged, rubbing sideways before slipping against each other and then stretching out again as they descended. They surrounded the vehicle, getting a taste for it, warning it not to misbehave. They hate disturbance and long for an excuse to strike at anyone, live or dead, seen or unseen. Their fangs reach out across the grounds, and if you step into their coils unwisely, they will trap you fast."

"What does that mean?" Delphine looked bewildered and a little scared. "Are you all right?"

"The tunnel is glittering with malice and paranoia. It will destroy strangers out of hand. Even friends are not safe, unless they know the right words and moves."

"You worked that out from the way the plastic fell?"

"Yes."

She looked back at him, eyes wide, then up at Theo. He shrugged. Delphine shook her head. "Holy shit."

"If their defenses are that tight, we have a problem," said Theo. "How to get into that place without being toasted?"

"Even I would not be able to simply walk in," said Itio.

"Yeah, they might have pressure sensors, proximity detectors or some other nonvisual shit in there."

"So what are we going to do?" Delphine sounded unhappy.

"Watch and wait," said Theo. "We might find a way in, and if nothing else, we can come back tomorrow with building plans or reinforcements or something."

She grimaced up at him. "Given that I don't seem to have any other options, maybe I'll try running with it. For the moment."

After an hour, Delphine was restless again, fidgeting irritably and occasionally muttering to herself. Eventually, she turned to look at Theo. "This is getting silly. Had any bright ideas yet?"

He frowned. "The best option might be to try

to scout the back of the building from the roof of one of the nearby properties."

"That sounds like a dangerous proposition," said Itio. "Such vantage points are likely to be under observation."

"At least we'd be doing something," said Delphine.

"We *are* doing something," said Theo. "We're thinking and observing." He ignored her pout and went back to studying the entrance.

A few minutes later, a burst of brighter light and the quiet growl of an engine announced a car turning into the road behind them. Theo looked around, and saw a dark-windowed sedan approaching their position slowly. "We could hitch a lift," he said thoughtfully.

Itio nodded. "Leave it to me, Theophilus. Keep out of sight." Before Theo could say anything, Itio was up and lurching across the sidewalk into the path of the vehicle.

"What the hell? He looks like a banker!"

Privately, Theo thought he looked more like a lawyer. As Itio stood up, his appearance had become indistinct, as if he were being seen through heat haze. The outlines of his body seemed to shimmer fluidly, the very shape melting. When he came back into full view a step later, he looked taller and stockier, and he was apparently wearing a smart pinstripe suit, complete with vest and tie. All he was missing was the briefcase.

"It's a trick," said Theo.

"A damn convincing one," said Delphine.

Theo nodded. "Yeah."

As the car pulled close, Itio suddenly launched himself drunkenly into its path and turned to face it, shielding his head with his arm. The car smacked into him, knocking him down, and Delphine stifled a shriek. Theo motioned urgently for her to quiet down and whispered "He's fine, watch."

The car slammed to a halt and the driver got out, cursing angrily. "Where the fuck did you come from, asshole?" He spit on the road. "You better not have done any fucking damage." He was a short, stocky man with a crew cut, wearing a cheap shirt and tie. He walked around to the front of the car and looked down at Itio, who was lying broken and still on the road. The driver scowled at him and kicked him in the ribs, hard. Itio didn't move. "You better pray you're already dead, you piece of shit." The driver knelt down beside Itio and pressed the side of his neck, looking for a pulse.

Itio's hand shot up and grabbed the man by the throat. He then pushed the man back, coming to his feet as he did so. The driver squawked, eyes wide with fright, as Itio shimmered and distorted again, melting back to his original appearance. He pushed the driver backwards easily and sat on the man's chest, clamping the other hand over his mouth. The driver struggled but couldn't get away. Itio pushed his head back hard against the asphalt and bent down close to the man. He said something and the man froze, scared. Itio continued talking quietly, and the man started shaking his head, a look of horror creeping over his face. He started thrashing again, increasingly wildly, but Itio just sat on him, holding him down and talking to him insistently. Eventually, the man went limp and started shuddering, his eyes staring blankly. Theo got the peculiar impression that the man could see right through him.

"What the fuck is he saying?" Delphine looked unnerved, her eyes darting around anxiously.

Theo shook his head. "You don't want to know. Trust me on that. *I* certainly don't want to know."

Itio stood up, leaving the driver on the road, and came over. "If you would like to question the man, you should find him receptive."

"Thanks Itio. Let's go have a word." They walked back in front of the car, and Theo knelt down beside the twitching driver, grunted as the shotgun stabbed into his armpit, and shifted it to a less uncomfortable position. "Can you hear me?" The driver's mind felt like mush.

The man grimaced horribly. "I can hear everything. I can hear the end coming. I can hear you." His voice was coarse and ugly, a nasal blend of East Coast and Midwest.

"What is the procedure for entering the compound?"

"Questions and answers. Passwords. Well past words."

"Tell me the password."

The man convulsed, thrashing. For a moment, it looked like he was going to swallow his own tongue. Then he subsided and croaked something unintelligible.

"Again," said Theo.

"Reindeer Flotilla."

"Good. Why are you going to the compound?"

"Special order for a special girl, special girl for a special order. Make it stop. Please, it hurts. Make it stop."

"What special girl?"

"Need to know. I don't need to know. Got to get the lady her takeout."

Theo arched an eyebrow. "Who is the lady?"

"The lady was, the lady is. The lady holds the strings."

"What is the lady's name?"

The man's eyeballs rolled up into his head for a moment, and he gurgled. "Mistress."

"I mean what do other people call her?"

"Lady."

Theo shook his head, irritated, and moved on. "How many of your people are there in the compound?"

"My people. I have no people. I have nothing."

"Okay, then how many of the lady's people are there?"

"The hip bone is connected to the thigh bone. The thigh bone is connected to the leg bone. The leg bone is connected to the ankle bone. Hear the word of the lady. I am the lady's people."

Theo frowned and thought back to the warehouse on Nicolet Island. "How many of Liam and Matthew's people are there?"

"The dirty thirty."

"Finally." He looked up at Itio and Delphine. "This is like pulling teeth."

"Teeth and gums and tongue and lips and blood, all splashed around," said the driver numbly. "What a pretty picture."

"What weapons do they have?"

"All the death in the world, inside and out. Make it stop."

"I take it that means they're heavily armed," said Delphine.

Theo sighed. "What do you know about the operation here?"

"Come and go. No more. Operations. Cut it out, cut it off, cut it up. Business is good. Better than some others."

Theo looked at the man sharply. "Others?"

"Here and there, not everywhere. A handful, with one for luck. The lady holds the cold strings, and her puppets dance. The great and the good, the bold and the beautiful, the mad and the bad. There are warm strings too."

"Where are the other operations?"

"Around and about, through and beyond and between. The lady knows."

"Theo, is this getting us anywhere?" Delphine sounded impatient. "Another car might come or something."

He frowned. "I'm not sure. I don't like the idea of other operations. I don't know how reliable this guy is though."

"He is undoubtedly telling you the truth as he perceives it, for whatever it is worth. I apologize for leaving him in this state, but his consciousness was heavily conditioned. It had to be circumvented."

The driver chuckled throatily. "True. Here. Now. Just nonsense. I can hear the end. The blood sounds like rain. Please, make it stop."

Delphine glanced down at him thoughtfully. "Hey Itio, could you do that impersonation trick with him?"

Itio shook his head regretfully. "Sadly not, pretty lady. An individual contains too many precise details that have to be captured exactly. It is beyond me."

She sighed. "That's a shame. We have his car and his password. If we had his face too, we'd be set."

Itio grinned nastily. "That can be done."

"Take my face," said the driver. "Take my life. Kill me. Please. Make it stop."

Delphine looked slightly sickened. "You don't mean what I think you mean, do you?"

Itio laughed, and shook his head. "No, pretty lady. Not on this occasion. The man's mind is fragmented. I can direct it for a while. Theophilus?"

"If you don't mind, old friend, it sounds like a good shot."

Itio nodded. "Then it shall be done. Step clear, please."

As Theo and Delphine moved away, Itio lay down next to the twitching driver, turned his head toward him and started speaking softly. The man nodded once, and then Itio relaxed. The driver rolled over, lifted Itio's body and then stood up carefully. "Come, Theophilus," said the driver. "Open the trunk of the car and I'll put my body inside it."

Delphine gasped.

"I'll pop the trunk," said Theo, grinning. He walked around to the driver's door and hunted for the catch. He found it a moment later, and the rear compartment clunked open.

The driver walked around to the back of the car and gently laid Itio's body down. Theo thought for a moment, then carefully pushed the body over to one side of the compartment. "You'll have to get in there too, Delphine."

She glared at him. "Oh yeah? How come?"

"You don't know how to fade into the background."

She pouted. "Can't you hide us again, Itio?"

The driver shook his head. "I would not wish to rely on it. Much of my attention is taken up with directing this man's body. I am not sure that I would be able to provide reliable cover. Not until I return my awareness to my own body."

"Oh, all right. I'll get in the stupid trunk." She sighed, climbed up into the compartment and folded herself into the space, curling around Itio as best she could. She looked out at Theo. "This had better work, or we're fucked."

Theo forced a smile. "Like clockwork. Now don't move, and don't say anything. We may have to stop a couple of times, so don't worry. Itio or I will knock twice before opening the door. It'll be fine, and I'll see you in a couple of minutes." She nodded grimly and shut her eyes. Theo closed the trunk.

"I suggest you lie in the rear seat well, Theophilus. I will bring the front seats forward a little. That will maximize your cover in the unlikely event that they have devices capable of perceiving you."

Theo nodded and clambered into the back, rolling down into the space behind the front seats. The gun was jammed painfully into the small of his back. "It's pretty damn tight back here," he said. "If we have any problems, I'm going to be in trouble."

"If there are problems, Theophilus, we will all be in trouble."

"You know, going against Paschek and wedging myself into the back of a sedan in order to break into a fortified criminal operation, to rescue a mortal, on behalf of a fledgling I just met a few nights ago has got to be one of the craziest things I've ever done."

"One of the most important, too," said Itio.

"I don't suppose you'd care to elaborate?"

Itio shook his head and took the car out of neutral.

"Didn't think so," said Theo.

"Keep down," Itio said, turning into the next street.

Theo relaxed and stayed perfectly still, letting his mind and aura quiet down, and concentrated on picturing the back of the car as it had looked when it was empty. Gradually the image took hold, and Theo started feeling detached from the world, as if it were wrapped in cotton wool. He resisted the urge to look up and forced himself to remain passive and calm, allowing events to wash over him.

The sound of the tires changed as Itio pulled off the road into the grounds of the factory. It felt as if he were driving down a long, curved route. It was only a few moments before the car slowed however, and Theo heard the scrape of the plastic strips against the hood and windscreen. The car juddered to a halt, and there was a low whine as Itio lowered the window.

"Evening, Bill." The voice was male, muffled.

"Hi," said Itio, doing a fair imitation of the driver's cadence. "I'm here for the special collection."

"Which special collection?"

Theo tensed helplessly, desperately hoping that

Itio would remember that the driver hadn't known Milly's name. There was a momentary pause. "How the fuck should I know?" Itio sounded put out. "Some girl. She didn't tell me who it was, just to come fetch."

The first voice laughed. "Always the way, buddy. Always the way." Theo relaxed again. "Hey, are you okay? You sound croaky."

"It's nothing," said Itio.

"Sure, there's a lot of it around. You got tonight's password?"

"Reindeer Flotilla," Itio said pleasantly.

"Spot on, buddy. I'll neutralize Bay Two for you. Park it up, then go find Liam. See you on the way back through."

"You too," said Itio.

There was a quiet clanking, presumably the barrier being lifted and the spiked speed bumps retracting, and then Itio drove forward slowly, rolling the window back up as he did so. A few seconds later, there was another clatter of plastic. The car slowed momentarily, and Itio swore under his breath, sounding surprised. He started off again, drove a short distance and then stopped. He turned the engine off and waited for several long moments.

"I see you, Theophilus," Itio said quietly. His voice was strangled, like a ventriloquist's. "No one seems to be paying us attention. When I knock on your door, open it and slip out. Keep down by the side of the car, and stay quiet. Once we free the girl, I shall swap back."

"Okay," said Theo softly. "You'd better warn Delphine that she's not going to notice me, though."

There was a click followed by rustling as Itio got out of the car. Theo got ready to move quickly. About thirty seconds later, Itio rapped once on the door. Theo immediately coiled up, reached over to open it, grabbed his gun and slid out. The driver's door was still open.

Theo looked around quickly. They were in a large converted factory or warehouse. Dust-silted tracks cut grooves in the floor, leading out from the bay and back toward a wide central area. The bay walls were raised, providing some cover from the main floor, and there was a larger platform directly ahead, with a structure of some sort on it. If the height of the factory roof was an accurate guide, they were roughly at the center of the building. Two bays down, a number of people were thronging around a large truck. There was some sort of commotion going on, and it appeared to be claiming everyone's attention. He closed the door behind him, tucking himself up against the driver-side wheel, his mind full of empty concrete and black tire rubber.

"Good," said Itio. He left Theo there, walked to the back of the car and knocked twice on the metal of the trunk. He then came back to the driver's door, leaned in and thumbed the catch, before going back to the trunk again and pulling the compartment open. He leaned in and said something softly to Delphine.

A few moments later, she scrambled around the side of the car, looking wild-eyed. "Theo?" Her voice was the barest ghost of a whisper.

Theo nodded, then remembered she couldn't see him and murmured "I'm here."

"Itio can't hide me yet, right?"

"Right."

"Okay, I'm getting under the car just in case. Keep out of the way."

"Be careful," he said, impressed.

She nodded and slid underneath the vehicle, silent apart from one quiet, disgusted "Jesus!" Theo watched the warehouse cautiously, keeping an eye on the hubbub, and tried to stay patient. A few minutes passed, and a sense of unreality gradually crept up on him. The whole situation was so surreal that it was difficult to believe he was there at all.

"Th-Theo? Are you still here?" Delphine sounded terrified.

"I'm here, kid."

"Promise?"

"Yes, I promise." The penny dropped. "I think it's Itio hiding us again."

A moment later, the real Itio walked around the side of the car.

"My apologies if I caused any distress. You may both come out now."

Theo pushed the image of bare concrete and car tire away, let his thoughts and aura expand back out normally, and reached down to help Delphine get out from under the car. She smiled at him weakly, wincing as she came up into a crouch. "It's good to see you. You too, Itio. You're much cooler than that shitbag driver."

"Yes, it would have been pleasant to have killed him. He was a vile being."

Someone screamed loudly from the vicinity of the truck, and the chaos there intensified.

Theo looked around, then shrugged and stood up. "I guess this is as good a time as any." He reached down for Delphine's hand and pulled her smoothly to her feet. "Let's go poke around." He led her and Itio to the front wall of the loading bay, and up the short flight of steps that climbed up to the platform. It zigzagged across the floor, following the staggered line of the bays. A big red "2" was painted on the wall, clearly marking the bay number. A flimsy-looking metal door was built into the wall at the edge of Bay 1. It was ajar, and further away from the crowd a few bays down, so Theo made for it, keeping slow and close in. Delphine and Itio followed behind, staying near.

When he got the door, Theo paused and listened for a long moment. He felt unpleasantly vulnerable just standing there exposed, despite Itio's cloaking, so he held a hand up to warn the others to wait, pushed the door open and looked inside. He found himself at the end of a gray corridor, cheaply lit with dirty neon strip lights. It was empty and less open to casual observation, so he beckoned to the others and slipped through. They joined him swiftly, and he pushed the door nearly closed behind them.

Theo walked slowly down the corridor, watching

carefully for any signs of surveillance, personnel or other dangers. The passage they were in ran for about thirty feet before feeding into a similar one, but there were no other doors or features. They were about halfway along when Theo thought he heard something—half-heard was more like it—and stopped dead. Delphine nearly bumped into him but had the sense to keep quiet. Moments later, there was a clatter up ahead. Theo crouched down against the wall, his gun bumping against his knees, Delphine and Itio dropping to join him. He heard several sets of footsteps.

"So what did they give them, then?" The speaker was male. Young and dumb, by the sound of it.

"Who knows. Some crazy-ass upper." The second voice was rough, a blend of old tobacco, cheap whisky and bitterness. "The whole thing went to hell. They shot the doc so full of her own shit that she's still in a coma, and then they must have got bored, because they just killed the bagman. They were only around the corner, so the driver thumped the lockdown and brought them in for Greg and the boys to play with."

"Who's going to take his place now?" The men came into sight, one tall and chubby with long, bushy hair, and the other shorter and older, his bare arms covered in tattoos.

"Greg? Who fucking cares," said Tattoos. "He was a useless jerk-off anyway."

"It might be you."

"You shitting me? I'm not going for no crappy sideways promotion. Anyway, I'm happy downstairs. More fun."

"I guess. So where we going to fit them all?"

"Cram them all in six for now. We'll sort it out in a couple of days once three and four come clear." There was the noise of a door opening and a brief burst of chaotic babble from the main warehouse, and then the corridor was quiet again.

Theo glanced back over his shoulder. Delphine looked murderous, eyes in slits and teeth bared, trembling with rage. When she spoke, however, her voice was tightly controlled. "I remember that one with the tattoos. Seemed to think he was a bit of a catch." She made a visible effort to calm down.

"Yeah? That's interesting. He might be good to talk to." He nodded in the direction the men had come from. "We go down for the moment, though. Maybe he'll be back."

"So be it. This is where I have to leave you for a short time, Theophilus."

Theo looked at Itio in surprise. "What? Where are you going?"

"There are certain things that I have to attend to. Do not worry. We shall provide you with a timely distraction. Pretty lady, have faith. Your sister awaits."

"We?" asked Theo nervously. "You're not under the influence of that driver, are you?"

Itio merely turned round and headed back up the corridor.

Delphine looked at Theo. "Hey, you're the one who said he was nuts."

Theo suddenly felt nervous, defensive, as if he were back in London, on display in front of a hostile crowd. He realized Delphine was grimacing, and pulling her jacket tightly around herself. She noticed his look. "I... I know it's silly, but I feel kinda naked. It's nasty. Weird."

"It's Itio."

"Oh. Oh, I see. So I feel shitty when it starts, then feel shitty again in a totally different way when it stops? It wasn't that bad earlier. What's the deal?"

"No idea," said Theo. "Maybe we're just twitchier now."

"Yeah, well, I guess the stakes are higher."

"So lets get on with it. Come on."

chapter fifteen:
smash and grab

Theo stood up and walked swiftly to the end of the corridor, turning right. A room opened out a short distance in front of him, an ugly concrete thing. A circular metal stairwell ringed with a safety rail was dug into the floor in the middle of the room. Aware of the door at his back, Theo hurried into the room and stepped to the side, getting out of the line of sight. He pulled Delphine in after him impatiently.

She looked up at him evenly. "Tell me, Theo, do you have a plan for this?"

He nodded. "Stay out of sight and have a poke around, see what we can find out. I also want to grab someone for questioning. Then once we've got some material to work with, we'll find your sister, get her out, hook up with Itio again and have him drive us out. We can pretend Nathalie is the person he came to collect."

"What if we get seen?"

"I want to avoid that. The one thing I don't want to do is to get involved in a pitched battle."

She looked doubtful. "That's not much of a plan, really."

"This is a scouting mission, not an attempt to take down the whole operation. I suppose you could do better?"

"Yeah. I'd free any prisoners we find to cause some confusion."

He shook his head. "That's bound to set off alarms and draw attention, and it might make them lock the place down. We'd risk being stuck. Besides which, a lot of them would get killed."

"All hell is going to break out anyway if Itio really is going to cause a 'distraction.' Loose prisoners would work in our favor then, adding to the chaos. They wouldn't get killed, either. These guys are slavers, remember? Corpses aren't worth anything. I'm willing to bet that they have standing orders to avoid killing escaped prisoners. Those bastards who walked past implied as much, and the fuckers certainly used tasers or something on Nat and me when they snatched us."

Theo grinned ruefully. "All right, I'll tell you what. If the balloon goes up, we'll free as many people as we can and they can take their chances. Okay?"

"It's a deal."

"Good. In the meantime, if we get into trouble, stay out of the way. If we get into real trouble, use my shotgun." He passed it over along with a handful of shells from his pocket. "It holds six rounds. It's real loud, so it's a bit spectacular to fire. Don't use it unless you have to, and warn me first. Yell 'clear' or something."

She took the gun. "Okay. Thanks. What about you?"

"I'll be fine." He patted his hip. "I've got a knife." Delphine looked at him uncertainly, and he grinned back at her. He looked back up the corridor to make sure there was no one approaching, then made for the stairs. "Come on. Time to dance."

The metal staircase spiraled tightly down the inside of a rough concrete shaft. They treaded quietly. The stairs came to an end about twenty feet down. Theo left Delphine partway up the shaft and slipped down the few remaining feet.

A broad concrete tunnel started at the foot of the stairway and led off to a four-way junction. The walls and floor were painted an institutional shade of white, and everything seemed well lit with bright fluorescent tubes. Past the junction, he could make out a number of unmarked doors. There didn't seem to be anyone around. He called softly up the stairs to Delphine, and she came down quietly to join him, shotgun at the ready.

They moved out of the immediate area of the stairs, and Theo went on ahead to the junction, crouched down and looked out to the right and left. It was pretty much the same in both directions, with white corridors heading off for a short distance before turning up parallel to the one that they were already in. Theo waved Delphine up, and they dashed straight across the junction.

Theo made for the first door off the corridor, a plain, white-painted wooden thing without any obvious identifying numbers or marks. There was no handle or lock, and no noise coming from inside, so Theo pushed on it slowly while Delphine kept out of the way, looking tense. The door swung open soundlessly, and he looked in.

It was a large room, maybe thirty feet deep and twenty across, brightly lit. The floor and walls were tiled with some sort of white ceramic that reminded Theo of bathrooms and hospitals. The place was cluttered with all sorts of stuff. One corner appeared to serve as a small kitchen, with sink, work surface, and a full range of utilities. Another corner looked medical, although some of the instruments seemed rather threatening, and there were a couple of tall cupboards. Shelves all along one wall held a wide variety of equipment, both mechanical and electrical. Some pieces were extremely sharp. Large, industrial sinks ran between the shelves and the medical supplies. The center of the room was dominated by a couple of big, ugly-looking workbenches. There was no one inside, so Theo stepped in, nodding to Delphine to come join him.

She entered and looked around the room. It clearly pissed her off. "Nice pad. You take me to all the best places." Her voice was angry, but she kept it low. "I particularly like the way they've separated things out—powered items on that shelf, manual ones below it, and so on. Classy touch." She glanced over at him and grimaced. "Hey, don't worry. I'm cool. I just don't like it."

Theo nodded. "I know. Neither do I. For the—" He broke off, holding up a hand to warn her to keep silent. Had that been a faint ring of metal? Theo stepped back behind the door, pulling Delphine with him. A few moments later, he clearly heard a footstep. A few more seconds, and he was certain someone was approaching. The footfalls got closer and slowed slightly as they arrived. The door opened and the tattooed man walked in briskly. He let it swing shut behind him. Theo felt a rush of scalding heat that swept across his body like a wave as the blood seethed within him, the energy prickling his skin with goose bumps.

He surged forward away from the wall, and as the man started to bring his foot down, Theo grabbed him by the mouth and waist and lifted him off the ground. He swung him around to one of the wooden tables as the man's eyes widened in alarm, and then slammed him down onto it, knocking the wind out of him before he could shout. Theo held him to the bench, one arm pinning him down hard, and the other silencing him.

"Fuck, you're fast." Delphine sounded awed. "You were just this great big blur, man. Awesome."

Theo nodded at her impatiently, ignoring the man's frantic writhing. "That's very kind of you. Now, if you don't mind, a little assistance would be nice."

She propped the shotgun against the wall and came over to the bench.

"Thank you," said Theo archly. "Could—"

She punched the man in the nuts, throwing her weight behind it. He groaned and sagged back against the bench, the fight knocked out of him. She beamed and turned away, heading for the shelves.

Theo blinked. "That's not exactly what I had in mind."

She started back, hefting a heavy hammer over her shoulder and grinning nastily. "Oh. Really?"

Theo looked at her uncertainly. "Delphine?"

"Yes, Theo?"

"What are you doing?"

As she got back to the table, she jerked the hammer down onto the man's shin, just above the ankle. There was an unpleasantly wet crack as the bone broke. He shrieked into Theo's palm and tried to start writhing, only to stop again immediately.

"I don't think he's going to give us any more trouble." She walked up the table toward the man's head, smiling sweetly down at him. "Are you?" The man did his best to shake his head urgently. "Is that more like it, Theo?" She put the hammer down.

"I guess it'll do," he said thoughtfully.

"Good. Bear with me for a moment." She walked back to the shelves, picked up a large, cruel knife, and returned to the table. Putting the knife down for a moment, she undid the man's belt buckle, then pulled his pants and jockey shorts down to mid-thigh, exposing him. Theo looked at her, concerned. Ignoring him for a moment, she picked up the knife, slid it between his legs, and dug the tip into the flesh behind his scrotum. He froze, eyes wide with panic. She slowly pushed it in further, just enough to start drawing a trickle of blood, and grinned at the man.

Theo looked down at him—he was doing his best to shake his head wildly and scream protests—then back at Delphine.

She stared him straight in the eye. "What?"

"Isn't this a bit excessive?"

She shook her head. "No. I haven't even started yet. I told you, I *remember* this one. If you want me to stop, you'd better get him talking."

Theo looked at the man, who nodded frantically.

"If he screams," said Delphine hopefully, "I'm having his balls."

"I'll tell you anything you want," said the man urgently. "Please, just keep her off me. You want to know where the other one is? Room 12. You want to know where to find Matthew and Liam? Upstairs, in the offices. What do you want to know?"

Theo grinned slightly, amused despite himself. "What's the security in this section?"

"Locks, a couple of guys patrolling, alarms if a door is forced."

"What about in the rest of the place?"

"Oh man, there's alarms, loads of the boys have automatics, there are some cameras watching the bays, you know, all the usual shit. Most of the heavy stuff is facing out though."

"What about the offices?"

"What about them, man? Yeah, there's a guard on the door and cameras everywhere, if that's what you mean."

"And what ways are there to get out of the building?"

"Just the tunnel. Nothing else. Look, please just go easy, eh? I'm not going to give you any problems. I don't care if…"

Theo held his hand up, and the man went quiet. "Liam and Matthew are the bosses, right?"

"They run the place, yeah. Matthew reports to someone, Liam reports to someone else. I don't know who. Liam's the real boss."

"What about other sites?"

"Other sites? There aren't any."

Delphine twisted the tip of the knife a little, and the man yelped. "Stop lying, asshole."

"I'm not lying, I'm not lying. Jesus, man, keep her under control. I don't know anything about any other sites."

Theo shook his head. "Who do you deal with?"

"Uh, all sorts. Gangs, private collectors, anyone with the readies or some quality merchandise."

Delphine growled and dug the knife in a little tighter.

The man winced. "Hey, hey! I'm telling you everything, aren't I? I'm keeping my end of the bargain. Keep her off me, man."

Theo shot Delphine a warning glance. "What do you know about Matthew?"

"Matthew? Nothing. He's kinda weird, really unfriendly. The guys don't like him. He's got a few boys of his own though. Guess he likes to keep a bit of the operation to himself. There are some pieces of meat that his guys insist on taking care of themselves. I've got to leave them to it. He moves a lot of merchandise, so I guess he knows a lot of buyers."

"I see. What about Liam?"

"He's got a heavy rep. Used to be something bad in New York. Knows everyone, all the gangs, all the players. Got them all eating out the palm of his hand, too—one way or another. Even Matthew. He's square, though, unless you fuck up big time."

Delphine snarled. "This is getting weak. Where do we find Room 12, asshole?"

"Go to the end of the corridor and turn right, and it's down the hall. It's marked. There's no one else in there."

She looked up at Theo, a nasty glint in her eye. "Was there anything else, Theo?"

"Yeah," he said nodding. "Have you ever heard of 'The Lady?'"

The man shook his head. "No, nothing." He looked at Delphine. "I swear."

"What about a driver called Bill?"

"Christ, I dunno. I don't deal with that sort of shit. I'm stock control."

"Theo," said Delphine. "It's just being bitten by us that makes feeding pleasant for them, isn't it?"

Theo looked at her curiously. "Yes, as far as I know."

"Good. Hand please."

"Excuse me?"

She mimed clapping a hand over her mouth. "Hand, please."

"Hey, wait a fucking moment," said the man, eyes wide with fear. "You promised not to let her have me. What about…"

Delphine pushed the knife slowly into the man's body. He began a high-pitched scream, and Theo immediately clamped his hand over the man's mouth, glaring at Delphine. She ignored him and pulled the knife up, using all her strength to saw it through the man's groin. The hot, salty smell of blood filled the room, tantalizing.

Theo watched with growing alarm as Delphine bent down, clamped her mouth to the ruined flesh and drank greedily, blood gushing up around the wound and drenching her face. The man's struggles got weaker and weaker, until he finally went still. When he was dead, she lifted her face from the wreckage, wiped it thoroughly on his shirt, and smiled at Theo unrepentantly. "That's better. I hope there wasn't anything else you wanted to ask him." She started rifling through the pockets of his pants.

Theo sighed, worried. "Are you all right?"

She smiled. "Never better."

He shook his head. "Listen to me. You can't just go around doing shit like that to people."

"Yes I fucking can," she snapped, suddenly angry. "He was scum. He deserved a hundred times worse. You'll never know how much he deserved worse."

"It's not good for you."

"Yeah? It felt pretty damn good, I can tell you."

"It usually does," he said sadly. "It's a really bad path to start down, though."

"Drop it," snarled Delphine. "You're not my fucking mother."

"No," he said icily, patience wearing thin. "I'm the bloody idiot who's putting his ass on the line to keep you from destruction and to rescue your sister."

She sighed. "Look, I'm really sorry I snapped at you, okay? That guy... I don't want to talk about it. It's a one-off, though. I promise. I really appreciate everything you're doing, and I know I owe you everything."

He sighed. "I guess it doesn't matter. Please don't do that shit again."

"I won't," she said. "Promise. I'm fine now." The red stains of gore still on her cheeks and collar didn't add much credibility to her contrition. She straightened up and brandished a keycard. "This may come in handy. Come on, let's go get Nat."

"We'd better stash the corpse out of the way somewhere first."

Delphine pouted. "All right."

Theo picked the body up and bundled it into the bottom of the cupboards, closing the door on it firmly. "Far from perfect," he said. "It'll have to do, though. Hopefully we'll be out of here before anyone finds him."

"Sounds good to me," she said, fetching the shotgun.

Theo crossed to the door, pushed it open slowly and looked around. The corridor was empty. He stepped out, motioning for Delphine to follow, and cautiously headed left toward the top passageway. They were almost at the top junction when Theo heard the clattering of footsteps on metal from behind them. "People are coming. A lot of them, by the sound of it."

The nearest door had a viewing slot, and a sensor plate with the number 3 stenciled onto it. He crossed over to it quickly, suddenly nervous, and slid it back a little. A prisoner was inside, bound tightly into a straitjacket. He closed the slot again. "Let's try this one."

Delphine nodded and pressed the keycard against the sensor. There was a click. Theo pushed the door, and it opened easily. They piled inside and slid the door closed.

The straitjacketed prisoner turned to look at Delphine curiously. "Are you real?"

"No," said Delphine quickly, before Theo could say anything. She held the gun behind her back as best she could. "I'm not real. I'm a ghost. You're hallucinating, because of what they've done to you."

Theo looked at her, shaking his head. Outside, the clamor was getting louder as what must have been a group of people approached.

"Oh," said the prisoner calmly. "That's okay then. What have they done to me?"

"What haven't they done to you?"

"Very true. That gun looks big. Are you here to kill me?"

"No," she said, dropping her voice to a loud whisper. "I'm not real, remember?"

Theo could hear muted voices talking threateningly as they moved past the door. One of them sounded like the man that had been with Tattoos earlier.

"That's a shame," said the prisoner, matching her reduced volume. "I wish someone would kill me. I'm not allowed to kill myself. They even tied me into this thing to stop me. I'm so tired of it all. It's not as if I'm going to miss it when I'm gone. All I want to do is die. Is that so much to ask?"

"Hang in there," said Delphine sympathetically. "Things are going to get better soon."

"I don't want to hang in there," said the man plaintively. "I just want to be done with it. I don't want to have to remember this. It's not fair. I didn't do anything to deserve it."

"No one ever does," said Delphine with some feeling. "Shit happens. Deal with it. It happens to you, it happens to me, it just happens."

"But…"

"Look, if nothing else, you can give suicide a try when you get out of here. Someone might help you escape later. Try it. You might even get killed. If you don't, just live out the rest of the day, and when you get tired, you can decide whether to kill yourself depending on what the day has been like. Keep your options open, that's all I'm saying. Once you're dead, you don't have any options at all, and that's a really sucky place to be in. You think death is the answer, but what if it isn't? What if it's like this still, only worse?"

"I hadn't thought about that," said the prisoner. "Do you really think that's possible?"

"I don't know," said Delphine. "But that means it could go either way, right?"

"Yeah, I see what you mean. All right, I'll think about it, see if the risk is worth it or not."

The noise outside had faded again, the captives presumably bustled off to some cell or other. Theo beckoned to Delphine.

She nodded, then smiled at the prisoner. "You do that. Just do what I said, okay? Give it a try. I'm going to go now, but remember, I wasn't ever here."

"I'll remember," said the prisoner. "Goodbye. You're the prettiest hallucination I've had yet."

Theo opened the door and looked out. When he was satisfied that the coast was clear, he stepped out into the corridor, Delphine close behind. She waved to the prisoner as he closed the door. Theo looked at her quizzically, and she shrugged.

"I didn't want him to just kill himself. Why give them that satisfaction?"

"Sure," he said. "It kept him fairly quiet." He left her by the door and sprinted up to the corner of the junction, darting a quick peek out either way. It was empty. He nodded to her, looked again and turned to the right. Apart from the positions of the doors, it could have been the same stretch of corridor. It ran for about forty feet, then turned back to the right. They walked cautiously, trying to balance speed and stealth. The first door they came to, on the left, turned out to be Room 10, an identical set-up to Room 3, at least on the outside. Theo didn't stop to see who was inside. A few yards on, Room 11 was off to the right. He ignored that too.

"God, I hope she's okay." Delphine sounded strangled. "Poor Nat."

If she's there, he thought, but he kept his mouth shut. There was a faint hint of a noise up ahead. He froze, wary, Delphine doing the same a moment later. A small metallic clink came from just around the corner, on the edge of audibility. He gestured sharply for Delphine to crouch down against the wall, then jumped forward toward the corner, where a dark-haired guard with a stubby SMG was coming into view. Theo's muscles screamed as hot, powerful blood flooded into them, and the wild leap seemed to turn into a stately glide.

A surprised look stole over the guard's face as Theo shot toward him. Theo landed a couple of feet away, going down into a crouch, then sprang up at the man, his hand flashing out like a blade to smash the guard in the larynx. His neck crumpled, and the guard staggered backward. His finger locked convulsively on the trigger of the SMG, and a wild burst of rounds filled the space between them.

Theo was so close to the gun that the sound was muffled, but he felt the bullets ripping up the left side of his body. A couple went through his left hand, turning it into a useless, pulpy mess. Pain washed over him like a flood, but he forced himself to wall it away as best he could. He reached for the gun with his good hand, grabbed the guard's wrist and crushed all the bones to splinters in one smooth squeeze, leaving the man's trigger finger flopping uselessly.

As the guard staggered backward, Theo paused for a moment to concentrate on forcing blood into his wounds. The flesh responded instantly, an uncomfortable sensation of crawling and writhing as the tissues started to knit together, driven by relentless blood. The bullets were forced outward painfully as the wounds healed, and his left hand shrieked its agonized protest.

The guard drew breath to try to scream as the pain from his shattered hand reached him, but Theo darted forward, pinned him against the wall and tore out his throat. Time seemed to pause as beautiful fresh blood gushed into Theo's mouth, smooth and delicious. Theo drank heedlessly, replenishing the stores that he had burned, feeling himself infused with new strength as the bullet wounds continued to heal.

Suddenly there was a loud explosion and a bright flash. Theo looked around in time to see a second guard. Half his face was missing, and blood fountained from the wound.

"Clear," said Delphine sheepishly.

Theo bent back to the first guard and continued drinking. When the man was drained dry, he stood up and dusted himself down, poking at the fresh bullet holes in his jacket. "Ouch."

"That was *incredible*," said Delphine, a little too loudly, her hearing affected by the shotgun's report. "I thought you were fast earlier, but you were like an explosion or something. You kinda landed and then just erupted. The guy never even knew what hit him. Then your hand shredded, but it seemed to start rebuilding itself instantly, all the rips and tears shrinking and healing over before I even had a chance to scream. Jesus! No wonder you said you're a fucking SWAT team."

"It still hurt a lot," said Theo. "It was real close, too. He nearly fucked me up. Good shot, by the way."

"Thanks," said Delphine, smiling.

"There's no point trying to hide these bodies. Even if there was no one down here to hear the gunshots, there's no way we can clean up all the blood and muck splattered everywhere. We'd need half an hour with mops. We'll just have to tuck them up against the blind side of the corner here and hurry up." He looked at the streaks of blood clotting in her hair, and the smears over her cheeks, and said, "You look like shit. I hope your sister is feeling resilient."

"You look a lot like a slaughterhouse yourself," replied Delphine tartly, bending down to drag one of the bodies away. "Hey, do you want this guy's gun?"

Theo shook his head. "No thanks. I'm good. Never did get on with SMGs."

She shrugged, tucking the body away. "Whatever."

Theo shifted the other one, trying to convince himself that it might be possible for someone at the other end of the corridor to miss the blood drenching the pale walls.

As soon as her body was laid out against the wall, Delphine rushed to the door of Room 12 and slid back the viewing panel. "Oh my god. Nat." She sounded distraught. Theo came over to join her. She passed him the shotgun, fumbled the keycard out of a pocket and unlocked the door, then threw it open and rushed in. "Nathalie!"

chapter sixteen:
open house

Nathalie Decourt was genuinely identical to her sister, save for the small variation in hairstyle. Her face was untouched, but the rest of her naked body was covered in a tapestry of bruises, yellows and browns meshing with purple and blue to give her an almost mottled appearance. She was lying on a thin mattress on the floor of a small, bright padded room. She looked gaunt and scared, and flinched visibly when Delphine approached.

Delphine slowed, hesitating nervously. "Nat, it's me." Her voice was close to breaking. "We've come to rescue you."

Nathalie curled up defensively, bringing her knees to her chest and wrapping her arms around them. "Del? No. You're dead. I felt you die."

Delphine's face crumpled, and she dropped bonelessly into a stunned half-crouch, tears of blood streaking down her cheeks. "No, oh no, Nat, I'm still me."

"This isn't fair. I'm tired. Go away." Nathalie shut her eyes.

"Please," begged Delphine.

Nathalie ignored her.

"Nat, please." Delphine sounded totally broken, crying in earnest, talking as best she could through huge sobs. "I love you, sissy."

Suddenly Nathalie was crying too, and the next moment the girls were holding each other.

Theo turned his back to give them a little privacy and checked the corridor. It was still empty. He checked it again.

"It's really you, isn't it." Nathalie, presumably.

"Damn straight."

"Missed you."

"Missed you too."

"Cold."

"New shoes," replied Delphine enigmatically.

"Big?"

"Biggest." Delphine sounded resigned. "You?"

"Nuh-uh. Is...?"

"Yeah."

They started crying again. Theo tried to puzzle some sense out of the exchange but couldn't. The crying stopped more quickly this time, and then they stood up, Delphine walking over to Theo, putting a hand on his arm.

"This lump who's pretending to be discreet is Theo."

"Where did you score such a stud, Del?" Nathalie sounded awed.

Delphine laughed, but it was tinged with pain. "Hardly. He's not too bad though, for an asshole."

"Does that mean I can borrow him?"

"If you want," said Delphine. "It won't do you much good, though."

"Ladies," said Theo, turning around to face them, "I am glad that you are together again. We should get the fuck out of here, though."

Nathalie grinned at Delphine. "He's quite commanding, isn't he."

The lights dimmed and red alarm beacons started flashing. A klaxon started up, deafeningly loud. Theo immediately pulled back inside the cell, looking up and down the corridor cautiously for almost a minute. Nothing happened, but the alarms continued. Nathalie flinched back into Delphine's arms, cowering. Delphine held her close and stroked her hair, murmuring something in a comforting tone of voice.

"They're coming for us," said Nathalie shakily.

"I don't know," said Theo. "No one's in the hall. It might be our distraction."

Delphine frowned. "Either way, I think it's time to go."

***

Up in the offices, Matthew and Liam were going over some paperwork when the alarm sounded. They shared a look and waited for a few moments. Sure enough, the phone on the desk started buzzing urgently. Matthew looked at Liam, who shrugged and picked it up.

"Well?" He listened to the person on the other end, his face grim. Eventually, he said "All right. You know what to do." He hung up. "We're under attack. A small force is attempting to storm the compound."

Matthew frowned. "Mortals? Kindred?"

"Not sure. It better not be your bloody kindred doing things again without you knowing about it though, I'll tell you that. I'm going to get onto the floor and see what I can make out."

Matthew nodded silently, privately certain that it had to be something to do with Bell and the twins. It was time to take care of the problem. As soon as Liam was clear, Matthew stood up and headed out through the door.

Itio watched him go, a broad smile plastered across his face.

***

Theo led Delphine and Nathalie—now wearing his jacket like a short bathrobe—out of the cell and back to Room 11. Delphine passed Theo the keycard, and he swiped the door open. It was a bigger room than the two they had seen so far, but not by much. Three men and a woman were sitting inside, looking defiant. They were a mixed bunch, different ages and types. They were shackled together at the ankle. The older one glowered at Theo, then turned away pointedly.

Theo looked at them, then shrugged. "Do you want out of this crap hole?"

"What are you talking about?" The older one looked back up again.

Theo arched an eyebrow. "I'm letting you out."

"Why?"

"I'm starting to wonder that myself, given the welcome I'm getting."

"Why should we welcome you?"

Theo sighed. "Because I'm not with these fuckers, and I *don't* like slavery."

The four shared a glance. "Are you with a Japanese man called Itio?"

Theo blinked.

The spokesman shook his head. "Well why didn't you say so in the first place? Can you break these shackles off?"

"Of course," said Theo. He shook his head a little. Maybe it wasn't surprising that they were being odd— Christ knows what the poor bastards had been through. He did the others in turn, doing all the hands before kneeling down and releasing their ankles. All four looked immensely relieved.

"Thank you," said the spokesman.

"Sure," said Theo. "You're welcome."

"Good luck," said the spokesman as he stalked out past the girls. The others followed, heading up toward the bloodstained corner.

The last to leave, a man in his thirties, nodded to Theo as he passed. "You're all right."

"Thanks," said Theo wryly. He looked up the corridor, where the four were sprinting off round the corner.

Delphine looked at him curiously. "Did you follow that?"

Theo shook his head. "Nope. I'm as lost as you are. Maybe Itio has a cult of maniacs behind him or something. It's not unknown."

Delphine giggled. "I think he has a cult of maniacs inside him."

"Dare I ask?" Nathalie sounded amused, but wary.

"Gnarly," said Delphine. "You'll see. Him and Theo…"

Nathalie nodded, grinning.

"Hey," said Theo. "Let's move it, eh?" He went down to the next room and swiped it open. Two men were inside, looking frightened. They were unrestrained. "If you want to escape, now's your chance," said Theo. "You're free. Go for it."

They looked at him. A shockingly loud scream echoed down from somewhere, terminating in a frothy gurgle. They both flinched, as did Nathalie.

"It might be your best chance," said Theo encouragingly. He stepped away from the doorway, and left them to decide what to do.

They took the longer way back to the stairs, opening up eight more cells along the way. At Delphine's insistence, they also detoured briefly back down the central aisle, principally to free the straitjacketed man in Room 3, cutting him out of the restraint before encouraging him to make a break. Some of the prisoners were eager to grasp the chance. Others had to be told to get out, or were just left to sit. Most of them were young adult males in moderately reasonable health, but there were plenty of females too, all under thirty. Theo let Delphine and Nathalie speak to them. In all, it took about five minutes to work back around to the staircase.

Theo glanced up toward the wing that they hadn't opened yet, but it seemed someone had beaten him to it. The doors he could see were splintered wrecks, hanging limply off their ruined hinges. Shrugging, he made for the stairs, Delphine and Nathalie behind him. The staircase was clear, and he hurried up. It sounded like mayhem upstairs in the main plant.

When Theo got up into the room at the top of the stairs, he was surprised to find that the lights were out in the corridor to the junction. He paused, uncertain. Something wasn't right.

He advanced cautiously, motioning to Delphine and Nathalie to stay back in the room. Delphine ducked into cover behind the wall, pulling her sister in with her. The lights in the room went out, and one of the girls yelped briefly in surprise.

Theo's face prickled as the blood gushed into it, his eyes and ears stinging painfully. The world immediately became sharper and harder, distant details now clearly visible. Back in the room, one of the girls screamed, and the other started talking quickly but calmly. There was a faint outline of solid black in the darkness ahead. A figure, watching calmly. Blood poured into Theo's muscles, a hard, hot torrent, filling them with power and still coming, pushing him tighter and tighter. The world was slow as molasses around him.

He tensed quickly and sprang, and was utterly astonished when he didn't go anywhere. It felt like iron bands were clamped around him—arms, legs, torso—locking him in place. He glanced down reflexively. There was nothing around him but shadow. Up ahead, the silhouette held up a hand and writhed its fingers sensuously. Long, sharp claws left jet-black outlines against the darkness.

"I don't know how you got in here, Archon, but I'm almost impressed with your persistence. Stupid of you to come for the girl of course, but tenacious nonetheless." The voice was cold and mocking. Theo remembered it from the warehouse on Nicolet Island.

"Matthew." Theo started struggling to move,

fighting against the invisible bonds. It was useless, like trying to punch water. He was held fast.

"You should never have gotten involved in this matter, Archon. Far better for everyone if you'd kept your nose out of it. Still, it will be entertaining to kill you."

"Plenty of people have tried," said Theo.

"My word," said Matthew. "That odious traitor was right. You really are pathologically stubborn."

"There's no traitor." Theo tried to make his voice sound incredulous.

Matthew laughed. "Incredible! You are *still* fishing for information, even in the face of your destruction. It would give me great pleasure to indulge you, just to watch your expression as I told you his or her name, Archon. Alas, I cannot."

"Theo, we're being held by something," called Delphine.

"If you harm them…" said Theo menacingly. The blood in his muscles ignited in an explosion of fresh power, seemingly swelling as new strength built and built.

Matthew sneered. "I could snap them in an instant, but I'm not going to harm them, Archon. You are."

One of the lights in the far room flicked back on, and he was inexorably twisted round to face back down the corridor. He threw all his strength into breaking just one arm free, the muscles seething with stolen power but, incredibly, he still wasn't strong enough. Moments later, Delphine and Nathalie stumbled out into the mouth of the corridor, cocooned in pools of shadow.

"I thought I'd save them for you," said Matthew nastily from just behind Theo, his voice thick with bestial hatred.

"Fuck off," said Theo, growling. He strained so hard that his muscles burned and his eyes waxed red with blood, and, slowly, the force restraining him started to give.

Hot knives of fire sank into his lower back, ripping into him, and he howled in pain.

"Ah, you like that, don't you," said Matthew. "You'll love this, then." He growled, a low, writhing noise that seemed to burrow deeper and deeper into Theo's mind. It was maddeningly insistent, and it swelled and blossomed, calling to the rage within him. Red fog billowed up to engulf him, and his last awareness, as the frenzy took him, was that he was free at last, pushed toward a pair of juicy targets.

…leaping forward, fangs extended… knocking the prey easily to the ground… one, then the other… fingers hooked like talons to rip the throat out… sweet screams of pain, confusion and panic… cool, firm flesh under his hand… no longer struggling, just speaking calmly… readying to strike… cool, calm… readying to strike… calm… kindred…

Delphine.

"You're not going to hurt me, Theo. I know you won't. I have faith now." She sounded calm and collected despite Nathalie's panicked screams.

"He has no idea who you are, child. He's just toying with you, like a cat with a mouse," said Matthew, gloating. "You're wasting the last moments before he slaughters both you and your sister."

Theo winked at Delphine, shifted his weight onto his feet, which were either side of her, and pulled a grimacing face. She caught on immediately and screamed in apparent agony.

Matthew chuckled nastily, and Theo erupted, his whole body blazing as the blood slammed into his muscles like a hammer. Matthew's laughter stretched out impossibly, and Theo launched himself backward, the walls blurring around him. He landed on one foot, spinning himself around with the momentum, dropping into a crouch.

Matthew took a step back and managed a single

word. "How…"

Theo pounced on him, crashing into him like a hammer and ripping into his shoulder, fangs bared.

The thin vampire screamed and stabbed down with his clawed hands, raking Theo's back and neck with agonizing lines of fire. Theo flashed his hands up and grabbed one of Matthew's arms, twisting it back on itself and shattering it like porcelain. The blood surged within him, muscles howling. Matthew screamed again, and Theo tore into the vampire's neck with his fangs.

A rich draught of thick, potent blood gushed out, spicy with age and power. Theo gulped it hungrily. Matthew gurgled weakly. Theo bit deeper, feeling him go limp. Theo almost felt sorry for him—cold, isolated, archaically formal, another fool past his time and out of his depth. He wondered briefly what kind of a mortal Matthew had been, what hopes and dreams he'd had, what goals he had set for himself after his embrace. The last of the blood ran dry, and Matthew crumbled into dust with a peculiar rustling noise, like old leaves sighing in the wind. Whatever they were, his goals obviously hadn't been sufficiently compelling.

The lights came back on. Theo straightened up, dusting himself down.

Delphine got up off the floor and picked Nathalie up. She seemed shell-shocked. She looked at Delphine and then up at Theo, who winced. "Oh my god. You had me totally fooled, you bastards. And you were like a streak, man. That was awesome! Are you like some sort of ninja or something?"

Theo and Delphine shared a look.

"Hey," protested Nathalie. "I'm not stupid. I know there's some weird shit going on here, and I know you're part of it Del, but you got me out of that torture hole, and if it's good enough for you, then fuck, it's good enough for me."

Theo laughed, astonished. "Yeah, she's your sister

all right."

Delphine hugged her sister. "Was there ever any doubt? Hey, Theo, how are we going to find Itio? It sounds like madness out there."

"I think it's dying down a bit, actually. There's less gunfire."

"That's good, right?"

"Sure," said Theo. "Anyway, it'll make it easier to find him. I'll go sneak around and see what I can turn up."

"There is no need to resort to such feats, Theophilus." Itio was walking toward him from the loading bay area.

"Itio! Good to see you," said Theo. "Did you do what you needed to?"

"Yes, thank you."

"I'm sorry Itio," said Theo. "I'm forgetting my manners. This is Nathalie, Delphine's sister. Nathalie, meet Itio, an old colleague of mine."

"Pretty lady, I am delighted to see that you have found your sister, and that she truly is as beautiful as you are."

Nathalie and Delphine beamed at him in stereo.

"What's the situation like out there?"

"Under control. Several of the slavers escaped, but the rest have been pacified. We are free to leave without harassment. Pretty lady, you will be pleased to know that our unwitting accomplice has also been set free, shaken but none the worse for her misadventures."

Theo grinned. "Excellent." He dropped his voice so that Nathalie couldn't hear him. "I dealt with the kindred half of the leadership. He was using shadows, controlling them. That means Lasombra." The Lasombra were shadowmancers of old, a line of vampires that had helped found the Sabbat, a bloody sect that flouted the masquerades and traditions of the Camarilla. "Do you know of other Sabbat activity in the area that could be related to this?"

Itio shook his head. "Not offhand. It may be worth investigating further."

"Yeah. Tell you what, let's get out of here."

As they headed for the main factory floor, Delphine looked over at Theo curiously. "Hey, Theo, what happens how?"

He forced a grim smile. Before anything else, there was a lot of cleaning up to be done. The masquerade was in tatters in Minneapolis. Too many mortals knew far too much to be left alive. Like Nathalie. Theo turned to Delphine, fighting hard to keep the sorrow from his face. "Now it gets interesting."

**

It was a misty night, and it made the lights of the city look like candle flames twinkling far below. The effect was quite enchanting. The mist muted the incessant chirruping of the insects too, making the evening unusually peaceful.

The man finished his account of the evening's events and lapsed into silence.

His companion tapped her lips thoughtfully with a perfect nail. "Flock's failure is disappointing, but the Minneapolis operation was due for replacement anyway. I am more concerned about any information that may have been released."

"It's impossible to say at the moment," said the man. "We'll get some idea of what Bell knows when he reports to the primogen, of course, but he may hold back if he suspects."

"That cannot be permitted. Flock was told little enough, but he may have inadvertently learned more from his superior. We should err on the side of caution. Bell must be destroyed."

"He is resourceful," warned the man.

"Yes, so it seems." The woman shrugged. "It is time for decisive action. Recall the Overseer."

About the Author

Tim Dedopulos has been writing for over ten years and intends to continue for as long as they'll let him. He currently has more than 70 published works under his belt, most written under one of his various odd pen names. As well as the **Clan Brujah Trilogy**, he wrote **Tribe Novel: Glass Walkers** and **Hunter: Apocrypha**. He has also contributed to a range of White Wolf game lines, including **Hunter: The Reckoning** and the **EverQuest RPG**.

His other works include game material and fiction for a number of other roleplaying game lines—particularly the futuristic urban horror game *SLA Industries*—as well as a wide range of nonfiction books for a variety of publishers. Notable highlights (and lowlights) include *Wizards*, *Dirty Cash: Organized Crime in the 20th Century*, *Conspiracy Theories*, *The Ultimate Insults Book*, *Baking Soda Secrets*, and *The Complete Guide to a Good Abdomen (In Just Five Minutes a Day)*. The latter three always remind him uncomfortably of Troy McClure, and help to make sure that he never takes himself too seriously.

Tim likes to think of himself as a cynical dreamer, and firmly believes that most people are far too quick to give up on the magic in the world. When he isn't chained to a desk, he can often be found at pubs, gigs, stormy beaches, ancient hill-forts and other strange places. His website for this project can be found at http://www.midnight.demon.co.uk/brujah1.html. He'd love to know what you thought of the book, so please do drop by and say hi.

acknowledgments

I really hate writing in third person. It makes me feel like some sort of cheap fictional detective or something. So that's enough of that.

Several people really helped me immensely while I was writing this book. I've said it before, but I owe thanks to Philippe Boulle for his patience, and for being a superb editor. He deserves most of the credit for getting this book as good as it is. Really.

Similarly, super-special thanks go to John Sullivan and Gail McNeillie for always being there; to Dave Allsop and Jared Earle for having faith; to Angus Abranson, Max Bantleman and James Wallis for invaluable assistance; to Wheels and the Brayford clan (Chris, Jen, Haley and Megz) for feeding a starving writer and for use of the pool, and, not least, to Liz Sharma, for unwavering support. Thank you all.